GODDESS SHIFTING

SHIFTER LORDS

S.E. BABIN

OLIVERHEBERBOOKS

Sometimes you don't get it right the first time. Sometimes you rise from the ashes of the fire that nearly consumed you and try one more time...

CHAPTER
ONE

I was a puddle of bruises and regret. Barrett, my father, and Rowan stood over me, each wearing a different expression, ranging from guilt to regret to annoyance.

"You have to learn these things," Barrett said. He was the one who wore the guilty expression. "It's regrettable you had no Chimera there to show you the ropes when you came out of the initial fog. The things I'm showing you now are taught to our children."

Rowan's attention snapped to the man. "Careful," he warned.

The Lord was aware of Finn's obsession with me and what had happened to me in that field and afterward. I'd told him everything a week ago, even the parts that still shook me out of a deep sleep in a cold sweat during the wee hours of the morning.

Rowan had not been the same since. If Finn were still alive...

Well. The Chimera responsible for all of this wouldn't have been alive for very long, that's for sure.

Barrett was lucky he was allowed within a hundred yards of me, but I'd convinced Rowan that I needed the male's help, and the Lord had always been reasonable, at least when it came to me. As Chimeras went, I was stunted, unable to do much of anything one of our kind should be able to do, except shift. I once saw Finn pause time, turning himself into a whirlwind on the battlefield. Not all Chimeras could do the same things. Like the Lords, we each had a special gift that would eventually manifest within us, sometimes with devastating effect.

Mine had yet to be uncovered. For now, I could shift into anything, which was a handy gift to have, but I was pretty limited on other abilities.

Rowan bent and reached a hand out. I clasped it, reveling in the feel of his calloused palm against mine, and allowed him to help me up. Things between us were good, but the bond between us strained for release.

I was the only thing standing in the way.

He was my mate, according to Rowan, shifter biology and lore, and the constant tug toward him and the warmth in my chest when he was near. I was born of gods but mostly raised by humans, and there were no mates, only those we chose to spend our lives with.

So far, I'd chosen poorly twice. Not a great track record there.

My first husband was an unrepentant philanderer. Caelan was driven by duty and power, and I'd surpassed his threshold for acceptability in a partner and became a threat. Add Lugh's terrible magic and toss in an ex-lover, and Caelan tore everything down and burned it to cinders.

Rowan started as a friend and stayed a steady one, all the way up until I revealed my Chimera heritage and had to leave town. Then he became not only my friend, but something more. Something I was still figuring out.

Barrett scratched his chin and looked at my dad. "There has never been a fae Chimera before," he mused. "Maybe the inherent Chimera magic works differently when mixed with fae blood."

Dad tilted his head. He studied me and slowly nodded. "Good theory. We can test it tomorrow. Evie is exhausted and needs to rest."

Exhausted wasn't quite the right word. Two weeks had passed since Tess announced Caelan was marked for death. He'd shut my offer of help down as fast as I'd extended a hand and had cut off all contact with the other Lords about the matter. He only responded to routine communications or items dealing with other Lord duties, but he didn't respond to Rowan at all.

I refused to let Caelan die because he was a stubborn ass. As soon as we returned to Rowan's territory, I'd contacted Dad and Barrett and asked them to step up all my training. They'd happily obliged, and a few days later, they showed up and had been kicking my ass ever since.

"Tomorrow?" I asked.

Dad shook his head. "No. Rest and catch up on your duties. We'll reconvene on Wednesday."

My duties consisted of the grand opening of Little Shop of Florals and maintaining Rowan's land to ensure the spell still creeping across the landscape never gained a foothold here. I'd shoved it out once, but the damned thing was persistent. Next week, I'd be on Thorvin's land, purging his territory, and the week after, Ethan's.

Ben and Soren had not answered our request yet. Ben was as hardheaded as Caelan was, so he could go either way, but I was surprised about Soren. He had the strongest streak of self-preservation. Maybe he was waiting to see what happened in Thorvin's territory before he agreed to allow my help.

"Alright." I shook Barrett's hand and watched the Chimera

walk back to his vehicle. Simone and Garrett followed a short distance behind to ensure he left.

Hope and Declan were somewhere close, keeping a watchful eye on things, but I couldn't pinpoint their exact location.

Dad started to shimmer away, but I held a hand out to stop him. "Can I talk to you for a minute?"

Rowan stepped away. "I'll be in the main house seeing to lunch. Find me when you're finished?"

I nodded. Rowan dipped his head to my father and walked away.

Hiding a smile, I studied the former fae king. Rowan had never been as respectful to him as Caelan was, and it rankled my father. For whatever reason, though, I suspected he liked Rowan far more than the other Lord.

I couldn't help myself. "Unused to the lack of bowing and scraping?"

To my surprise, Dad laughed. "That male is not even a little bit frightened of me."

"Should he be?" I curled my fingers around Dad's elbow and tugged him toward the forested area. A soft shuffle of branches told me either Hope or Declan was close by.

"Allow me my privacy," I called.

The shuffling stopped, followed by a huff of annoyance.

Dad snorted. "Lots of ninja spies around this place."

I rolled my eyes. "Four of them, to be exact. Overbearing but sweet."

Another snort from the trees before the sound of someone dropping from a high distance thumped some distance ahead.

"We're alone," Dad said after a moment. "Or at least free of shifter eyes and ears."

I let out a slow breath and let my shoulders relax.

"Very little privacy can grate on beings like us," Dad guessed.

"They're worried about Caelan and this damn spell. No matter that there's no trace of it here."

"Would it be better if they were nonchalant?"

I shot him a dark look. "You know the answer to that."

"Shifters are nosy creatures by nature," Dad said with a smile. "Even if all this wasn't going on, you're the fae queen and a Chimera, two things they've never experienced before. On top of that, their Lord is very territorial toward you, and there is an unfinished mating bond. Those two things send a shifter's protective nature into overdrive."

I'd been wanting to ask him a question for a long time and tried to figure out a way to ask without being so blunt, but there was no soft way to go about this. "Do fae have mating bonds?"

Dad stopped walking, jerking me to a stop with him. His eyes went all swirly. "Why?"

I blinked. "Um. Because I'm curious. If I'm sort of a shifter but also fae, does one bond supersede the other? If a mating bond exists for shifters, but both of those shifters have fae blood, is it possible for one bond to exist but for them not to be fae mates as well?" I pressed the space between my brows. "It's all very confusing."

Dad exhaled a heavy breath and gave me an exasperated look. "You think too much," he muttered.

"Don't I know it. Why are you being squirrelly about it?"

"You don't have one with Rowan?" His eyes were still swirling.

"Not that I know of."

"You would know." Dad shook his head. "I've seen it knock grown men to their knees."

"The answer is yes, then?"

He sighed and tugged me down to the grass. "We do have

them, but they are exceedingly rare. No bond is something to take lightly, but a fae bond is...more." My father's face grew inordinately sad. "If you decide not to accept the young Lord's heart, you can still walk away from this."

Rowan had said as much. Eventually, I'd have to make a decision. Drawing this out was painful for both of us, but if I let it go on too long, it would turn cruel. Rowan deserved someone to love him with their entire being. I was too damaged to see beyond a few days from now, and with Caelan's life on the line, I found it difficult to focus on much else except fixing that problem.

"If a fae mating bond forms and is offered and accepted, you will not so easily escape that magic. Your power will be forever linked together, and if one of you dies, the other will never be the same. With Rowan, even if you accept the bond, there are things that can shatter the magic. Not so much with our people."

"Is there a possibility of two bonds?" I mused.

"I've never heard of such a thing. But..." he rubbed his hand over his face, "there has never been a fae and Chimera hybrid. I assume the bond would combine into something we've never seen before." He studied me for a long moment. "Is there a reason you're asking?"

I shrugged. "Curiosity mostly." A true statement, but also not the entire truth. I'd been feeling things lately. Odd things. Things that made me want to latch onto Rowan like an alien Facehugger and hold on for dear life. My magic felt *hungry,* and I was getting a little itchy in the britches for more than friendship. It was making me twitchy, and Rowan knew something was up because of his excellent senses and because he was not an idiot. Was it the shifter bond, or was something else happening, something more fae than animalistic?

"I like knowing the odds of things," I continued, "but I

wondered if the shifters have them, why wouldn't the fae? Or at least something similar."

Dad chuckled. "They do exist, but our people can be inherently selfish. They are also tied to their lands, and only the most power hungry explore beyond their boundaries for any long period of time. If you rarely leave your home, the odds of finding a mate are substantially reduced."

"You and Mom weren't mates?"

Dad's eyes flickered with grief before he shook his head. "The female is the one who initiates the bond. She is always the first to feel the power rising, and she is the one who accepts or denies the chosen person."

"Will the male feel the bond too?"

"The possibility of one, yes. The tug would be quite powerful, but someone like Rowan, who knows that you've already been chosen, might confuse it for the shifter bond. That too holds powerful magic," Dad acknowledged, "but he holds no power over the other. In this, the woman 'wears the pants,' as the humans like to say. It's very possible there are more bonds refused than accepted, simply because the female does not want a partner. Fae women can be choosy when it comes to melding their lives with another."

"Like Mom?"

Dad laughed, but the sound held a twinge of sadness. "Yes. I failed your mother in many ways. She has never been a forgiving woman with errors of the heart, but when it came to you, one strike and I was out."

My heart ached for them, but it warmed me to know how fiercely Mom had protected me, even if I wished she made different choices. I patted Dad's knee. "I'm sorry. Maybe once things calm down, she'll see I can take care of myself and warm up to you."

Dad snorted. "Your mother has another in mind. I am a page in her history she is fond of but never plans to revisit."

I wasn't touching that one with a ten-foot pole or any pole, even if it belonged to someone else. Neit had been after Mom for a while now, and as far as I knew, those two were still involved in a merry chase. I liked the god. He was fun to tease and easy on the eyes. But calling him Dad?

Too far.

"If there are so few bonds, how does marriage work in the fae lands?"

Dad rose and helped me up. "Same as a normal marriage, I assume. Choosing a partner is difficult, no matter what or who you are. We're all fumbling around through life the same way everyone else is on many things. The lack of a bond does not preclude someone from living their life to the fullest."

I frowned. "What happens if they find their mate during their marriage?"

"I've never heard of such a thing. Maybe the bond goes dormant when they sense a partnership like a marriage. Such a thing is no mating bond, but it's a bond all the same." He put my hand around his arm. "Come. The young Lord is preparing lunch, and I can hear your stomach growling. I'll walk you to the Keep and return on Wednesday."

I leaned my head on his shoulder for a moment. "Thanks, Dad."

Cernunnos let out a soft sigh and started walking.

The ancient grump loved it when I called him Dad.

TWO

ROWAN

Something was wrong with Evie. She was twitchier than normal, a little more prone to temper, and...she wanted to jump my bones but was resisting with the willpower of a godsdamned monk. I could smell her desire and felt her eyes on me when she thought I wasn't looking. While good for the ego, the way she was looking at me made concentrating on anything way more difficult than usual.

I swore I would give her the time she needed, and I'd been extremely careful not to push boundaries. My touches were those of a close friend, sometimes straying into deeper intimacy when she encouraged such. But there had been no more trapped in the hole serious make-out sessions.

Much to my regret.

She watched me now, her heated gaze burning against my back as I chopped lettuce. If she didn't stop, I wasn't going to be able to turn around for a while, for fear she'd see exactly what those looks were doing to me.

"Need some help?" Her voice was huskier than usual.

My grip tightened on the knife. "Lettuce is the last thing we need. If you want to get the tea and some glasses out, that would be helpful."

Evie rose and passed by me, reaching to open the cupboard. Her hair swayed, exposing the pale line of her neck. The sweater she wore lifted, revealing the curve of her waist.

Gods above.

Her mysterious and ever-changing scent teased my nose. Sometimes she smelled of jasmine and honeysuckle, other times of dirt and green things, and when she used her Chimera magic, she smelled of ancient power and violence, mixed with a tinge of floral. Today, she smelled like peonies and snow.

I didn't realize I'd stopped chopping until she slowly turned to me. Her rose-colored lips parted. "Everything alright?"

Evie's eyes were azure pools, her cheekbones high, her jawline sharp. A pulse beat in her throat, and a hint of desire entwined in her scent.

I was dying a slow death as I drowned in the possibility of pleasure. "I'm fine." If she wanted to continue playing this maddening game, I'd play it with her. We'd see who broke first.

I was nothing if not completely focused on seeing this thing to its inevitable conclusion. Evie would be mine, come hell or high water. But this felt more than that. This felt a little dangerous, and I wasn't sure why. Not in the way that I thought she'd harm me; more in the way of us barreling toward something we could never extricate ourselves from, and even more serious than a mating bond.

If there was something more serious than that bond. I'd never heard of something trumping a shifter's mate bond, but I'd be a fool not to believe there were more things in heaven and earth than were dreamt of in my philosophy. Or whatever the hell that Horatio guy said.

"You're still not chopping," Evie said.

"You're staring at me," I responded.

Her lips twitched. "And you're staring at me," she countered.

"Hmm. I suppose we were staring at each other. Is there anything you want to discuss?" My gaze dropped to her lips.

That sexy pulse in her neck sped up. More desire entangled in her scent.

Yep. She wanted me. Bad.

Fuck. Yeah.

"Why would there be?" Her face was innocent, but two spots of color rose in her cheeks.

"I don't know," I said, "but you can always talk to me if you need to." I leaned closer, so close I buried my nose in the crook of her neck and inhaled her scent. "About anything. If you want anything from me," I said with a long pause, "*anything* at all, I'm always happy to oblige."

Evie's breath caught. "What could I possibly want?" Her voice held a tinge of panic.

I smiled against her skin. "I wouldn't know. I'm many things, but I've never been psychic."

That place in my chest where Evie lived warmed like molten metal.

"I'm fine," she insisted and pulled away, holding two glasses in her hand. Evie's smile was shaky as she turned and hurried to the table.

I hid my smile and started chopping again. "Alright," I said amiably. "The offer's always open. No matter what time of day or night. I'm always ready and willing to offer any services you desire."

A soft choking noise cut off.

I swallowed my laugh and kept chopping.

CHAPTER

THREE

He knew. Godsdammit. He knew I wanted to throw him down and do terrible things to his person, and the bastard was teasing me about it. I closed my eyes and tried to concentrate on the window display I was putting together, but I was hard-pressed to think about anything but the feel of his lips against my neck.

What was wrong with me? I'd consummated my relationship with Caelan when I was so drunk on power, I probably would have humped a tree stump if it gave me a come-hither look. But Rowan had done absolutely nothing but exist. He'd been careful with me and never initiated anything too intimate, his touch enough to keep me balanced. Rowan understood touch starvation far better than Caelan had. When Caelan touched me, it was about desire. When Rowan touched me...

I swallowed hard. When he touched me, I felt like no matter what happened, I'd find safety with him.

Why shouldn't you jump his bones? came that dark little voice inside my head that usually only came out in the deep dark night. But today it was early. Way too early. And that was a problem.

I'd taken dinner in my room tonight, refusing Rowan's invite to eat together for fear I'd jump on him like a ravenous beast.

"Get it together," I muttered. I was not a teenage boy for crying out loud. I was a full-grown woman in total control of her emotions. Acting like an ovulating madwoman was a fast way to send everything on its ear.

Plus, there was a consequence to us moving farther than touching, and Rowan had warned me about it after our meeting with the Lords. If we consummated our relationship, there was a very good chance the mating bond would finalize. We would be linked forever.

I wasn't totally against the possibility, but I wasn't all for it either. Not long ago, I'd promised myself to Caelan, and this felt like a betrayal. Even if he had treated me with cruelty toward the end.

But this...whatever this was, I didn't know how much longer I could hold out against it. I needed a distraction. I thought going to the shop might work, but I'd spent most of my time daydreaming about Rowan's hazel eyes and clever fingers.

"Aaaargh," I groaned, tossing a handful of rose petals up in the air.

A key sounded in the door. Seconds later, a dark head poked around the corner. "This town is as nosy as Joy Springs." Moira grinned and locked the door behind her.

After tossing her purse down, she came over and brought me in for a tight hug. Her cool cheek pressed against mine. "Maybe nosier," she said with a roll of her eyes. "Everyone is *very* interested in Rowan's little Floromancer."

I sighed and slumped onto one of the new chairs. Dad had transported every single thing from the old shop to the new one, but there were certain pieces I couldn't look at without seeing Caelan. The chairs and couch were the first to go, donated to one of Rowan's shifter's young daughters who'd just gotten her first apartment.

Moira and I went to an artisan furniture store and found our new ones within seconds of walking in. The artist, loyal to the bone to Rowan, had all but tried to give them to me, but I insisted on paying. However, the woodworker refused to take full price, even when I tried to argue about it. I ended up paying a fraction of what they were worth, and the guilt remained.

Now, once a week, I put together a fragrant and gorgeous flower arrangement and delivered it to his shop. He tried to return the first one, but when I let a sliver of the Chimera out, he laughed and acknowledged he was beaten.

I figured we'd be square in about twelve months.

To Rowan's consternation, I bought the couch online because I couldn't afford to give away another year's worth of flowers.

We were alone in the shop. Tess and Ash were out apartment hunting, though neither was in a hurry to move from Rowan's Keep. Ash was happy as a clam, and Tess had made another banshee friend none of us had seen yet.

Rowan had already said they could stay permanently if they wanted to, but both of them felt guilty about it. I planned to talk to them soon, but I knew how they felt. Rowan's cottage was amazing, but it was a little small for my plant collection. Eventually, I knew I'd start itching for a bigger space and a spot of land of my own.

Moira made herself a cup of tea and brought me a steaming mug of coffee. She kicked off her boots and curled her feet under her, watching me with those wise dark eyes.

"How are you?"

"Better, but still a remedial student."

Moira snickered. "No luck being a badass, all-powerful Chimera?"

"Hardly. According to Barrett, I have 'adequate' shifting abilities."

Moira cracked a laugh. "What an ass."

"But the rest of my abilities are non-existent. They think it might have to do with my fae blood."

"Good theory," Moira mused. "Allowing your powers to merge is how you learned to control the Chimera in the first place, right?"

I nodded. "Yes, but now I have no idea what to do. Unfortunately, wiggling my nose or snapping my fingers just makes me look stupid."

She sipped her tea. "You'll get it. You always do." Moira's eyes glittered. "Now tell me about Rowan."

If I had something to throw at her, I'd throw it. "What about him?"

Moira grinned. "You like him. A lot. I can tell."

"Yes, but I'm not ready for anything more. Caelan..." I trailed off.

"Fucked you up," Moira said unrepentantly. "Big time." She lifted a slender shoulder in a shrug. "Understandable. But honestly, Evie, he's always been a growling dick."

I blinked at my friend.

She cackled at my expression. "He has, and you know it! Caelan was always pushing you to the brink, encouraging you to do things you weren't sure about. Getting out of your comfort zone isn't always a bad thing if it helps you grow. But Caelan violated your boundaries and pushed you beyond what you were ready for. Even so, he pushed you to be something you were not."

I was speechless. Moira plowed on, her pale hands wrapped around her botanical tea mug. "Then," she added, "he got super pissed off when you surpassed him."

At my furrowed brow, she held up a hand. "Not finished."

I clamped my lips shut.

"At first, he was all, *'Whoa, look at my badass girl. She's the best!'* And then you did your whole thing against the tree. Super hot, by the way, and the flowers in that spot grow all four seasons, no matter the weather. Well done, Evie."

Crimson heat touched my cheeks.

"Even after the tree, he was cool Caelan, but I saw his face that night." Moira leaned forward, a serious expression on her face. "I saw the way he looked when you came out of the tree and burned that fucker to the ground. There was a moment when your back was turned, and you raised your hands and destroyed the thing that had tried to destroy you, and Caelan's expression was terrified. He knew right then that you were the more powerful one, even if he tried to hide it and work through it. Even after knowing you, knowing you would be loyal to him and his people forever, he couldn't deal with it. And that was when he started making you feel like shit about things. Tiny things, a word here and there, an odd look." Moira gave a sharp shake of her head. "And I knew I was hearing the death knell."

Tears swam in my eyes. I opened my mouth to speak and found I couldn't form any words.

Moira's smile was sad. "I'm glad you found your way out. I'm glad you're here. I'm glad Rowan was there to help you pick up the pieces. You don't have to do anything with him that you don't want to do. But don't wait forever. That man is a good one, a really good one, and he would walk away from everything if you demanded it from him. But if you don't want this, if you don't want him, you need to call it soon."

"I think we're fae mates," I blurted, the words escaping before I could hold them back.

Moira's hands shook. She set her tea mug down. "Holy shit," she breathed. "Are you sure? How do you know?"

"I—I'm not sure. And I don't know. I've been feeling this *thing* when he's around. This feral tug toward him, and it's different from that thing in my chest."

"It doesn't feel evil or dark?" Moira's eyes narrowed. "No other sense of magic around it?"

"I've already checked. Multiple times." And I had. "The magic is coming from inside me. And it wants Rowan. Bad."

Moira pressed her lips together. "My gods, Evie. You're horny for Rowan, aren't you?"

"Stooooopppp," I begged.

"Like *horny*, horny. You want to throw that man down and violate him, don't you?"

"Please shut up."

Moira snickered. "Alright. Let's talk this out. Two, let's call them species, are tugging you toward each other. Don't you think that's the biggest sign the universe is ever going to send you?"

"It's more complicated than that." I closed my eyes.

"Oh," Moira breathed. "You feel you're being unfaithful to Caelan."

A silence fell between us. "That's the dumbest fucking thing I've ever heard," Moira said after a moment. "That fucker had his head and other things buried the gods know where in Rachel."

I winced.

"No. You need to hear this. It's been months, Evie. Caelan treated you like shit, was unfaithful, and then mocked you over it." She plowed through my attempts to interrupt her. "And before you say, '*Moira, Lugh tricked him. He wasn't in his right mind,*' we all know he was in his right mind enough to say all the horrible shit he did afterward, right? And we all know

Lugh's type of magic could never force someone to do those same things if they were truly in love with their partners. Caelan had one foot out the door already when Lugh fucked with his head. He might have stayed. In fact, I think he would have because he wanted to be king, but eventually, he would have torn everything you built down and crushed your heart in the process. Rowan is the one who took you from that place and helped you rebuild your life. If you want to go take that delicious hunk of man meat to pound town, you go home right now, flip your hair, and I guarantee that man will go feral."

"Moira," I breathed.

She snorted. "I've been saving that all up for months."

"Obviously. So...you weren't a big fan of Caelan then."

Moira rolled her eyes. "I liked him just fine for a Lord. Hell, I like him better than Soren. But I sensed the moment things changed. Now I think he's a coward and a petty little man for not using his words to end the thing between you before he destroyed anything good you two had."

I had a lot to think about. Moira had always been a blunt kind of friend, but she rarely spoke to me like this. Not with this heat. "You're a good friend," I said softly. "But I'm not going to pound town with Rowan. I'm not ready. If we go that far, the mating bond will probably finalize. I want to be sure. Things are moving too fast."

"Ah," Moira said. "Okay. That makes sense. This time, there are consequences to pound town. Can you do butt stuff?"

A laugh cracked out of me. "Ass."

She grinned and nudged my thigh with her toes. "Just keep it as an option. You'd be surprised at all the undiscovered nerve endings."

"Shut up and finish your tea. I need help putting the window display together."

Moira laughed and winked.

With her, I always knew where I stood. She was the best friend a girl could have.

Even if she was the kind of friend who suggested doing butt stuff.

FOUR

The next morning proved overcast and cooler than normal. I had several things I needed to do to get the shop ready to open, but today was a perfect day to curl up beside the fire and read. Doing that sounded way better than going into the store.

Maybe I could go in and work half the day, then spend the rest of the day rotting on the couch. I shrugged on my heavy cashmere cardigan and took my coffee to the backyard. Squirrels chased each other through the trees, shaking spring blossoms from the limbs, sending them floating down into a shower of fragrant color.

There was no yard here at the cottage, only Rowan's expansive land as far as the eye could see. My claim would remain for as long as it took for the spell to diminish, something Moira and I were working on. When Tess and Moira burst into the Lord's meeting, Moira never got the chance to tell me the origins of the spell, something she found out when she made a brief return to Joy Springs.

Everyone was too distracted with the screaming banshee to worry about where the spell came from, but when we returned to Emberwood, Moira told us she was almost positive the spell came from Joy Springs. Someone there had started the entire thing, more than likely working with one of the many gods and goddesses who enjoyed trying to screw up my life.

We were relatively positive Caelan had nothing to do with it since both he and his land had become infected, but we weren't ruling anything out.

The sound of soft footsteps revealed Rowan coming around the corner, holding his own coffee. His eyes crinkled at the edges.

"You're up early." He took the seat beside me, the scent of pine and wild things following him. Rowan dressed more casually here than when he was with the Lords, preferring jeans and pullover sweaters or athletic wear when he was indoors. His shaggy brown hair was in worse disarray than usual, but his hazel eyes sparkled. This morning, his green pullover was—I reached over and drew the material into my fingers, rubbing them together—a blend of cashmere and silk. Nice.

Rowan chuckled. "Does it please Your Highness?"

"Very much so." I eyed him. "Do they make them for women? I've tried to find the cashmere silk blends and strike out a lot. Thrifting isn't what it used to be."

Rowan shook his head, amusement tipping his lips up. "Even with my new wardrobe of all natural fibers, you still make me feel like an environmental wretch sometimes."

"Every little bit matters. I like the thrill of the hunt. If I really want something and can't find something comparable at the thrift store, I'll purchase new. But things like cashmere and wool are usually plentiful in the secondhand market." I eyed his pullover. "I might make an exception for that, though."

"I'll text you the name of the shop later."

"Thanks." We sipped our coffee in silence for a little while. I liked sitting with him like this. He had a steadiness that was uniquely Rowan. The Lord lived in the moment, especially in the morning. There was nothing out there so stressful that he couldn't sit down and have a cup of coffee. Most mornings, he drank that coffee with me.

"Are you heading into the shop this morning?"

I stretched my legs in front of me and wiggled my sock-clad toes. "I need to, but it's such a wonderful, overcast day that lazing in front of the fire sounds amazing, too."

Rowan grinned. "Bears like to laze, you know."

"I know one bear who's far too attached to that spot in front of his fireplace."

"No regrets," Rowan said. "It's warm and cozy." He wiggled his eyebrows. "You could join me there sometime, if you wanted."

"Hmm. Have you ever tried the spot in the cottage?"

Rowan tilted his head and thought about it. "Can't say I have, but there's no cozy rug in there to lie on."

I snorted. "Says who? You haven't been inside in a while."

His eyebrows lifted. "If there's a cozy rug one grizzly bear can avail himself of, he would be happy to give another fireplace a try."

"Good. How about we meet for lunch here at one?"

"Done. I'll have Hope move some meetings around."

My heart did a little leap. "You don't need to do that. We can always try again another day. I know how busy you must be."

Rowan gave me a quelling look. "When a beautiful woman asks you to try out their rug, you try out their rug." He laughed at my expression and picked up my hand to press a kiss against the back of my palm. "Life is meant to be experienced as it comes. Plans have their place, and work is just work, Evie. If I have the chance to spend my time with you or people I care about, I will always choose them. Besides, the Lords have too many damn meetings anyway, and ninety percent of them are mostly so they can bluster about shit that doesn't matter."

My palm tingled where his lips had touched me. "If you're sure."

"If you're not here at one, I'll break into the cottage and use the rug anyway, so make sure you're here."

I snorted. "It's your cottage. You can come in anytime you want."

He scooted his chair to the side so he could face me, his expression serious. "No. The cottage is on my land, but it is yours for as long as you choose to use it. I will not avail myself of the facilities." His lips twitched. "But I will be here sitting on your porch, so you better be here."

How did he always manage to say all the words I needed to hear? "I will," I said softly.

"Good." He took a sip of his coffee. "Hope needs to go into town this morning and offered to drive you, if you're interested. She's leaving at nine."

My car was here, but Tess and Ash were using it for now. Neither would tell me what happened to theirs, and I had a terrible feeling whatever it was had to do with me. "That would be great. Ash is supposed to be looking at a car this week."

Rowan's jaw tightened. "Have him hold off. He and Tess will be receiving a check in the mail soon for the damages their vehicles sustained during Lugh's reign of terror."

"I knew it," I whispered, guilt flooding me. "Neither one of them would tell me what happened."

Rowan exhaled heavily. "Lugh had nothing to do with it. The check is coming from Caelan's Keep. His shifters got a little overzealous in Rachel's presence."

My chest tightened at the mention of the woman's name. She had a lot to do with what happened to me and Caelan, but so did Lugh. And so did Caelan. And if I really thought hard about things, I had a little bit to do with how things ended, too.

"I'm surprised mine wasn't damaged."

"Yours wasn't downtown. The damage was localized. Either way, that never should have happened. I negotiated what I hope is more than a fair amount." His lips twitched. "They should be able to purchase whatever they want, within reason."

I reached over and took Rowan's hand. "Thank you."

He inclined his head. "Your people are my people now. I'd do the same for anyone."

"Thank you anyway." I sighed and tilted my head up to look at the cloudy sky. "I love the cottage, Rowan, but I was thinking I might need more room soon. Can you put me in touch with a realtor or direct me where to go downtown?"

He was silent for a long moment. "Of course."

"I plan to stay for at least a few more months, but if you haven't noticed, I have an indoor plant problem."

He smiled. "You want a larger space, maybe a screened in porch?"

I nodded. "Maybe I could design something this time. I always wanted to have a place built around my power. Might be nice." A tree growing through the middle of the floor would be cool, but I'd have to ask Dad about the logistics of something like that.

Rowan shifted, stretching his long legs before him. "We have a talented Pack architect living in the dorms. I'm happy to ask him to meet with you."

"Gotta find the land first and figure out a budget. The shop wasn't doing as much business over the last several months after everything happened."

Rowan's face darkened, but he held his tongue. "How about you build on my land?"

I blinked and stared at him. "You've already done so much

for me. As soon as we figure out who's responsible for that spell and get rid of it, I'll turn your land back over. As much as I love being here and nurturing these woods, I need to have a space of my own. Everything I do here affects you and your shifters." A chuckle slipped from my throat. "And you already have several females pregnant. Eventually, they'll stop thanking me."

Rowan shook his head. "Shifters have trouble getting pregnant. Your presence remains a gift to them." A sly grin curled his lips up. "Besides, they all have the ability to curb their urges, they just don't want to."

I snorted. "The Keep is going to be so cute in a year. There are going to be so many cheeks to squish."

"Evie." Rowan leaned forward. "Let's work out a deal. Even if you choose not to accept what is between us, you are good for this place. My shifters love having a Floromancer around, and we've never had one as powerful as you. My land is happy. I am happy. We can come up with a deal where you buy ten or more acres, and I can knock off some of the price if you agree to continue tending the territory once your claim is gone."

"And the mating bond?"

He laid a hand over his heart. "My hope is you accept the bond between us one day. But if you don't, you will have to stop tending the land. You'll keep your piece of property and still live within the boundaries of my territory, but you won't be able to come onto Keep land without the bond starting up again."

"I am not a cruel person, Rowan. And that sounds cruel. Losing your friendship will break my heart, but if I don't accept the bond and choose to live here..." Tears filled my eyes. "I wouldn't do that to you. I can't say whether I'll accept or not. I feel it here, every time you're close and sometimes when you're not." I touched that space in my chest where Rowan lived. "But I'm not ready. We know there's something between us, something good, but what happened before—" I cut myself off and took a moment to gather my thoughts.

"Caelan broke my heart a little at a time until the pieces lay in a mixed-up pile. I still haven't figured out where all the pieces go yet." To soften my words, I reached out and took his hand. "The work is slow, but it's happening."

He scooted his chair closer and touched my cheek. "You're doing the work. That's all that matters." Rowan tapped his knee. "Let's do this," he said suddenly. "Agree to stay in the cottage for six months. I'll see about renovating to add a large, screened porch and another room for your plants." I opened my mouth to argue, but Rowan shook his head.

"The cottage is for Keep use. A screened-in porch is always popular with shifters, and an extra room can be turned into whatever a new tenant might want. Six months, Evie. Let's see where we are then. By then, things should be resolved with the spell, and you will have had time to deal with Caelan."

His offer was a good one. Much could happen in six months, and the extra time would allow me to figure out what was going on with this insane tug I kept feeling toward him. If this was a fae bond or something else...six months was enough time to make a plan.

His thumb traced the back of my palm, sending heat down my spine. Every time he touched me, I wanted to straddle his lap and run my fingers through his hair and—

Rowan's eyebrow rose. "Evie?"

I cleared my throat and pulled away. "Six?" I asked, my voice a little too high-pitched.

A slow grin spread over his face. "Six months."

I could do six months. "Agreed."

He held out his hand. "Shake on it?"

"Are we businessmen making a backroom deal?"

Rowan waited. With a loud sigh, I shook his hand.

"Good. I'll send Harry over tomorrow."

"Harry?"

"The architect. He'll sketch out the new areas for you."

"I'd like to do something for you."

Rowan shook his head and stood. "You breathed life back into the Keep, Evie. You've given my shifters gifts beyond their wildest dreams. The least I can do is make your living quarters a little more suited to your magic." He leaned over and tucked a piece of stray hair behind my ear. "One p.m. You. Me. A warm fireplace and a rug."

With a wink, he turned and walked away.

CHAPTER

FIVE

ROWAN

Six months was the first thing I could think of, and I blurted it out like a desperate teenager begging a girl to go to the prom. I should have asked her for a year. Or five. Or forever.

Half a year was not a long time to convince a woman she should choose you. Our bond was still there, still strong, still incomplete, but something between us had changed.

In my favor, if the change in her scent when I touched her was any indication.

I had to do this slowly but thoroughly. Caelan tap danced all over her boundaries and pushed her when he should have let her choose to come to him. I would not make the same mistake. We were two different men. Two different creatures swam in our veins. I'd woo her thoroughly.

I'd already started. Taking care of her was easy, though I had to be careful how I went about things. Evie dealt in trades, services, or money. She wouldn't accept anything for free or if she thought someone was going too far out of their way, so I couldn't give her anything, even if I really wanted to.

As far as building a house on my land, I would sign

hundreds of acres over if she wanted them. But she wasn't wrong about the bond. If she owned property within my territory and rejected the bond, things would be extremely difficult. We wouldn't be able to see each other anymore, and her touch on my land would slowly fade.

Six months would make or break us.

I had to ensure we didn't break.

AT TWELVE FORTY-FIVE, I was sitting on Evie's front porch, holding a small bag of clothing. Hope had put together an enormous charcuterie board and a plate of sea salt and caramel brownies.

My heart pounded in my chest, and I chuckled at my nerves. This was Evie. I knew her inside and out, but I was still nervous as a kid talking to a pretty girl.

Evie was far more than a pretty girl, and when Hope pulled around and dropped her off, and Evie slid out of the car, my mouth went dry.

She smiled, her entire face lighting up when she spotted me, and I couldn't stand up for a few seconds. The way she looked at me sometimes knocked the wind out of me.

Evie turned and waved to Hope. My Omega sent me a telling wink before pulling away.

Then it was just me and Evie.

Her smile widened when she saw the food. "I'm starving!" She handed me her keys and picked the board and brownies up, peeking inside to see what goodies I'd brought.

With shaking fingers, I unlocked the door and held it open. Evie's scent hit me in the face. Her place smelled like flowers and growing things, and when she breezed past me, she left the scent of peonies and roses in her wake.

Every muscle in my body went taut.

Maybe this was a bad idea.

"Brownies!" Evie squawked. "Who made these?"

I shut the door behind us, her scent enveloping me. "Hope." To my relief, my voice wasn't strangled.

She went straight to the kitchen and brought down two plates. "I'm assuming you want some."

"A bear never turns down food."

She sent me an impish grin and turned away to fix our plates.

I poured us both a glass of the blueberry green tea she kept in her fridge and brought them to the living room. Evie came in with plates piled high. "Give me a minute?" she asked. "I want to get out of my work clothes."

"Of course."

She hurried to the back. I let out a heavy exhale and tried to get my head on straight. We were friends. That was all she was ready for now, no matter what I smelled when she looked at me.

Evie would have to come to me.

She came back out wearing loose joggers and a blue off-shoulder sweater that looked like cashmere. I was still crap at identifying fabrics, but it looked soft, and my fingers itched to touch it to find out if I was right. Her hair was tied up in a high ponytail, and she'd removed her makeup, leaving her face soft and bare.

Holy. Mortal. Hell.

I'd never seen her look this peaceful or innocent, and it was doing terrible things to my emotional state of mind, not to mention my physical state.

Evie set down her e-reader and spotted my still full plate. "You didn't have to wait!"

"My mother would have smacked my hand if I started eating without you."

She smiled and curled up next to me on the couch. Her feet were bare, and her toenails were unpolished. No jewelry that I could see, except the pendant she rarely took off. The sweater's style showed off the damaged tattoo she had yet to fix. The sight of it roused anger within me for how she'd sustained that wound.

If she hadn't put Lugh away in a place he couldn't escape from, I would have put him in the ground. The urge to hunt him down anyway made my eyes glow.

Evie's brows snapped together. "Rowan? Everything alright?"

I offered what I hoped was a reassuring smile. "Yes. Sorry. I was distracted by something else."

Evie nudged me with her bare foot. "Get distracted by all the yummy prosciutto on your plate before I steal it."

I yanked my plate from the table before she could reach over and steal a piece of meat. "Ha. Get your own, you monster."

"You'll let your guard down soon enough," she teased, stuffing a piece of cheese in her mouth. "Mmm. Tell Hope thank you. This is wonderful."

"Her brownies are even better. She has a cult following within the Pack. If anyone smells those, we might have some visitors."

"I shall defend my land from all brownie threats, foreign and domestic," she vowed, her eyes glimmering with amusement.

Her foot still rested against my thigh as she happily munched. Her plants shivered and shifted, the soft rustling sounds inevitably Evie. No plant life could be within her vicinity without being profoundly alive. As her power grew, so did the natural world's reaction to her, and I didn't think she even noticed. Evie was one of the few people completely unaffected by her staggering depth of power. While her training was sporadic, every time she flexed her magical muscles, her power grew substantially. I, like most of my shifters, could smell it on her. Pretty soon, she would rival her father in power, if she didn't already.

But right now, she was merely a hungry woman with a book and a mission to not do a single thing but enjoy herself for the rest of the evening.

And I was a man blessed to spend time with her.

HALF AN HOUR LATER, I was in bear form, lying on my side in front of a crackling fire on a surprisingly soft wool rug. Evie lay curled against my side, her head resting on my front leg. She held her e-reader above her face, concentrating on some novel about a handsome prince and a wicked woman. Her scent tangled in my nose, and the bond between us pulsed with light.

I had a million things to do, none of them more important than this moment. Satisfied and happy, I shut my eyes and drifted into sleep.

The soft thump of something landing against my side awoke me. I had a moment's disorientation before the scent of flowers alerted me to where I was. Evie's home had plunged into night, but the soft glow of incandescent light cast the room in gold. Her soft, even breath told me she was asleep.

With a quick flash of light, I shifted and pulled Evie into my chest. She was out like a light and made no protest. With my other hand, I reached for my bag and slowly eased my joggers on, doing my best not to wake her up. Her silky hair lay scattered over my chest, and her face was peaceful in repose.

Her breath had barely interrupted its rhythm, even with my awkward attempt at dressing, giving me insight into how exhausted she must be. I eyed the couch, large enough for both of us, but I'd have to jostle her quite a bit to move her. A quick glance at the clock over the fireplace told me we'd been asleep for hours. After ten now, it was too late for dinner, and really too late for much of anything other than going back to sleep.

I might be a shifter, but sleeping on the floor all night was not appealing. Extricating myself from Evie took a bit, but soon I was able to stand and scoop her into my arms. She mumbled something, but I held her to my chest and carried her over to the couch, sitting with her in my lap until I could situate us once more.

Her eyes fluttered open once, shining a clear, azure blue. "Rowan?"

"Shhh," I reassured her. "I got you."

"Mmm." Her eyes fluttered shut.

I lay behind her and pulled her closer to my chest, tucking her body against me. My arm wrapped around her waist, and her head rested just under my chin. It didn't take long for me to fall back asleep, nestled against the woman I loved.

CHAPTER
SIX

Soft light streamed from the living room windows. A leanly muscled arm lay slung over my waist, warm breath tickling my neck. A familiar smell washed over me.

Rowan.

How had I gotten from the floor to the couch? I remembered reading my book and how warm and soft Rowan's fur was, and not a thing after that.

But this was the most rested I'd felt in months. I let out a soft sigh and smiled, content to lay here for a while longer.

Dad and Barrett would be back over today, and that wasn't something I was looking forward to, but training was a necessary evil.

Rowan shifted against me as he came awake. His arm tightened, dragging me even closer. I huffed a laugh. Sometimes he was such a bear.

"Morning," I whispered.

Rowan answered by placing a warm kiss behind my ear. Every nerve in my body went taut at the touch. His fingers flexed against my stomach. Another kiss lower on the side of my neck. My neck arched, allowing him better access.

Rowan's breath went ragged. His teeth teased my earlobe, dragging a moan from me. He went still, let out a wicked chuckle, and did it again. Fingers slid over bare skin, dragging up over my abdomen, brushing against the underside of my breast.

That strange magic inside me came roaring to life, screaming *Mine* in my head over and over again. I went pliant in his arms, reaching back to drag my fingers through his hair. Rowan shifted me onto my back and loomed over me, hazel eyes bright with gold. He dipped his head and claimed my lips in a hot open-mouthed kiss. I met the demand, opening my legs to allow him to settle in between them, the evidence of his want pressing against my core. His clever fingers slid downward, past the elastic of my joggers and found—

Rowan let out a violent curse as his hand found only bare skin. "Gods, Evie."

I dragged my hands down the front of his bare chest, that magic still screaming inside my head. Rowan looked at me, swallowed hard, and let his fingers drift lower, sliding into the slickness of my folds.

My lips parted, breath caught.

"Your eyes," he murmured, dipping his head for another kiss. Our tongues tangled, his fingers stroking a rhythm beginning to drive me mad.

"Rowan," I moaned.

He slipped a finger inside, sending my hips bucking. A ragged cry tore from my throat, swallowed by Rowan's lips. He put his mouth on my neck and dragged a kiss down my collarbone, his other hand pushing my thin sweater up.

His hot tongue swept over the peak of my nipple, and those clever fingers continued to work.

Oh gods. "Rowan, I'm—We—" My back arched from the couch, ragged gasps and moans dragging as a crescendo built within me with every clever touch.

"So fucking beautiful," Rowan murmured. His thumb swept over my clitoris, tipping me over the edge. Stars burst behind my eyes. My throat went hoarse as I bucked against his hand. Magic swept over the room, a blast of power that shattered the windows, and still pleasure held me in its wicked grip.

"Evie," Rowan moaned, his body highlighted in power the color of watermelon tourmaline. "Gods."

My hands swept down his broad back and pushed at his joggers. He sucked in a breath as I slid them down.

"Evie."

I pushed at his chest until he was on his back. Looming above him, soaked in power, Rowan's eyes went wide with desire.

"Your eyes, Evie. They're different."

I slid down his body, exploring every scar and lean muscle with my lips. Rowan sucked in a breath as I went lower. "Evie, we don't—"

"Shut up," I snarled.

Rowan let out a bark of hoarse laughter, which quickly turned into a shout when my lips closed over the tip of him. His hands buried in my hair as I tasted him. Desire pooled in my core, even after the release that had rocked me only moments before.

My hand slid around him, reveling in the hard, silky feel of him. All thoughts other than Rowan's pleasure flew out of my head. All my doubt was gone, the only thing to focus on was him. Our eyes met. Rowan's heavy-lidded with pleasure, a ring of molten gold around his irises, and mine casting a strange azure-gold glow over his body.

My hand stroked up his shaft, and my tongue swirled around the silky head.

"Fuck. *Evie.*" He gritted his teeth and arched his neck. A low moan came from his throat as his hips bucked. I worked him, reveling in his pleasure. His scent drowned me, and I sensed the moment he lost control.

A sharp shout ripped from his throat. Claws slid from his fingertips, the sound of fabric tearing as release found him. Magic snapped between us, tightening that bond, but deeper, more ancient magic swirled around us, waiting for that moment when we joined as one.

Even when the sound of his pleasure quieted, and I collapsed against him, I still wanted him. Rowan reached down and dragged me up, holding me against his chest, my head tucked under his chin.

Silence dragged on, the only sounds in the room that of our ragged breath.

"Fuck," he breathed after a few moments. "I—I didn't mean to get carried away."

"Rowan?"

"Mmm?"

"Shut up."

He snorted. "How about this?"

I tilted my head up to look at him.

"How about we do that every single day from now until eternity?"

I chuckled, even as my cheeks burned with embarrassment. "I didn't mean to be quite so forward. My magic rose, and instinct led me."

"I like your instincts."

I lightly smacked him on his chest.

He tilted my chin up. "Seriously, though. You can touch me anywhere, anytime, any way you want to. You can interrupt any meeting, shut the door, and have your way with me. I don't care who I'm speaking to or what I'm working on. Shit. I don't even care if you turn my computer off. Let everyone else know how lucky I am."

I smiled against his chest. "There's something I need to tell you."

Rowan stilled. "Okay?" He didn't sound worried, but what I was about to tell him was a little weird. "Is it about that other magic that keeps reaching out for me?"

I jerked my head up. "You feel it too?"

"How could I not?" His eyes crinkled with a smile. "Whatever it is has a serious crush on me. And your eyes get super weird, especially today."

I groaned. "Are you familiar with fae mating bonds?"

Rowan went very, very still. "Some. They aren't very common."

"I think I'm experiencing one." I cleared my throat. "With you. It's a little disconcerting."

His fingers stroked down my back. "Huh. How about that?"

I peered at him. "You aren't even a little bit freaked out?"

His brow furrowed. "Why would I be? I didn't think double bonds existed, but to have the opportunity to be mated on both sides of my nature is an honor few, if any people, ever experienced." His chest lifted in a sigh. "I'm in love with you, Evie. I have been for a while."

My heart stuttered. I suspected but hearing him say the words brought my world to a screeching halt. He loved me. Without conditions.

"I'm all in. I would never say no to this magic, or whatever it is that calls me to you. I feel it in my chest, but I also feel that strange tug. The magic feels like some sort of compulsion spell drawing us to each other. I can sense this intellect looking at me through your eyes sometimes." He chuckled.

"And every time I sense it, I can smell your desire kick up a few notches."

I squeezed my eyes shut. "Gods."

Rowan clicked his tongue. "Don't be embarrassed. Desire for one's potential mate is the highest compliment. There's a period when the mating bond completes that turns a male into a complete rutting machine."

He laughed at my expression. "If you let this happen between us, don't be surprised if I'm jumping out of corners, reaching for your skirts."

"I don't wear skirts."

"Just keep wearing no underwear in those joggers, and we won't have a problem."

"Rogue," I said with a chuckle.

He brought me in for a tighter hug. "You have training this morning?"

I groaned. "Yes."

He stroked a hand down my hair. "I have a few meetings later on. I'll meet you outside in a few hours if you want."

I nodded. "Sounds good."

Rowan made no move to leave. "Bears have an inherent lazy streak," he mused. "It can be quite problematic."

I pressed a kiss against his chest. "Oh? How lazy?"

His fingers drifted down my back and cupped my rear end. "Never too lazy for that."

My lips curved, but everything we'd just done sank in. I was playing with fire and gods, was it difficult to stop. "Rowan?"

"Hmm?"

"I care about you. Very, very much. I'm not sure what the future holds, but right now, I hope you're in it with me."

He let out a slow breath. "Me too, Evie. Me too."

CHAPTER
SEVEN
ROWAN

I was good for nothing in the back-to-back online meetings I had. Visions of Evie sliding down my body and putting her mouth on me haunted my thoughts so much that Soren snapped at me.

"Rowan! Godsdamn man. Are you alright?"

Ethan smirked at me through the computer screen, though he stayed silent. Caelan's black look almost made me laugh.

Thorvin kept his face blank, but even stoic Ben seemed annoyed.

"I'm fine," I snapped, annoyed that I had to leave Evie to deal with political bullshit. Again. "Momentarily distracted, that's all. What were you saying?"

Soren's lips twitched. "We need to hold another in-person meeting, this time away from Caelan's territory. Ben's territory is available."

We met in the same place ninety percent of the time. Soren was making an unusual request. "Why not Caelan's?"

Ethan's amused expression faded. "There are concerns of dark magic workings swirling around his territory. Caelan will not attend this one." His lips twisted. "An anonymous source sent a message to my assistant."

Caelan's teeth pulled away from his lips in a snarl. "I'm sitting right here, you assholes."

Ethan's fingers tapped on his desk. "Then perhaps you should heed our concerns and allow the Floromancer to help you."

Caelan's furious gaze. "Just like Evie helped Rowan this morning?" His mocking tone made the other Lords tense. We were behind computer screens, none of us in the same room, but I still wanted to rip his throat out just the same. Bears and wolves didn't get along in the wild for one main reason. We were both predators. At best, we coexisted.

Caelan and I had once been good friends. I mourned for that part of our shared past, even knowing we'd never get those days back. He treated someone I loved horribly, forcing me to stand back and watch. While I never directly intervened, I tried to steer him on the right path with her, even knowing she and I might have something if allowed to explore things.

After this morning, it was all but a certainty we were meant for each other. With the revelation of the fae bond...I found myself, for lack of a better word, gobsmacked, I'd been so fucking blessed.

I refused to let him get under my skin. Instead, I allowed a slow, satisfied smile to curve my lips up.

Soren choked on a laugh. "Gods, man. Are you itching for a fight?"

I ignored him and focused on Caelan. "She did help me. Repeatedly." The sounds of her ragged breath and low moans, and the way her back arched when she took her pleasure...gods. I wanted to stalk outside, throw her over my shoulder, and do it again and again and again, until she was sated and weak.

Ethan closed his eyes. Ben scrubbed a hand over his face and sighed.

"You should see my land, Caelan." I closed my eyes and inhaled. "It's stunning. When she's happy, everything around her blossoms. My shifters, my personal lands, my entire territory." I opened my eyes and let a little gold flow in. "Me."

Claws slipped from Caelan's fingers. He moved them off the desk into his lap, but he couldn't hide the gold rising in his eyes. Satisfaction and loathing warred within me. Caelan would come for me one day.

I would be ready.

Ethan cleared his throat, a warning look in his eyes. "We'll meet four days from now. Evie is due on Thorvin's land soon. Once the results of that experiment are apparent, we'll discuss what comes next. Caelan, you are always welcome to attend our meetings, provided you are free of any *extra* influence."

Caelan turned his attention to Ethan. "You might be taken in by the Floromancer's supposedly gentle nature, but she is the fae queen. Her people have been trying to exert their influence on our lands for years now, and even if she's not complicit, they are using her to steal our territory right out from under our noses. Mark my words. She will be our downfall." His golden gaze met mine. "You are the most vulnerable. Allowing her to claim a large part of your territory leaves you vulnerable. She can rip it right out from under you and what would you do?"

I studied him, noting the slump in his posture and the exhaustion etching lines around his eyes. Even through a screen, I could see Caelan was having a difficult time. "She could do that to any of us at any time, or have you forgotten Donovan and the subsequent lesson she taught Dario when he tried to usurp her rightfully claimed territory? If you think that way, then none of us is safe."

"Then you welcome our floral overlords?" Ethan asked dryly.

Soren barked a laugh.

I held my hands out. "I'm merely pointing out what Evie could do if she had the proper motivation. She has sworn she will release our territory once the magical threat is passed. I, for one, believe her."

"Because she's your mate," Ben growled.

"We are not formally mated," I pointed out. "Things are going in that direction, but I will not force Evie into anything she's not ready for." A pointed blow at Caelan. "If she chooses not to accept me, we've already agreed she will return the land and refrain from additional Floromancy within Keep grounds."

Ben's brow furrowed. "You'd allow your mate to walk away from you?"

"I don't *allow* Evie to do anything. She's her own person. We all know how the bond works. I choose to believe she will accept me, but she is dealing with the unfortunate after-effects and trauma that comes from prior relationships."

Caelan let out a derisive snort. "And yet, she's fucking you."

I smiled. "You see my point," I said mildly before turning to Caelan. "I've already promised to take you to task for speaking about Evie that way. This is your last warning."

Caelan's smile was full of teeth. "Any time you want to go, brother. I'm ready."

"I stopped calling you brother the day you abused a woman whose only crime was loving you too much."

Silence fell like a stone. "Send me the meeting details," I snapped. "Other than that, I hope to hear from no one for the next five days."

I cut off the call and leaned back in my chair, willing my breath to steady before I went out to see Evie. She'd sense my anger, especially now. While our bond wasn't complete, I could now sense her exertion outside, as well as her annoyance. No doubt she could sense my fury.

I closed my eyes and took a few deep breaths. Caelan and I would come to blows one day. I had no doubt, but it would not be today.

Once I could focus without wanting to smash my fist into something, I rose and went outside.

EIGHT

I collapsed in a puddle of sweat. "Whyyyyyyy?"

Dad snorted and sat beside me. "You're thinking too hard."

I glared at him. "Honestly, that should be a boon these days because most people don't think. And here I am thinking too hard and being punished for it."

"Magic is will, not thought."

"I'm going to punch you in the kidney." I sighed. "But I'm too tired right now. I'll punch you tomorrow."

"Thoughts are polluted," Dad continued. "I'm hungry. I'm thirsty. Why does my sock feel weird? My couch needs new throw pillows. I need to work out more. I forgot my water."

"Are you a frazzled Mom?" I asked. "Your internal monologue is weird."

He sighed with barely concealed impatience. "It's an example of all the thoughts running through someone's head on a daily basis."

"Will, on the other hand, is demand. You're in one place now. You demand to be somewhere else. The magic responds. Boom. You're here, then you're there. You must clear your mind of the pollution and ensure only your will responds. Once you master that, you will find your fae magic, outside of your Floromancy, much easier to command. You've already conquered the natural world. Even now, the grass and flora bend to you. Fear prevents you from mastering the other."

"Can I not master anything for a bit?" I begged, spitting out a piece of grass.

Barrett was sitting against a tree texting something on his phone. "You don't have much time. The swans have disappeared, and with them all our leads are gone." He lifted his gaze. "It's not a stretch to think they're amassing their forces to come after you."

A shiver rolled down my spine. I'd told Moira some time ago I planned to kill them all if they came after me. Time had not mellowed that thought. Reaching me at Rowan's Keep was all but impossible unless they had outside help.

I felt rather than heard Rowan coming toward me. Heat colored my cheeks, making my dad raise an eyebrow. His lips twitched, but he held his tongue. Thank the gods for small favors.

"If the swans set foot on my lands, it's a declaration of war." Rowan took one look at my dirty face and grass-stained clothes and frowned.

He and Dad had a brief stare down before Rowan glanced at Barrett. The Chimera hadn't moved from his place against the tree and was giving Rowan a curious look. Then his gaze went to me before he inhaled a soft gasp.

"Oh," he said thoughtfully. "Things make a lot more sense now."

Rowan straightened. "Do we have a problem?"

Barrett snorted and waved a nonchalant hand. "Not even a little bit. I wish you both good luck."

I rolled to a seated position. "You couldn't sense anything before?"

Barrett chewed on the side of his lip, his eyes sparkling with amusement. He cleared his throat uncomfortably. "Contact of a certain kind sometimes strengthens bonds in our kind." He coughed to try to keep from laughing.

My face went crimson.

Barrett grinned. "I see it is the same for shifters and possibly fae."

"Gods," I groaned and covered my face.

Rowan let out a wicked chuckle. "You can assume recent contact adds a certain flair to all shifter senses." He winked at me.

"Rowan. Shut. Up."

He plopped down next to me and ruffled my hair. "You can't hide much when it comes to a mating bond, Evie."

"I don't want to hide it, maybe just not talk about—" I waved my hand around. "The other stuff."

Rowan leaned in and whispered in my ear, so low Barrett couldn't have caught it. "We don't have to talk about it as long as we do it again. And again. And again. For practice." His teeth caught my earlobe, sending liquid heat through my entire body.

Dad jerked his head at Barrett. "We're done for the day."

The Chimera and my dad walked away, both chuckling under their breath.

When they were out of sight, I launched myself at Rowan, tackling him to the ground. He caught me by the hips, delighted laughter shaking his chest.

"Rowan!" I loomed above him, my annoyance draining at the happy look in his eyes. "Damn you," I grumbled.

A second later, I was kissing him, and he was kissing me back. His hands tightened on my hips, and things below the belt tightened, and gods help me, I was in *so* much trouble.

I pulled away, breathless. "What is happening to me?"

The amusement faded from his face. He rolled me over, gently pinning me beneath him. "My hope is you're falling hopelessly in love with me, just like I am with you." He kissed my throat. "And once that happens, my hope is that we can both have our pants off at the same time."

A surprised laugh broke from me. He grinned and kissed me again. I ran my fingers through his thick hair tugging the strands gently. Rowan's eyes went golden.

"Do that again," he whispered against my skin.

"Oh," I murmured. "You like this?" I tugged a little harder. Rowan bit down on my collarbone, gently but hard enough to leave a slight impression.

"*Oh*," I breathed in an entirely different way.

He lifted his head, curiosity in his glowing eyes. "No one has taught you where the edge of pain ends, pleasure begins?"

I blinked up at him.

"Hmm." One of his eyebrows went up before a dark chuckle escaped him. "You and I are going to have so much fun." He kissed me once more and rolled off.

I wanted to pull him on top of me again and ask him to show me. As if sensing my thoughts, Rowan's smile became edged. He held a hand out to help me up.

"I want you to stay with me tonight."

My throat went dry. "In the Keep?"

"Or in your cottage. Either way, I want to wake up with you in the morning."

"Rowan." I wanted to. So badly. But we obviously were having a hard time keeping our hands off each other.

"I will never ask you for more than you're willing to give. But I enjoyed sleeping with you, and I want to do it again. If we decide to fool around—" His eyes sparkled. "I will let you lead."

He bent his head and whispered in my ear. "I'll even let you tie me to the bed, so my hands won't wander."

My breath caught.

"Or, if you're concerned about your hands wandering, maybe you're the one who should be secured."

"Gods," I choked. "*Rowan*."

He laughed and tugged me toward the Keep. "Come. Lunch awaits. Your mother called me earlier and requested entrance to the Keep a few days from now."

"Wow. Mom is being nice." Cliona could walk right through Rowan's wards if she chose. Sometimes she did, but she usually tried to play by the rules.

"I am not Caelan." There was an edge to his voice that made me still.

"Did something happen?"

He pulled my hand to his lips and pressed a kiss to my wrist. "Our meetings together rarely go well. Nothing to worry about. Posturing is inevitable with the Lords."

He held the door open for me. Lunch had already been spread out on the table. Comfort and routine were doing much to heal my body and soul.

With a smile at Rowan, I took a seat and dug in.

Mom and Moira showed up at the door a few nights later grinning like thieves after a successful mission.

I frowned. "Do I need to worry about this?"

Moira's expression grew innocent. Too innocent. "Worry about what?"

Mom held up a bottle of booze and a large thermal bag. "I brought taco fixings!"

Both women breezed in. Moira dropped a kiss on my cheek and followed Mom to the kitchen. When Mom opened the bag and started pulling things out, I inspected the meat very thoroughly after her joke about fae eating people for dinner.

She clicked her tongue. "Honestly, Evie. It's ground beef. The other one is grilled chicken."

Moira dug through the cabinets until she found a cocktail shaker, then started mixing an alarming number of ingredients inside.

"Just checking," I said. "One can never be too sure."

"Plus," Mom added, an evil glint in her eyes, "you don't use that kind of meat for tacos. That's more steak night fare."

Moira snickered.

"I'm not sure when to take you seriously anymore."

"Just get the sour cream out of the fridge, will you?" Mom rolled her eyes and unpacked the rest of the bag. She'd even remembered to bring cilantro.

Once we fixed our plates, Moira brought over three drinks and set them on the coffee table. I clicked on the fireplace and turned on some music. We didn't speak all that much until we finished.

"What is this?" I asked Moira, swirling the pink drink around in my glass.

"Some kind of raspberry mixed drink. I can't remember the name. Delicious, right?"

It really was.

Mom took a sip. "I'll have that recipe. You have my number."

"I'll text you."

I watched Mom and Moira with trepidation. "Are you two hanging out without me?"

Moira laid a hand over her chest. "Evie! I would never."

Mom grinned. "You've been a little busy, darling, trying to save the world and whatnot."

"I can't believe it. Mom and my bestie going on girl's nights without me." But I wasn't mad. How could I be upset with either of them? Everything I thought I knew about Mom had been wrong, and Moira deserved all the friends she could make. She'd spent so long taking care of all of us and working at the shop that her social life had suffered, big time. If she and Mom wanted to hang out, who was I to begrudge them? For years, Moira was terrified of her. If she liked Mom and enjoyed hanging out with her, I'd never get upset by any time they spent together.

Moira leaned over and put her head on my shoulder for a moment. "Cliona is helping me with the extra magic from that night."

My stomach lurched with guilt. The extra magic happened at Caelan's Keep when Rhona, another female Chimera, tried to kill me. Magic had been flying everywhere, and Moira had been exposed more than anyone else. The power had manifested in curious and sometimes disturbing ways, the latest when she pulled a god from the fae lands into ours, though now we suspected Lugh had taken advantage and helped that along some.

As messed up as that time was, Moira's magic snafu had resulted in me finding out exactly what kind of person Caelan was and spearheaded our subsequent move here. One night had a serious butterfly effect on all of our lives, though my spirit was more settled than it had been in months.

"How's it going? Can you get rid of the excess?"

Mom and Moira exchanged a glance. "No," Mom said slowly. "Things aren't quite that simple."

When were they ever?

"Much like you, Moira possesses unique DNA." Mom looked like she wanted to say more but held her tongue. "Exposure to our magic manifested within her body in curious ways. Since she can't rid herself of the power, she has to learn how to handle it to the best of her abilities. And she's doing well."

"No more pulling gods from the aether," Moira said with a wince.

Mom snorted. "Yes, well, Lugh had a lot to do with that one. Most of us aren't looking for opportunities to screw up some lives."

"I'd like to meet those people," I muttered.

Moira poured me another drink. "Me too, sister."

Mom shook her glass at Moira. Once we were all refilled, she kicked off her shoes and studied me. Mom and I looked a lot alike, so it was almost like staring into a mirror. "Tell me, darling, what is going on with the delectable Lord I scent all over your home?"

Moira choked on her drink.

Mom grinned. "The bond between you is brighter. Have you decided to accept?"

I tipped up the drink and downed it in one go. Moira's eyebrows rose, but she was a great friend because she refilled me without a word.

"No," I said slowly. "I haven't decided one way or another. But I like him. A lot."

Moira got it. "But you liked Caelan too, and look what happened."

I nodded. "They're not the same. Not even close. But Rowan is a Lord. I'm hesitant to take that step because this one is far more serious. Caelan and I weren't mates. Now I know we were never going to be. This feels much more serious."

Mom nodded. "You're right. But haven't you considered what a mate is?"

I stared at her. "Um. Someone you're tied to for eternity?"

Mom gave me a look and downed her drink. Moira let out a soft laugh and poured her another, then got up to make another pitcher full. My head was already feeling a little buzzy. Mom had brought the good stuff.

"Bring the extra tacos over!" Mom called. "We're going to need them."

"Ooh! There's a tin of brownies by the coffee pot!" I added.

"Hell yeah," Moira said.

While she was in the kitchen, Mom leaned forward. "Your definition of a mate is simplistic. While you are 'tied to them'," she made insulting finger quotes, "it's not a punishment. You want to be with them. A mate is not a boyfriend or a fiancé, or even a husband. A mate is the piece you've been missing your entire life. The universe, if you will, has elected to give you a special gift in living form. This gift is meant to complement you in all the best ways, support you in your endeavors, love you without conditions, and, to steal a phrase from the humans, rock your world in the best ways."

Moira brought over a fresh pitcher of drinks and all the taco stuff. We all dug in because no one could ever have enough tacos.

"Caelan basically steamrolled you to get you to date him, but who was there the entire time gently guiding you and supporting you? There was no bond between you until recently. You finally let go enough to trust him, and the universe responded. Rowan is not Caelan," Mom continued. "He is the furthest thing from that man you can get."

"But am I a gift to him?"

Moira's drink sloshed over the side of the rim. "Shit." She mopped it up while also gawking at me. "Are you serious?"

Stupid magical booze. Tears burned the back of my eyes. "I'm a mess," I admitted. "Rowan is kind and steady and..."

"So fucking hot?" Moira added helpfully.

"Smoking," Mom agreed, kissing three of her fingers like a

lusty Italian lady. "Those pullovers he wears? Gods!" She fanned herself. "What is going on under those?!"

"Mom!" I knew exactly what was under those and she was not wrong, but Mom should not be lusting after...

Her knowing grin made me snort.

"Caelan was handsome, too."

"Sure," Moira agreed. "All the Lords are. But being handsome is a matter of genetics. Anyone has the potential to be handsome. Being hot is an entirely different matter. Rowan is on another level. He's smart, strategic, funny, wise, and the way he looks at you..." Moira let out a low whistle. "He's the kind of guy that would bend you over a fence and make you forget your name."

I burst out laughing.

Her cheeks had turned pink from all the laughter and booze. "I'm serious. Caelan would be all broody and shit about it and probably make you work for it. Rowan would have your skirt up in five seconds if you gave him a come-hither glance. Bears see honey and go for it. Rowan is like a sexy cartoon bear, and he is out for *your* honey, Evie. No one else's."

Mom was laughing so hard she had to hold her stomach.

I confessed to what we'd done earlier, keeping it PG-ish because Mom was there. Some people might be weird about talking about certain things in front of their mothers, but I didn't know her as a child, not really. She hadn't been there. Mom was fae and sexuality was second nature to them. They were not like humans.

"That's why the bond seemed stronger." Mom wiggled a finger at me. "You're playing with fire, darling. If you don't want to accept the bond, you might want to stop with the hanky-panky."

"I want to accept it," I admitted. "But everything feels too soon. I was about to marry Caelan only a few months before."

Moira reached for my hand. "In other circumstances, I would agree with you. But what you have with Rowan is not a boyfriend/girlfriend relationship. The man is your literal mate. No one controls when that happens. Very few people get to experience this." Her eyes softened. "Of all the people I've known in my life, you deserve this the most. Who gives a shit what anyone thinks? If you want to accept the bond, you should."

"There's one more thing." Moira poured me another drink. Maybe I'd go and get some of those drops from Rowan later. From the fuzziness in my head, I'd need them.

Mom and Moira leaned forward.

"Other magic is tugging at me. I think it's a fae bond."

Mom sucked in a breath, her azure eyes wide. "Are you sure?"

"Well, it's never happened before, so I can't say with complete certainty, but being around him makes me feral." I'd always been drawn to Rowan because he put me at ease. But now, I wanted to claw his clothes off every time I saw him.

Mom slowly nodded. "I cannot say with any certainty because I've never experienced a bond with another, not a mating bond, anyway. But I know a few who've been lucky enough to experience one. When the bond is forming, there is an overwhelming draw to the other party. I believe it takes a while for the male to feel the tug. If Rowan already feels the shifter bond, it's possible he won't notice the other, if that's what this is." Mom frowned. "Would you mind if I looked?"

I'd never allow Mom to use magic on me because I was afraid of her. Things had changed, but the thought still made the abandoned child rear up.

She blinked and leaned back. "Apologies, Evie. I should not have asked." Mom looked down at her lap. "There will always be wounds and jagged edges between us."

Her hurt was palpable.

I reached for Mom's hand. "No. I'm sorry. I—" A heavy sigh escaped me. "The past is difficult to escape, and we still have a lot of work to do. Please. Look. I'd like to know what you see."

Mom glanced at Moira for some reason, and what she saw there must have reassured her because she scooted her chair closer and placed her hand on my cheek. She closed her eyes, and a gentle, cool magic swept through my body. Mom's magic reminded me of Tess's, but I felt no fear as she looked within me. She knew many of my secrets, and I had nothing I felt the need to hide.

When she pulled away and the last of her magic slipped from my body, Mom opened her eyes and gave me a wobbly smile. "You're right," she said quietly. "A fae bond builds within you as well as the shifter bond." A slight furrow formed between her brows. "They've melded together in the center. I'm not sure what that means yet, but both are strong and pure."

She took both my hands. "You are on the brink of something so pure and beautiful, Evangeline. Do not let the wounds you've been dealt prevent you from opening yourself to what the universe believes you deserve."

My lower lip trembled. Moira's cell beeped, ruining the moment. She winced and pulled out her phone, her mouth pursing as she read the text.

"Everything okay?" Mom asked.

"Sirena is asking to see us."

"The gelato lady?" I asked in confusion.

Moira gave me a look. "We both know Sirena is a hell of a lot more than just a gelato lady."

"She has your number?" I was having trouble catching up.

"Duh," Moira said lightly. "How else would I know what the gelato specials are? She refuses to keep her social media updated."

"And yet, she texts you?"

Moira waved a dismissive hand. "If only you knew how much money I have in my emergency gelato fund."

"What does she want?" Mom, coming in with the real questions.

"She has information for us and won't give it to us over the phone."

"Could it be a trap?" Mom downed another drink, and Moira, on autopilot now, picked up the pitcher and refilled our glasses.

I was pleasantly buzzed, just about to tip over into full on drunk if I had much more. "Everything is a trap," I said glumly.

"But if it's not, and she can lead us to whoever's doing this," Moira mused. "That'd be worth the potential of danger, right?"

"What if we run into Caelan?" The thought made me shudder.

"He won't recognize you," Mom said. "Unless you get too close. I'll put glamours on all of us."

Moira refilled her own drink. "I want to be blonde."

"Ooh. I'll be a redhead," I volunteered.

"Maybe I'll go as one of the swans and see what happens," Mom mused.

I gasped and pointed at her. "Genius. See if she has any besties that want to discuss mass murder and kidnappings."

Moira snorted. "Yes, as one does during natural conversation."

"What do you think?" Cliona asked. "Should we go? I'm happy to transport us. We can check on Evie's land, see what the horny gelato maker wants, and stop by and get some of that delicious soup Marnie makes."

I eyed her. "You know who Marnie is?"

"I care about the woman's soup more than the woman,"

Mom said. "Witches have never been high on my trust list. They've always got something brewing."

We fell silent. Moira was the first to groan. "Is that why gods never tell jokes? Because they're terrible at it? Gods, woman."

"Mom." I rolled my eyes. "You have to know how bad that was."

Cliona's eyes twinkled. "Let's take a trip. You got a thermos, Evie? A big one? Moira will mix up more drinks for us."

Moira stared down at her empty glass like she was surprised she held anything. "Um. Sure. But I'm feeling pretty buzzed. Should we slow down?"

Mom snorted. "I've got drops in my purse. No need to worry about hangovers."

Moira frowned. "I'm not worried about tomorrow. Not too much anyway. I'm worried about us going to a hostile area after we've had—" She unsuccessfully tried to count on her fingers and gave up. "Many drinks."

"What's the worst that could happen?" Mom said.

Had she met me?

NINE

I felt the second Evie left the territory. My fork clattered to the ground, and I lurched from my seat. Hope and Declan stared at me as I dashed outside and ran the short distance to Evie's cottage. When my knocks on the door went unanswered, I let myself in using the key and did a quick sweep to make sure she wasn't home.

An epic taco disaster lay spread over her coffee table, and the telltale smell of Cliona's famous booze wafted from the table. I also smelled Moira's presence.

My lips twitched. What had they gotten into?

Declan and Hope knocked and came inside. They scented the same thing I did, but Declan laughed out loud. "Where do you think they went?"

"With Cliona yanking them around the world? Could be anywhere." I wasn't worried. The bond between us lay content and silent. We were far enough along that I'd probably feel something if she got into trouble. The more worrisome part was, depending on where they were, I might be too far away to assist.

I pointed to the bottle on the table. "If Cliona ever offers you any, make sure you don't have any plans for the next several hours."

Declan picked up the bottle and sniffed, jerking his head away a second later. "Gods, man. What the hell is in this stuff?"

"No idea, but it's powerful." Cliona's booze was fast becoming legendary in shifter circles.

"From the look of things, your lady and her dubious entourage drank enough for a spring break frat party." Hope's eyes danced with amusement. "This is good for her, Rowan. She's beginning to live again."

Declan agreed. "She came here looking like death warmed over." He clapped a hand on my shoulder. "You and your lands have put a spark back in her eyes. Try not to fret. If anything happens, we'll find her."

They were right, but I still couldn't help the frisson of worry winding through my gut. If she were here and close, I could protect her. If she were on my land, every one of my people would rise to defend her. I closed my eyes and let those thoughts drift away. She was a goddess, for crying out loud. And a Chimera and a powerful Floromancer. Why was I beating my chest like a Neanderthal when she could very well defend herself?

"There you go," Hope said with a smile when I opened my eyes. "You were about to take the misogynist path for a moment. I saw it in your eyes."

Declan barked a laugh. I sighed and ran a hand over my face. "She's my mate, man. I want to wrap her in bubble wrap and keep her by my side all the time."

Hope's smile was soft. "It's fine to think that way, as long as you realize Evie is four times as powerful as you are and would kick your ass if you tried."

A rueful sigh escaped me. I rubbed that spot in my chest and sank onto the couch. "Yeah. But she's still Evie. The world has hurt her too much."

Hope sat beside me and nudged me with her shoulder. "She's healing, Rowan. It's a process."

I looked at her and saw the woman I always knew she could be. Hope was attacked years ago and left with physical evidence of the attack that had shattered her self-confidence. When Evie claimed my land, every single shifter in the territory had received an impromptu healing, including Hope. The stubborn scars that had come to define her were wiped away in an instant. Once they were gone and Hope no longer saw that defeated woman in the mirror, things had changed for her too.

I let out a shuddering breath. "I know. I'm sorry."

Hope's laugh was soft. "Never apologize for worrying about someone you love. Evie is probably out there having the time of her life. She'll be home soon. And you have her phone number. Text her if you get worried. But not now. Give her some time. She's with her mom and Moira. She's safe."

Having a mate was not for the faint of heart, that was for sure.

TEN

Cliona handed Moira something that looked suspiciously like a blunt.

"Mom," I hissed. "What the hell is that?"

"Something Hazel and I have been working on in our spare time."

Moira took it and lifted it to her nose to smell. Her eyes lit up. "You naughty little minxes. Is this weed?"

"What the fuck?" I whispered. We sat in the town square watching people walk by. On the surface, nothing in Joy Springs had changed. But there was a taut tension in the atmosphere now. Little laughter rang in the town square and things weren't as busy as they normally were.

"You can't light up here," Moira said. "Texas is weird about drugs and basically anything fun." She tucked the handmade cigarette into her pocket. "But when we get to Evie's, game on."

Despite where I'd grown up, I'd never smoked weed or done any form of drugs, mostly because they didn't work on a paranormal's metabolism. But if that thing was anything like the booze coursing through my system giving everything a light haze, we were all in for it once the stuff went to market.

"I brought half a dozen," Mom said.

Moira cackled. "Your mom is so cool."

"You both need a handler," I muttered, but I couldn't stop the laugh bubbling from me.

"How long are we going to sit here?" Moira asked.

"Long enough to see if we're being set up," Mom said.

She'd glamoured us within an inch of our lives. Mom had gone for a sophisticated silver-haired look. She'd shrunk her height down several inches and turned her long flowing hair into a sleek, silver bob. Her eyes were now a pale blue peeking out behind dark rimmed glasses.

Moira was blonde and willowy with pale amber eyes, and I was a red-haired, curvy vixen. We needed to do this more often. Playing magical dress up was *fun*.

Sirena's gelato stand was several feet away, far enough away where she wouldn't catch our scent and give us away. Mom could put up a shield, but that might make people suspicious, wondering what we were trying to hide.

Caelan's scent was nowhere to be found, and there was no sign of any shifters. Fortuitous for us. Their noses were too sensitive to miss our presence. Getting kicked out of Caelan's territory meant any shifters we ran into would become immediately hostile. Anger rose in me, and it took a moment for me to calm down.

Moira reached over and touched my knee. She'd always been sensitive to my moods. Vampire senses or some other inherent magic she refused to talk about. "He's not here," she assured me. "I don't think he's been to town for a while."

Interesting. Caelan was normally very involved in the goings on around town.

Mom sat up straight. "Sirena's line is gone. We can approach if we hurry."

Moira and I followed Mom over to the gelato truck. Sirena's

eyebrows rose when she spotted us, and when we got close enough, she burst out laughing. "Nice glamour," she said quietly, leaning out the window of her truck.

Sirena was gorgeous and she knew it. The siren had night black hair and vivid sea foam green eyes glimmering with a keen intellect. With a body that could stop traffic, she possessed her own dangerous brand of magic. Topped with her stunning beauty, she could be a dangerous foe.

None of us wanted to tangle with her. I think it helped that the gelato she made and sold from her food truck was as close to magical as something inert could be.

"Moira always wanted to be blonde, but it's not going quite the way she thought it would," I said.

Moira patted her hair. "Not one single person has approached me and asked me to have fun."

Mom rolled her eyes. "Can you meet now, witch? Every second we spend exposed leads us closer to discovery. We cannot stay long."

Mom's words would have sounded sharp and cool if she hadn't been wearing a grin and swaying back and forth on her feet.

Sirena's eyes narrowed. "Cliona! Are you...tipsy?"

Mom's eyes widened comically. "No!"

The siren slid a narrow-eyed look our way. Moira and I stayed silent.

"What's in that thermos?"

"Coffee," Moira blurted.

Sirena's lips twitched. She produced a coffee mug from thin air and held it out the window. "Mind sharing?"

Mom swore under her breath. "Fine, you aggravating witch. We'll share as long as you tell us what we need to know." She gestured for Moira to pour some in Sirena's mug.

Moira barely poured her any.

Sirena's brows lifted. "Meet me in an hour on Evie's land. You'll have to open a door to let me in."

"A temporary door," I said. "One-time only, and you'll be under full guest rights. No funny business, Sirena. I'm too tired to deal with fae shenanigans tonight." My buzz was wearing off, and that was annoying.

Sirena's eyes flashed. "Fine. It won't take long, but I can't be seen with you. One hour. I'll come in on the back side."

"Watch for shifters. They've been testing the wards for weeks now." I could feel them pinging in the middle of the night and early morning hours. Not every day and not all of the time, but enough to be annoying. Dad had gone over to shore up the wards and had assured me none but the most powerful of mages would be able to shatter them, and the last time they had a mage that powerful, Arthur was king.

If I'd ever felt confident in anything, it was that statement. So far so good. The wards were holding well with no weak spots, and Caelan could not access my land no matter how hard he and his people tried.

But Sirena asking to enter was...odd.

Once we ordered gelato and wandered away from the food truck, we walked through the town square, careful to avoid getting too close to anyone. Twenty minutes before Sirena was due, Mom motioned for us to enter the forest through a concealed path.

By then, almost everyone had gone home, and ninety percent of the shops were shut down, leaving us free from nosy small-town gossips.

With a final check to ensure we were alone, Mom gestured for us to grab hands. "We'll pop right into the backyard."

A tingle of magic over our skin and we stood close to the back porch. My land hummed in my senses, joyous at my presence.

I touched my fingers to the ground and sent a soft glimmer of magic into the soil. "I promise I'll tend to you in a bit."

I straightened and wiped my fingers on my pants. Mom walked closer to the fence and closed her eyes. "Two shifters prowling the backside of the property. They've sensed nothing amiss. Might be better if we went inside."

Moira pulled out her key and opened the back door. We tiptoed inside, and I went through the house ensuring all the blinds were down. Dad had left the lamps in the living room on. The soft warm glow cast a comforting golden haze over the living room and kitchen area.

But the air inside was a little stale. Frowning, I went over to the kitchen and cracked open a window, then to the living room and opened two more.

"I'll close them before we leave." The place was empty of almost everything, but a few chairs, an old coffee table and some mugs left over in the cabinet. Dad had transported most of my things to Rowan's, leaving only necessary things I might need if I ever had to come back. I walked through the rest of the house to check on everything and noticed nothing amiss.

I'd loved this house for so long, and being back here made my chest ache. I thought I'd finally found a real home, somewhere I could plant true roots and live out my days.

Funny how things could change in a heartbeat.

Caelan's scent lingered in the bedroom and living room, a faint tinge of his presence left behind, reminding me of better days. He wasn't a bad person or a bad Lord, though he'd certainly felt like one when I'd been in the thick of things. Everyone, given the proper fuel, could lean toward cruelty, and I, through no fault of my own, had been that fuel for him.

Seeing me opened the wounds of his own lack of self-confidence, his worry I'd somehow usurp him and steal what he'd gain or won. Instead of seeing me as a partner, he started seeing me as an obstacle. Once that happened, everything about me became flawed.

I was no longer angry about what happened. How could I be? None of it was my fault. Not my genetics, or my power, or my inheritance. Mostly, I felt a deep sense of exhaustion and disappointment, though the second was slowly disappearing under Rowan's careful ministrations.

The disappointment wasn't over losing Caelan, more that I'd finally opened my heart again only to have it crushed under the weight of another's insecurities, and that it had so effectively ended my way of life.

The possibility of something better, cleaner, purer beckoned to me if only I was brave enough to allow it to blossom.

A light hand landed on my shoulder, shaking me from my thoughts.

"It's only a house," Moira said quietly. "You'll make more memories elsewhere. Better memories."

I smiled at Moira. "Rowan asked me to build on his land."

Her eyes were dark and solemn. "Oh Evie. What if you don't accept the bond?"

"He will grant me the land, but I cannot step onto Keep land again. Things will become difficult for us. The friendship we have will end."

Moira nodded. "Don't build at all for a while. Give it some time."

"We agreed on six months."

"Wise. By then, your heart and mind will be your own again and no longer tangled in the what ifs."

"I don't miss him," I said. "Only what could have been." My fingers ran over the burnished wood doors as we walked through the hallway. "Though even that feels foolish. None of what I thought would be could have ever happened. Not with me being the way I am and Caelan being him. One of us would have had to fundamentally alter ourselves.”

Moira let out a heavy breath. “I can’t love like you do, Evie. I never have been able to.”

I glanced at her sharply. Her smile was faint. “This does not mean I don’t love. I do. But I don’t allow myself to crack open the door of my heart to anyone. Only you, Ash, and Tess. You are the only ones I allow myself to love.”

I watched her for a long moment. “You liked Soren.”

Her eyes crinkled as if I’d made some secret joke. “Soren will always be a passing fancy. His heart is a stream, while mine is an ocean. If I ever open myself to the kind of love you might have with Rowan, I fear I’ll drown both of us.”

I stopped walking and turned to face her, my heart aching for my friend. Cupping her face in my hands, I rested my forehead against hers. “Whoever gets you to open your heart to him will gladly drown with you, Moira. You are my fiercest, most loving, and devoted friend, and you deserve all the happiness the world will bestow upon you. Only the most worthy will win your heart, but do not close yourself off from the possibility. There is a man out there who will move heaven and earth for you. I promise.”

Moira closed her eyes and put her hands over mine. “I have what I need. I don’t know if what you say is true, but it would have to be someone incredible for them to shake me from my path.”

“Someone meant for you wouldn’t try.”

We stood like that for another moment until I felt a touch on the wards.

“The booze stealing siren is here,” Mom called.

Moira snorted and stepped away. “Let’s go see what that man stealer wants.”

I linked arms with her and opened a door in the wards to let Sirena in.

CHAPTER

ELEVEN

LEMM

"Well," Mom demanded, cutting a fierce figure as she loomed above Sirena.

The siren, however, was less impressed. "Sit down, Cliona. You're hovering like a grandmother."

Mom's eyes narrowed. "One day, Sirena, pow, right in the vagina."

Moira let out a loud laugh.

The Siren clicked her tongue. "Might want to try a different area. That thing can take a licking and keep on ticking. Plus, it's my moneymaker."

"Ugh, gross." I held up a hand. "Can we steer the topic of conversations away from vaginas, please?"

"Your mom started it," Sirena said with a glitter in her eyes.

"I'm stopping it. Why did you text Moira?"

Sirena sipped her booze and sighed. "I know all of you can feel the blight on our land."

We all nodded.

"Our current Lord is powerless to stop the spell. He has refused all offers of help and rumor has it, he's sequestered in his Keep bringing in experts of all manner to assist."

73

"But none are helping," Moira assumed.

"Exactly. I don't know how much any of you know about Sirens, but we have an affinity with water. With that comes some handy gifts. Sound is vibration. Sometimes I catch snippets of conversation that happen around water. I'm limited, distance wise, but if I'm close enough and receptive, I will sometimes pick up things that are meant to be private."

Note to self. Do not have any conversations near water if Sirena is in a fifty-mile radius.

No one said a word. Sirena smirked and continued. "You are looking for a female goddess."

No one was really surprised by that. We already suspected. Mom rolled her eyes. "We know."

Sirena nodded. "Thought you might. You're also looking for a female witch."

Mom and Moira exchanged a look.

"Is that all?" I demanded. I suspected that too. "This wasn't worth coming all the way to Joy Springs."

Sirena speared me with those vibrant eyes. Magic glittered in the glowing depths. "That witch is well-known to you."

Dread pooled in my stomach. I only knew a few witches, one who would never betray me, leaving only—

"Marnie. Perhaps her sister Twyla as well, though she was not mentioned." Sirena settled back against the chair and watched us.

Mom swore. "The one time I find the best soup in all the realms and now I can't frequent her shop anymore because she's a lying bitch!"

Moira closed her eyes and slumped against the wall. "Shit," she breathed. "Are you sure?"

"Positive," Sirena said. "Evie's stunt in the town square shocked everyone, but those two especially. They are from the old school of witches, those who remember how dangerous and powerful Chimeras are. You'd do well to do a thorough check of your belongings when you return home. If you haven't already looked through everything, I would search for charms or bags, anything that might not belong. They were *aggrieved* when you revealed what you are."

Mom was staring hard at the siren, close to mean mugging her. "Why are you being so helpful?"

Sirena smirked. "Ever the suspicious one, Cliona."

But Mom wasn't letting her deflect. She crossed her arms and waited.

The siren clicked her tongue. "Fine. Since Evie's absence, it has become glaringly obvious that our Lord might not be powerful enough to protect us from what is coming. The shifters are less sensitive to magical disruption, but those of us with fae blood feel the poison seeping through the land. Most of the magic is centered on Keep property, which is odd, but none of us want to wait around to see if we remain unscathed. Something is happening, and Caelan is completely unprepared and refuses to accept your help."

My eyes narrowed at her knowledge, but Sirena scoffed. "We talk, Evie. All of us know you tried more than once to help him. We also know he refused every time. When his lack of concern became apparent, our people started to move away. Others are thinking about it. The business owners are the ones who are stuck because we've made our lives here. I'm a little more flexible than the rest, but I like it in Joy Springs." Her eyes flickered. "My kind are not always welcome. I've never felt less in this place."

I digested her words, empathy rolling through me for her, something I thought would never happen. "Where is everyone going?"

She shrugged. "Some have gone back to the fae lands. Others have asked for sanctuary in other Lord's territories. I have not decided where to go yet. My hope is to stay here, but Caelan's rule is on shaky ground. I need to be in a territory with a strong Lord. Such is the nature of my kind." A thin smile before she looked down at her hands.

My eyes met Mom's with the slightest hint of softening in them toward Sirena. But the siren wasn't off the hook and wouldn't be unless her information proved reliable. Marnie was the last person I'd suspect of performing magic so anathema to the world. She and her sister were Hedgewitches, paranormals who worked hand in hand with the earth to nurture all its bounties. Magic like the one poisoning the grounds seemed out of character for her.

"How good is Marnie with glamours?" Moira asked.

"Decent, but if you catch her inside the restaurant, you've got a better chance of escaping her notice. Too many magical signatures in there to filter much out."

I looked to Mom for confirmation, who nodded. "But is that where she'd cast such a dark spell?" I asked.

Sirena chewed on her bottom lip. "I'd lean yes. She wouldn't want that sort of darkness seeping into her home."

"Wouldn't her customers sense a spell like that?" Moira asked. "Magic seeps into everything and leaves a trace behind. But the magic she's doing would leave more than a mark. Her more sensitive customers would know."

"She has a workshop out back," Sirena said.

Moira and I exchanged a look. A dark chuckle slipped from Mom's lips.

"You thinking what I'm thinking?" Moira asked.

"How bad do you want that soup?" I asked Mom.

We grinned at each other.

• • •

I SENT Rowan a text as Mom adjusted our glamours to include putting us in darker clothing so Moira could slip into the back while we distracted Marnie inside. Twyla was the wildcard, but we'd figure out a way to get her out of the back to let Moira snoop around.

I didn't want to tell Rowan where we were—plausible deniability and all that. My message was short and to the point.

Safe. With Mom and Moira. Sorry I didn't tell you before. Spur of the moment. Looking into some leads on the project we're working on.

Hopefully he'd realize what I meant.

His response came back almost immediately. *Thanks for letting me know. Hope told me to play it cool and not text you like a nagging wife.*

I smiled. *Text me anytime you want.*

Dangerous words. You're going to create a monster.

I like monsters.

Moira snorted. "Quit texting your boyfriend and get your shoes on."

"He's not my boyfriend," I said hotly, though my cheeks were burning.

"Yeah, yeah. He's more." She rolled her eyes and tossed me one of mom's illegal cigarettes. "Stow that, so if one of us gets busted, it won't be a felony."

I snatched the offending thing from the air and tucked it into my bra. "Mom has no respect for the criminal justice system."

Mom scoffed. "Mood altering substances have been part of the world since the dawn of time. It's stupid to prosecute over them. Put the murderers and rapists away. Leave the herb smokers alone."

"Here, Here," Sirena said. Her eyes held a curious light. "Do those actually work for people like us?"

Mom grinned. "You get us what we need, siren, and I'll share our stash. Help us get in and get out without raising the alarm, and we'll come back here and show you exactly how well they work."

Sirena stared at Mom for a long moment. "You know what?" she mused. "Why the hell not? It's been a long time since I've engaged in mischief for mischief's sake."

Mom and Sirena discussed a plan while Moira and I had another drink. When they finished, we had a shaky but viable plan. Moira would do most of the heavy lifting. She was faster and sneakier and had a resistance to magic stronger than most. Mom, Sirena, and I would serve as the distraction. Mom and I would go for Marnie, and Sirena would ensure Twyla stayed out of Moira's hair.

As plans went, this one was not the best, but we had Mom with us. Until I learned how to transport people, she'd get us out in a hurry if we needed to make a quick exit.

I took Moira's hand. "All we need is evidence to implicate Marnie and Twyla. Find it, grab pictures if you need to, then get the hell out of there."

Moira squeezed my fingers. "Don't worry. I know what I'm looking for. If she has anything there, I'll find it."

"There has to be," Mom said. "A spell like this has to be renewed. Otherwise, the energy would run out and become stagnant. She has to feed the power on a regular basis."

Sirena's attention sharpened. "You think she's using sacrifices?"

Mom's expression was somber. "If I had to guess. Something this damaging requires a stronger source of energy than anything herbal can provide."

My heart sank. "Marnie corrupted herself over her own prejudice. All those years of good work only for it to end like this."

"Her own fault," Moira said. "She's known you for years. If you were evil, she would have known. Her magic is too sensitive not to. The woman helped you multiple times." Moira shook her head. "I don't understand her thought process. Does she think you all of a sudden became evil?"

"Little is known about Chimeras," Sirena said. "Humans are not the only ones prone to hate things they do not understand. Marnie is old enough to remember when Chimeras last walked the world." A thin smile. "As am I. Just like bad people, there are bad Chimeras. Evie has been among us long enough for us to see the difference."

Moira made a disgusted noise. "All the events, all the times Evie went out of her way to help someone, and this is how they thank her."

"Caelan is not helping," Sirena said. "His casual dismissal of their relationship made waves around town and contributed to their general dislike of Evie." Her glance was apologetic. "They are used to following their Lord's lead on things, regardless of whether he's right."

"Regardless," Mom interjected, "tonight we find out whether Marnie is responsible. Then we make a plan." Her azure gaze slid to Moira. "Do nothing tonight but gather evidence. She will know someone was in her workspace, but take this and drench yourself before entering. The perfume will help muddy your scent and disrupt any spells to help differentiate the scent. By the time it dissipates, we will be long gone."

"Why didn't you do this when we first came?" I asked.

"Because smelling like a streetwalker on a busy Friday night in a crowd gathers too much attention. Moira will smell like one only to confuse the witch's senses." Mom flicked a hand toward the door. "She can shower when we return."

Moira plucked the bottle from Mom's fingers and popped the lid off to take a whiff. "Good enough."

I leaned over to smell. "White Diamonds."

Sirena shuddered. "The perfume of the 80s. Everyone's mom smelled like that and strutted around like they were on Dynasty."

"That shit could clear out a room in a hurry," Mom added. "Perfect for tonight."

Moira pocketed the bottle and adjusted her black beanie. The hat made her look like a sophisticated cat burglar. With her pale hair and night-dark eyes, Moira was the epitome of a creature of the night.

"Ready when you are," she said and gave me a cheery wink. Her cheeks were flushed with color.

I laughed. "You love getting into trouble."

Moira grinned. "We always had to be so careful when we were living here. This is the first real chance I've had to raise a little hell."

Mom held her hands out. "We'll come in at the edge of the forest, so no one sees our arrival. Remember, Moira. Get in and get out. Call to me when you're ready, and I'll transport you back to Evie's house."

Moira nodded.

"Alright then. Join hands."

A moment later, in a dizzying lurch, we stood in a dense forest, surrounded by trees. Mom stepped away and peeked out to see if the coast was clear.

"Come," she hissed.

Moira went the other way, cutting through the forest to come out on the backside of Marnie's restaurant. The rest of us walked through the square, our conversation inane in case there were curious ears. When we arrived at the restaurant, I sent a quick text to Moira to let her know.

If things were going to fall apart, it would happen within moments of us entering.

When we opened the door, the comforting scent of home cooking washed over us. Mom let out a low curse. "Maybe I'll get an enormous thing of soup to freeze," she muttered.

"If Moira sees a recipe book, she'll probably steal it," I whispered.

Mom brightened at the thought of petty theft, especially if it netted her the soup recipe.

The door shut behind us with a solid thud, sealing us inside. Thankfully, the place was busy, filled with townspeople and tourists. I recognized some and kept my eyes averted. Curious gazes watched us for a moment before returning to their own spaces. Their eyes lingered on Sirena the longest. Unsurprising. The siren was stunning, and part of her power was luring men in.

Marnie stood behind the counter. Twyla was nowhere to be seen.

"Follow me," Sirena whispered.

We stayed a foot back and smiled at Marnie when Sirena introduced us as some of her old friends. "Where's Twyla tonight?"

Marnie jerked a thumb over her shoulder. "In the back. There was a run on baked potato soup, so she's prepping a new batch." The witch frowned. "We haven't been this busy in ages. Not since—" Her gaze flickered over us before she frowned. "Well, no matter. The customers are a blessing."

"Well, you're in luck again, because these two heard about your famous food. They're dying for some of the soup." Sirena motioned us forward. An almost undetectable breeze swept over us. Sirena's work to keep our scents from reaching Marnie's nose.

Clever.

I let Mom do the talking.

"Erm, yes," Mom said in a posh British accent. "I'd love

some of the baked potato soup to go, the largest serving you have."

As Mom ordered an outrageous amount of food, I sent Moira a quick message.

Twyla's in the kitchens. Mom ordered enough to feed an army. Should keep them busy for a bit. Good luck.

I tucked the phone away, only to hear Mom still ordering.

"And you, Glinda? Is there anything else?"

I almost choked at the name she used. Good witch, my ass. "Erm, you got everything," I said, in a warbly high-pitched voice.

If Marnie didn't see right through this, she was either very tired or completely clueless.

The witch gave us an odd look but sent the purchase through. "Might take a bit. Twenty minutes okay with you?"

"Fine with us," Mom said. She handed over a few bills and waved the change away.

We found a seat toward the back. I sagged against the cushioned back. "I don't think I'm cut out for subterfuge like this."

Mom reached over to ruffle my hair. "You're made of the earth, where all the good and plentiful things come from. I'm made of dust and wind. Far more suited to this kind of work." She slid a look at the siren. "And this one is made for the sheets."

To my surprise, Sirena burst out laughing. "You make me sound like a common harlot, Cliona. We both know I possess far more specialized skills." She clicked her tongue. "In case you didn't know, I'm an old thing, Evie. I no longer have to feed as often. A bite and a nibble here and there will feed me for months."

Sirena had never shared anything about her power. I leaned forward. "Months?"

At her nod, I plowed on. "When you say a bite or a nibble, what does that mean exactly?"

Mom sent me a warning look that made Sirena chuckle. "She's young, Cliona, and I don't mind answering. It's not often that I am allowed to hang out with the youth."

I blinked. "Is that because you bite them?"

Sirena grinned. "Those days are behind me. I only bite with permission now."

At my wide-eyed look, she chuckled. "During relations, an energy transfer occurs. When I was still learning, the transfer only occurred via completion. My powers are honed far better than my younger brethren. Now, I can receive energy through touch or kissing."

I studied the hand she'd held not long ago.

Sirena grinned. "Not to worry. You will feel if I ever try to take energy from you."

"Plus, I would kill her," Mom chimed in.

I glanced back and forth between them. They were smiling at each other, but their smiles held sharp edges. Mom did not sound like she was kidding, but Sirena seemed unconcerned. Did they have history? Was this a frenemy sort of relationship? Both options seemed viable.

"Let's change the subject," I said slowly. "Before this turns into a showdown."

Sirena snorted but sat back and turned her attention to me. "You look well, child of the gods. The other Lord's territory agrees with you."

"Lots of glorious greenery out there," Mom murmured. "Evie blossoms where there is life."

Sirena grunted in agreement. "I was surprised when you moved here. Every territory needs a Floromancer, but there's a reason those in the past never stayed long."

"Most didn't get involved with their local Lord," I muttered.

Sirena's eyes twinkled. "Yes, there's that."

My phone dinged.

Got it.

I leaned close. "She's ready."

Mom straightened. "Marnie almost has our order ready."

I stared at her in disbelief.

"What?" Mom sounded affronted. "This is the last time I'll ever get that soup. I'll get our girl. You get our order."

Mom grinned and breezed out the door just as Marnie called Sirena's name. We walked up to a counter full of carefully packaged goods. I stared at them, wondering how we were going to carry everything, when Sirena took out a large picnic basket decorated with pearlescent seashells and carefully started packing everything.

"I wish I could do that," I said wistfully.

Sirena gave me an odd look. "You can, child." She handed me over the final bag that wouldn't fit. "We'll talk on the way."

Sirena smiled at Marnie and turned toward the door. When we were outside, she looked over her shoulder. "Let's get out of sight. Marnie is in the back quite often. We won't have much time until she discovers someone has intruded into her space."

We hurried toward the place where we came in. Mom was already waiting for us. Her face lit up at the bounty we carried. Without a word, she grabbed us both by the arm and whisked us away.

CHAPTER

TWELVE

Moira looked decidedly green around the gills when we went inside. Her hair was tied into a wet and loose bun on the top of her head, and she'd found a pair of old joggers and a tank I'd left behind.

Mom produced a long cardigan out of thin air. Moira gave her a grateful smile as she shrugged into it, tugging it close as she curled her legs under her on the couch.

"We'll talk while we're eating," Mom announced.

I helped get everything ready, Sirena assisting by opening one of the bottles of wine left behind.

When we were all settled in, Moira pulled out her cell. "She's guilty. Her scent is all over everything, but I didn't sense Twyla's. It's possible she knows about what's going on, but she had no hand in the creation or application of the spell."

Mom took the phone and swiped through the images, her lips thinning the further she went along. "Do we take this to Caelan or handle this ourselves?"

Sirena leaned over to peer at the photos. "Since you two are persona non grata, this might be easier to hear coming from me."

85

I shook my head. "Caelan is the kill first, ask questions later kind of leader. Marnie is only half the spell. We need to find out who she helped."

Moira nodded. "Agree. But how do we get that information?"

We all looked at Sirena. She blinked at us. "Umm. Marnie is going to know something is up after tonight. I, a siren who has very few, if any, friends, came in with two unidentifiable women, and it was just a coincidence someone broke into her private shop on the same night?" She winced. "We all know Marnie isn't that dumb."

A thoughtful look stole over Moira's face seconds before a slow smile tipped her lips up. "Then we make it look like she wasn't the only one affected."

Everyone, meet my devious friend, Moira. "You want to make this look like a rash of burglaries?" I chewed on my lip. "Good plan, but it may further weaken Caelan's hold on power."

Mom snorted. "So?"

"As Lords go, he's not the worst." I shot Mom an exasperated look. "He's kept crime down and his people all live in relative comfort. What happens if someone like Ethan comes in?"

Moira's brow furrowed. "Ethan has flaws, but he's not a bad Lord either."

My eyebrows rose at her defense of the unlikable Lord. "I thought you didn't care for him?"

She snorted. "I don't, but none of the Lords are as bad as Donovan. They all have different styles, and Ethan can be trying, but in my opinion, and overlooking how he treated you, he might be a better Lord than Caelan."

Interesting. I was going to tuck this conversation in my back pocket and reexamine it later. "You think Joy Springs might be served better with another leader?"

Moira shook her head. "No. I'm saying I don't give a shit

what happens to Caelan. If he can't hold his territory and loses it to another Lord, I won't shed any tears."

I blinked. "Um. Alright." Moira was rarely one to be so openly blunt in front of people other than me, Ash, or Tess, but she obviously had unresolved feelings over what he'd done to me.

"A rash of burglaries, then," I said after a moment of tense silence. Sirena watched Moira with a thoughtful look. "Are you really going to steal anything?"

Moira nodded. "Yes, but I plan to put their things around town. Still a burglary, but a temporary and confusing one."

"Messing with their minds even more and making Caelan look completely inept," Mom theorized before she grinned. "I like it."

We all looked at Sirena. She shrugged. "I'm with Moira. If Caelan can't hold his territory, he shouldn't be a Lord."

"Then let's go steal some shit," Moira said. "After I finish eating."

MOIRA HIT FIVE STORES, including the one that had just opened in the place where mine had been for all those years. Caelan hadn't wasted any time in filling the empty storefront. At first, the knowledge stung, but that chapter of my life was over, even if Caelan and I still had some unresolved issues, mainly his dying land. I'd come to terms with the end of our relationship.

In that store, Moira had taken her time, carefully rearranging almost everything in the front room and taking some of the more expensive jewelry from the case. I didn't ask where she put anything she'd taken. Moira assured us the pilfered goods would be found within 24 hours. In the other stores, she took one or two hard to miss things and broke a few windows.

I winced at that, but Moira assured me the cost of repairs

would be taken care of. The specifics of how remained trapped inside her deviant little brain.

"Tomorrow," Moira said, stretching her lithe body out on the couch, "Caelan will wake up to chaos." A slow smile tipped her lips up. "Well deserved."

Sirena's wicked chuckle made the hair on the back of my neck stand up. She was more than a woman. The siren was human sexuality in monster form.

"If I had any idea of how much fun you all could be, I would have come around a lot sooner."

Mom gave the siren a dark look. "And we're all the better for your lack of attention."

Sirena winked. "I believe you owe me a little something, Cliona."

Mom rolled her eyes and fished out one of her magical cigarettes.

"No smoking in the house!" I barked as Mom tossed it over.

"No fun," Sirena pouted.

I pointed to the back door. "Out."

The siren waved the joint at us and glided outside.

"The gods help us," Mom muttered. "That woman is insufferable."

Moira burst out laughing. "You two have some history. Care to share?"

Mom sighed. "No. I would not. Let's wait for the siren to finish up and get the hell out of here."

"Can we trust her?" Sirena had never moved against me or done anything to make me worry about her loyalty. She had no loyalty, and I liked knowing that more than being kept in the dark and wondering if she'd strike me when I was weak.

Mom shrugged. "In this case, I believe so. She was telling the truth about her kind not being accepted." She sighed. "Sirens are universally hated."

Moira sat up. "Because of the whole sailors jumping to their death thing?" She rolled her eyes. "Stay away from small islands in the middle of the ocean. Like it's hard."

I got up and peered out the window. Sirena was sitting in the middle of the yard. A small orange light flickered close to her mouth. Guilt speared me.

"She helped us tonight. Maybe we can give her a break. Just this once."

Mom's lips thinned. "She's not to be trusted, Evie. Don't think she's your friend."

I snorted. "I rarely think anyone is my friend. But we can wave our white flags. Just for tonight, can't we?"

Moira rose and linked our arms together. With her other hand, she pulled out the joint Mom gave her and wiggled her eyebrows. "How safe are these wards?" she called out to Mom.

"Unbreakable," Mom assured her. She held the door open for us. "I'll be back in a minute."

I glanced back. "Everything okay?"

She brushed a hand over my hair. "Everything is fine. Back in five, I promise."

She disappeared in a shower of light. Moira and I walked outside and sat in a semi-circle by Sirena.

Her eyes lit with surprise. She waved the joint at us. "Your mom is a godsdamned genius. Do you know how much of this we have to smoke to even get a buzz?"

Moira grinned. "A lot."

Sirena laughed. "Your mom is already a rich woman, but this on top of her booze?"

The siren shook her head. "Icon status."

Moira pulled out a Zippo and lit the joint. The sharp scent of the herb filled the air. I'd never been around drugs. My human friends in high school used illegal substances, but I was never interested. Why would I be if they never worked?

Mom reappeared in a flash, standing next to—

I got to my feet and launched myself at Rowan. He caught me with a sharp laugh, large hands spanning the backs of my thighs.

"Hi," he murmured against my neck.

"Hey."

Moira let out a wolf whistle.

He turned to Mom. "Caelan can't see me here," he said quietly. "I'm no longer allowed in his territory."

Mom shook her head in disgust. "A small glamour will tweak your appearance." She waved her hand and a shimmer of magic appeared around Rowan. I glanced at Mom quizzically when I couldn't see a difference.

"Only Caelan and his people will see something else. The spell won't last longer than a few hours." Her eyes glittered with amusement. "When he sees you, he will see a young blond man. Just think. If you and Evie make out, Caelan will think she's dumped you too."

Mom laughed and walked away, going over to join Sirena and Moira.

Rowan's hands were right under my rear end, cupping the backs of my thighs. "Hey," I said again, quieter this time.

His hazel eyes crinkled at the edges. "Missed you."

Our gazes locked. "I missed you, too."

He pressed a soft kiss to my lips, gentle and tender. I resisted the urge to tackle him to the ground. "Should we join them?"

I wanted to say no, to ask him to take me home so we could be alone. I ran my fingers up his neck and let them tangle in his hair. "Moira has a joint. Mom's newest experiment."

Rowan's eyes lit with a ring of gold at my touch. His surprised laugh warmed me from the inside. "Does it work?" Was his voice a touch rougher?

I lifted my shoulder in a shrug. "We're about to find out."

His eyes narrowed. "And you?"

"I grew up knowing they wouldn't work on me, so I was never into them."

"Never worked on me." He hitched me higher and walked me over to where everyone was sitting.

Instead of letting me go when he sat, he turned me and settled me in between his legs. His arms were wrapped around my waist. I leaned against his chest and when I had settled into his warmth, I realized Rowan made me feel safe, *really* safe. I never had to worry about what I said or did, or what I looked like. I didn't have to fear what my future children might become or worry whether they'd become monsters. They wouldn't. Not if they were made with love. The thought made something tight uncurl in my chest.

Unbidden tears sprang to my eyes.

Rowan leaned forward. "You okay?" he whispered in my ear.

I nodded, not trusting myself to turn around.

Mom's eyes settled on me. A soft smile curved her lips at the way Rowan held me, the way he was unconcerned with what other people might think. He fit in so well with everyone and was well liked.

Why couldn't I take that final step?

Sirena blew smoke rings and let out a satisfied sigh. "You've outdone yourself, Cliona."

Moira lit hers, took a few puffs, and passed it over. I stared at it for a moment. "What the hell," I whispered, and joined in, passing it to Rowan when I was finished. Mom had her own, so Rowan passed it back to Moira.

Mom snapped her fingers. A small firepit appeared in the middle of our makeshift circle. Another snap and a cheery blaze lit, the sound of wood popping and crackling lending a cozy feeling to our gathering.

"Now we're talking," Moira said, coughing a little before she passed the joint back over.

We were silent for a while. I was digesting the night's events and wondering what our next steps should be when a slow, languorous feeling crept through my body. All the stress and worry fell right out of my head.

"Oh," I whispered. "That's *nice*."

Rowan's chest rumbled with a laugh. "How much would you charge for this?" he asked Mom.

"Family is always free," Mom said. Her words were a little slower and her eyes a little more glittery.

Sirena clicked her tongue. "And me?"

"Full price," Mom said. "Plus fifteen percent."

Sirena showed her teeth. "Honestly, Cliona. You can't possibly still be mad after all these years."

Mom sighed. "I can't be mad at much of anything right now. Ask me tomorrow."

Moira snort laughed. "What did you do to her?"

Sirena sighed. "I flirted with her boyfriend."

I gasped. "Dad?"

The siren rolled her eyes. "Yes. In my defense, everyone flirted with Cernunnos."

"Were you friends before this?" I looked at Mom, who watched Sirena with the intensity of a leopard about to pounce from the brush.

When Sirena winced, Moira let out a chortle.

"Noooooo," I breathed. "Were you two besties?"

Mom took another hit and squinted at the siren. "Besties. I've never heard that word, but yes, we were what the humans called best friends."

"Sirena, you ignorant little cow," Moira murmured.

I belly laughed. Rowan's amusement rumbled against my back. He shifted and brought up a knee, allowing me to lean back a little further. I laced our fingers together. Rowan stroked his thumb over the back of my knuckles, sliding down the back of my hand toward the wrist.

I felt good. Relaxed, happy, and secure. I can't remember the last time I hadn't stressed about anything. This stuff Mom brought was dangerous. If I had access to it, I'd never get anything done. I'd curl up with Rowan and waste the day away.

I tilted my head up and watched him. He dropped a kiss on my nose. "Feeling good?" he asked, his voice a low rasp.

"Mmmm." I liked hearing him talk. With my other hand, I reached up and stroked the line of his jaw, my thumb sliding over his bottom lip. He was the most beautiful thing I'd ever seen.

Rowan's eyes crinkled. "We have an audience," he whispered. "But I'm not going to care if you keep looking at me like that."

"You make me feel safe. Cherished. I love who I am when I'm with you."

Rowan's eyes turned gold. He bent to kiss me when magic flared against the wards.

His head jerked up. Mom let out a soft curse.

"We have company." She rose and straightened her skirts, approaching our unwanted guest. "Lord Caelan, we are in the middle of a private gathering."

"You're on my land." Rowan and I turned to see Caelan prowling back and forth at the back of the property, stopped by the glowing wards.

"No," Mom said. "The fae has claimed this land. It belongs to my daughter, the fae queen. Your territory begins where hers ends."

Caelan slammed his hands against the ward again, his eyes widening when he spotted me. Confusion lit his face as he took in the man holding me—Rowan under a glamour.

A derisive laugh broke from him. "Why am I not surprised by another man holding you? Does your Lord know?"

Rowan's arms tightened around me in warning. I didn't know if he'd give himself away if he spoke.

Mischief reared its marijuana-soaked head. "My Lord knows everything." I ran a proprietary hand over Rowan's thigh, higher and higher until I reached the apex of his thighs. I pressed a kiss to his jaw and nipped his chin.

Rowan sucked in a sharp breath and closed his eyes. He tilted his neck to give me better access.

"Every single touch, every single word, Rowan knows."

Caelan's eyes glowed with fury. "I judged you correctly," he growled. "Who is he? Someone who can help you get wherever you need to go?"

I pressed my nose against Rowan's throat, then replaced it with my mouth.

He went pliant under my hands. I licked up the column of his neck and nipped him again.

"Gods," Rowan whispered, so low only I could hear it. "*Evie.*"

"Yes," I said to Caelan. My eyes glowed azure blue, casting light over our skin. "This man is sexy and powerful and doesn't give a shit what my womb can or cannot do for him." My fingers wove through Rowan's hair, the silken tresses sliding through my fingers like satin.

Caelan slammed against the wards again. I laughed and turned to straddle Rowan. His hands wrapped around my waist.

"You faithless *bitch*," Caelan seethed. "I will call the Lord and tell him exactly what you're doing."

I grinned at Rowan. My body felt both connected and disconnected, warm and supple. "You should," I said to Caelan. "Describe in great detail what we're doing tonight." I bent to kiss Rowan. "He's a little voyeur and likes to know what I'm doing with my body."

Our tongues tangled, the taste of him setting my nerves on fire.

"Leave, Lord," Mom commanded. "You have no dominion here."

"Your daughter is doing a fine job of making an enemy out of me."

Mom laughed. "My daughter did nothing but love you when you didn't deserve it. She fought by your side and would have died there. As far as I'm concerned, you did her a great favor. She's no longer your concern, and if you're smart, you'd leave her alone."

I heard the words, but Rowan was busy sliding my shirt up and running his hands over my bare back.

Words fell away when his hands moved up and his thumbs brushed the tips of my nipples through my bra.

"We should go," Moira said, choking on a laugh. "Before we all get a little too voyeuristic."

There was more whispered conversation and shuffling before Mom touched my shoulder. Rowan's hands stilled. "He's gone, but I wouldn't linger outside." A pause. "I've furnished your bedroom. Text me in the morning and I'll be back to get you."

A shift of wind and silence fell.

Rowan opened his eyes, showing me the telltale gold that would have given him away to Caelan. I leaned over him, my hands on his powerful chest. "I want to taste you. Everywhere."

"You say the sweetest things to me." Rowan's smile was slow and lazy. He rose up and claimed my lips in another searing kiss. He pulled away, amusement glimmering in his golden gaze. "We must be careful tonight, Evie. Our senses are dulled by pleasure and drugs. I want to touch you everywhere, take you against every surface, but if we go that far, the mating bond will seal."

His thumb brushed the undersides of my breasts. I lifted my arms up and raised an eyebrow. A wicked chuckle was his response as he slid my shirt over my head. Rowan wasted no time in removing my bra, his lips and hands everywhere.

"I'm serious," he murmured against my skin. "I won't let you go that far, no matter how much you may want to."

I wanted to. Gods did I want to.

"I smell your desire. I feel it tugging me into you." Rowan's nostrils flared.

"We can do other things. A lot of things, I hope?"

In response, Rowan wrapped his arms around me and leapt to his feet. "Yes, you beautiful, wicked thing. We can do *a lot of things.*"

Several hours later, we lay in a tangle of limbs, our breaths rasping and hoarse.

"Mom is an evil genius," I rasped.

"Gods," Rowan murmured. "*Gods.*" His hand tangled in my hair, and he tugged me closer, claiming my lips in a bruising kiss. "Can you imagine what it might be like if—"

He cut himself off.

My head was clearer, my thoughts cohesive, and even in a haze of pleasure, clarity struck me like a lightning bolt. I rolled on top of Rowan, straddling him, and laced our fingers together.

He blinked up at me in surprise. "You may have to give me five minutes, darling."

I snorted. "I'm in love with you, Rowan."

His eyes went liquid gold. "*Evie.*"

I shook my head. "Don't doubt this. I don't. I'm scared of what comes next. I'm scared of a permanent bond. I feel guilty about what happened with Caelan, but I do not doubt how I feel about you." I swallowed hard. "I'm not ready for a mating bond. Not yet."

He watched me carefully, his body tight like a drum.

My lips curled into a soft smile. "But I will be."

Tears shimmered in Rowan's eyes. "Yeah?" he whispered.

I nodded. "Yeah."

His smile was bright and wide. "Thank the gods," he whispered, reaching up to cup my face. "You are everything I've ever wished for, Evie. My people love you. My lands love you. I love you. Always." His thumbs stroked my cheeks. "The first time I ever saw you, I choked on jealousy. Caelan and I were friends, and I would never have dreamed of doing anything improper. Even when I saw things between you hanging by a thread, all I wanted was your happiness, even if it came at the expense of mine. But seeing what Caelan was doing to you slowly broke my heart. When I carried you away from this place, I couldn't think of anything other than protecting you and helping you heal. This, where we are right now, wasn't even a sliver of hope in the back of my mind, not with the way he'd broken you. I only wanted you to live again. Lying with you now, holding you skin to skin..." His voice trailed off. "This is more than I ever thought I deserved."

Tears spilled freely down my face. Even when we were only friends, Rowan knew exactly what to say to me. "You are a precious gift to me," I whispered. "And now that we are here, and we know how we feel about each other, we should never speak of Caelan again. Not in this context. He is a part of my past that brought me to you, so in a messed-up way I have to be grateful."

Rowan's eyes crinkled. He tugged me down to kiss me, and when we broke apart, a soft laugh escaped him. "I noticed you long before Caelan did."

I stilled and lifted my head to peer at him. "When?"

"I traveled to Joy Springs frequently and spent a lot of time in the downtown area. Occasionally, I would spot you through the window of your shop. I wanted to come talk to you, but it was bad form for another Lord to encroach on their host's citizens. In fact, dating one's citizens sets a dangerous precedent." His eyes crinkled. "That is why I hope to marry you. I do not like to set dangerous precedents."

My heart melted. "You should have talked to me."

His eyes glowed. "Should I?"

I nodded. "I'm not sure if I would have been nice to you, but I would have remembered you."

He laughed. "I've never met someone with such a disdain for authority."

I pressed a kiss to his shoulder. "You're cute, so I might have held back some vitriol."

Rowan snorted and rolled over, trapping me between his arms. "Just cute?"

I pretended to mull but lost all my coyness when his lips began traveling down my skin.

Soon after I was a quivering mess, and that golden thread between us grew ever brighter.

CHAPTER

THIRTEEN

Mom didn't say a word about our disheveled state when she popped in to pick us up. She took us straight to Rowan's doorstep, kissed my forehead, and nodded solemnly to Rowan. "I'll come again when you are well rested."

An amused glitter lit her eyes from within. "There is much we need to speak about."

She disappeared in a shower of magic, but not without a wink.

"I like your Mom," Rowan said as he pushed the door open. "She's an odd juxtaposition of prim and completely out of control."

I groaned. "She is. I wonder if there are other fae moms out there who grow weed and brew magical booze in their spare time?"

Rowan laughed and headed straight for the coffee pot. I sank into one of the kitchen chairs and watched as he brewed a new pot. He worked with efficiency, the muscles in his forearm flexing as he tapped out the used filter and refilled a new one. His hair was a little messy and a sexy five o'clock shadow turned his jaw dark. My heart beat a little faster, and I had to resist the urge to walk over and run my fingers over his skin.

Rowan glanced back at me with a raised eyebrow. "Struggling, Evie?"

Heat touched my cheeks. I cleared my throat and looked down at the table. "I am not sure what's wrong with me," I said hoarsely. "We spent the entire night doing..." I waved my hand around. "Things."

His grin tightened something deep inside me. "More than things." Rowan shook his head. "We came really close, Evie. I'm not sure how much longer we'll be able to halt this if you keep looking at me like that."

I closed my eyes. "Sorry." A breath escaped me. "Can you stop looking so yummy?"

Rowan poured a pitcher of water into the reservoir and snapped the filter into place. He flipped the switch on and turned, walking over to me. Without a word, he snatched me up from the chair and tossed me over his shoulder.

"Rowan!" A squeal of laughter escaped me.

He slapped me on the rear, the sound making a loud crack. "Hush." His voice was harsh and guttural.

Every muscle in my body went liquid.

Rowan kicked his bedroom door open, slammed it shut behind us, and tossed me onto the bed. I lay there with wide eyes on him as he tugged his sweater over his head.

"Oh gods," I whispered. That unfamiliar fae magic rose and swirled around me, wanting to claim Rowan as our own.

His eyes turned gold as he reached for me and tugged my jeans off. With a flick of his fingers, my underwear tore at the sides. He shoved the silk away and buried his face between my legs.

A keening cry rose from my throat. "*Rowan.*" My hands clutched the bedsheets as he explored me, his warm tongue touching me in the spot that made it hard to concentrate on anything.

His hands went under me and lifted my hips, and he rose onto his knees, holding me in place as he feasted.

Stars burst behind my eyes, the first prickling of release clawing at my skin. My breath turned ragged and uneven. I couldn't stop murmuring his name.

He shifted, holding me in place with one hand as his fingers slid through my folds, one sliding inside me.

"Evie," he said against my skin.

The orgasm took me by surprise, sending me up and over a cliff of unfathomable pleasure.

My vision went black, and Rowan, the gods bless him, didn't stop what he was doing, wringing every drop of pleasure from me. My voice went hoarse and ragged, and when he finally released me, I realized I wasn't ready to be done.

I reached for him, deftly undoing his jeans. They slid over his hips, along with his underwear until he was bare before me.

I lifted my eyes. "Yes," I said.

Rowan went still. "Evie."

I scooted away from him, higher up on the bed and opened my legs. "Yes," I said again.

He closed his eyes for a long moment, his jaw clenched so tight I could see a beating pulse. When he opened his eyes and our gazes locked, a frisson of delicious fear rolled over me. Rowan prowled toward me, one hand reaching out to snatch me by the leg to draw me closer.

I gasped as I slid along the sheets. Rowan settled himself—

"Lord." A knock on the door.

"Go. *Away*." Rowan's voice was animalistic.

"I am sorry—" Hope's voice. "But there's something you and Evie have to see."

"Godsdammit, Hope. *Right now, a fucking nuclear war can wait.*"

I pressed a hand over my mouth to keep from laughing. Rowan sounded both pissed off and desperate. And I made it worse, by taking him in my hand and pumping him slowly. He hissed and pulled me closer.

The sound of a baby's cry made us both freeze.

Our eyes locked.

His closed in defeat a second later. "Godsdammit," he snarled under his breath. "Give us a minute."

"Of course, Lord."

Declan's hoot of laughter made my cheeks burn. They were shifters. They knew exactly what we were doing in here.

Rowan's furious curses as he dressed made me laugh out loud. I hurried as well, stumbling when I first slid off the bed. My legs were weak and I was still quivering with anticipation and desire.

Rowan pushed me against the wall and nipped at the column of my throat. "This is not over, Evie. Not by a long shot. The next time I take you, it will be completely. You will scream my name and beg me for more. And when the bond between us threads us together, I will make you my wife before the gods and my people."

I lifted my eyes to his, stunned at his words, but unable to resist making a joke. "Hmm. I still haven't decided how cute you are yet."

Rowan's flash of teeth and glowing irises made me laugh. I reached down and cupped him, leaning forward to gently nip at his bottom lip. "And I won't be the only one screaming, Lord."

Rowan closed his eyes and let out a slow breath. "You're a godsdamned witch sent from hell to vex me."

Reluctantly, he stepped away and adjusted himself. I

grinned and slapped him on the rear before reaching for my shirt.

Once we were as decent as we could make ourselves, we stepped into the hallway. Rowan laced our fingers together and led us to the kitchen. Hope and Declan sat at the table, a car seat between them.

A smile started to form on my lips until I spotted something extremely familiar about the baby. I dropped Rowan's hand and hurried over, my heart in my throat as I gently lowered the blanket draped over the handle.

An adorable baby blinked up at me. Big blue eyes, pale skin, and dark hair, she was the cutest thing I think I'd ever seen.

But that wasn't all.

Powerful magic beat from the baby's heart.

Chimera magic.

This little child was a Chimera infant.

And that should have been impossible.

CHAPTER

FOURTEEN

ROWAN

I noticed the magic in the instant Evie did. Her hands shook as she lifted the baby from the seat and cradled her in her arms.

My chest tightened at the sight. As much as I should be worrying about this recent development and how it might affect things, I was still trying to shake off the anger about the interruption.

We'd almost mated. The beast inside me, usually pretty genial, was as pissed off as I was and making it known. My emotions roiled and I had to resist the urge to hand the baby back to Hope and haul Evie over my shoulder once more to take her so we could finish what we started.

A gentle hand pressed against my forearm. Hope. "Do you need a moment?" she whispered, her eyes filled with concern.

My nostrils flared and I willed my fury into submission. The golden light sweeping over the room faded little by little until it was gone. A sharp shake of my head, and Hope nodded.

"Again, Rowan, I'm so sorry. Couldn't be helped."

Declan was staring at me with barely suppressed mirth. Asshole.

105

Evie swayed gently from side to side, speaking to the baby in nonsensical words. Her messy hair fell over one shoulder. She smelled like me, as she should. We'd been tangled together for the last sixteen hours. If I had my way, we'd be tangled together for sixteen more.

Evie covered the baby with the blanket in the car seat and lifted her gaze to me. "This should be impossible."

I shook my head. "Maybe the mother is human."

Evie's brow furrowed. She brushed her fingers over the baby's cheek, releasing a tiny thread of watermelon tourmaline colored magic. Her eyes glowed a brilliant blue before dimming. She shook her head. "Full chimera."

Declan spoke up. "Still not impossible. Fertility rates are usually low within Keeps."

We both ignored Declan's knowing smirk. My Keep was about to have a historical baby boom after Evie's magic had saturated the land and turned every single shifter here into feral, horny beasts.

Hope snorted.

"But," Declan continued, "many of our shifters are full-blooded, even with human mothers. Genetics are funny things. This could be how the swans turn their curse around."

Evie frowned at the baby. "I have to assume they've already tried mating outside their race."

Hope rolled her eyes. "Don't be so quick to give them the benefit of the doubt. Many shifters refuse to dilute their blood-lines, no matter that doing so could save their kind."

"I have no idea how to take care of a baby," Evie murmured, more to herself than any of us.

Hope rose and walked over to Evie, leaning forward to brush her fingers through the baby's hair. "Our Keep has a larger population of women than any other." She lifted her shoulder. "And our men are no slouches, either. It takes a village, Evie. We all love babies. This little thing will want for nothing."

Evie sucked in a sharp breath. "You want to keep her?" Her eyes shimmered with tears. "A Chimera baby?"

Hope stared at Evie for a long moment, her lips tightening. "I am sorry you ever experienced hatred for what you are. She's a child, Evie. Of course, we'll keep her." She smiled at her, and touched Evie's hand. "Look at that sweet little face. Everyone is going to eat her up."

A shuddering breath racked Evie's slender form, breaking my heart in the process. I'd kill Caelan twice over to prevent him from ever shattering her self-confidence like he'd done before.

"I don't think we should tell Barrett." Evie glanced at me. "I'm not sure why. Just a feeling."

"Then we won't." I walked over and held my arms out. Evie gently handed the baby over and hovered as I rocked her from side to side.

I hid my smile. "She's lovely." Large, guileless blue eyes stared up at me. "Maybe five months," I murmured, turning my attention to Hope. "Did they leave anything for her?"

Hope shook her head. "Just the baby, the seat, and a note tucked inside the blanket."

She slid over a cream-colored envelope. The front was blank, and I got no scent from the paper or the ink when I held it to my nose.

"I tried, too, and couldn't pick up a scent. Whoever this was knows what we are."

The note was written in a spidery, feminine scrawl and only had one word.

Protect.

The rest was a blurred ink line.

"And they know Evie is here. Where was she?"

"Right outside the Keep by the main house. They didn't trip the wards."

I lifted my gaze. "Who found her?"

"Declan on one of his rounds."

"Anything else?" I asked my Second.

"A trail that disappeared abruptly. Small footprints—a woman, if I had to guess. No scent trail anywhere." Declan shook his head. "The damnedest thing. Extremely difficult to hide scent from our kind."

"Could be fae," Hope mused. "Or a fae spell."

"I'll call Mom in a little while." Evie's fingers trembled as they stroked the baby's cheek. "She's too little to eat baby food, isn't she? We don't have any formula, and there aren't any new mothers here who might spare some milk—"

Evie was spiraling. "Someone will go to the store."

"What if she's allergic to formula? What if—"

"Evie." I gave what I hoped was a reassuring smile. "Babies are resilient. We'll figure things out."

She let out a shuddering sigh. "Right. Of course." Evie squeezed her eyes shut, but not before I saw the suspicious moisture. "I'm sorry. I just—I've never even held a baby before. She's so small."

I knew Evie would be a good mother the moment I met her. Now, seeing her fret over a baby left on our doorstep, my belief only solidified into stone. One day this might be us. I hoped this was us. For now, this child was a complication I wasn't sure how to handle.

A cute complication, certainly, but a complication, none-theless.

"I'll send a few of the den mothers," Hope said. She nodded to me and touched Evie's shoulder. Declan rose and followed behind, winking at me once he was past Evie.

I shot him a dark look. Declan's dark laughter followed him out, leaving Evie and me with the child of a stranger.

Neither of us spoke for a while. Our mingled breaths were the only sounds in the room, that and the baby's soft suckling noises, and the rasp of skin against cloth as she waved her hands all around.

Evie turned and sank into the closest chair. "Gods," she murmured, a rasping laugh shaking her shoulders. "A baby. Sometimes I feel barely capable of taking care of myself."

I placed the baby back into the car seat and went to my knees in front of Evie. My hands rested on her thighs. "Stop selling yourself short. You are amazing and loving, and everything I ever wanted. Someone entrusted us, *you*, to take care of this child, to ensure her safety. And I can think of no one better equipped to do so."

A tear slipped down her face. I reached up to brush it away. "I'm sorry we were interrupted." She ruffled my hair and mustered up a smile. "We were about to get to the really good stuff."

Warmth suffused me. "To be continued."

"I hope so."

"I've never meant a promise more," I swore to her.

CHAPTER

FIFTEEN

Mom arrived right when Hope returned, her face a mask of worry when she saw what I was holding. Her gaze snapped right to the bundle in my arms, eyes wide with surprise.

"My gods," she murmured. "A baby Chimera." Mom blinked a few times, then shook her head as if to wipe the thoughts whirling through her head away. She came closer and held her arms out for the child.

I let Mom hold her. She swallowed hard as her arms wrapped around the baby, and our eyes met. "How?"

"Someone left her outside the Keep." My voice caught. "She should be impossible."

Mom's eyes filled with tears. "Perhaps a human mother. Or some other fluke of genetics or magic." Her fingers brushed over the baby's face, magic making Mom's eyes glow. "Or maybe you are not the last living female Chimera."

I'd thought the same thing when I saw the baby, but if there was another female alive, why wouldn't she announce herself, at least to me? Why would she leave her child alone and defenseless? What if someone hadn't found her and the cold had taken her? The month was still cold enough to harm a child as young as this one.

"Barrett swears I'm the only one."

Mom shook her head. "Or he has his own reasons for keeping her secret. Do not trust him until you know for sure. He is an unknown player in this game."

I scrubbed my hands over my face. "Too bad I don't know the rules in this damned game."

The door opened, and Moira walked in, stomping her feet on the rugged mat. "I heard we have a new and adorable visitor."

She gasped when she saw Mom. "Oh my gods," she moaned. "Look at those adorable little dumpling cheeks!" Moira bent over the baby and grinned. "Hi!"

The baby let out a gurgling laugh, taking us all by surprise.

Moira's laugh was the happiest I'd ever heard, bright and sunny. There were few things more innocent than a baby. Soon we were all laughing, which made the baby laugh harder.

Moira reached for the baby. "May I?"

Mom nodded and handed her over.

"Oh my goodness," Moira breathed. "I haven't seen a baby in so long. And I've never seen a Chimera. She seems like just a regular baby."

"We all look like regular babies when we're born," Mom said dryly. "Unless our main form is an animal. While I've never seen a Chimera child, I can only assume they're the same." Her face took on a contemplative look. "Though it's wonderful to know for sure that Chimeras can be both made and born."

My heart leapt into my throat. The baby was perfect. She had all ten fingers, all ten toes, her laughter was pure and innocent, and her smile was adorable and gummy. This child was everything a baby should be. I could have one, a baby just like this.

Mom took my elbow and led me to a chair. "Sit, honey."

I sank into a seat and stared blankly ahead.

Moira picked up a chair and set it close to me. She sat and scooted my way until our knees touched. "Hey." Moira's dark eyes were warm and edged with sadness.

A sob bubbled from my throat. Rowan's warm hand landed on my shoulder and squeezed gently. He brushed a kiss against my temple and jerked his head. Hope followed as he left the room.

Moira angled the baby so I could see her sweet face. "Caelan is a shit."

"Don't cuss in front of the baby," Mom said.

My lips twitched.

Moira rolled her eyes. "Caelan is a S-H-I-T." She stuck her tongue out at Mom. "He made you doubt who you were at your core. This would be your baby. But better. Not saying she's not perfect, because she is. She's a baby. All babies are perfect. She's not Evie perfect though. Add fifty percent of Rowan to that and you've got a kid competing for the cuteness crown."

A smile wobbled onto my face. "I'm completely off kilter today. Everything seemed so far away. Children were always one day, or maybe in the future, or I'll see when I meet someone nice. And then Caelan and I decided not to take any precautions because shifters had such a low birth rate." I let out a ragged breath. "Looking back, that was the moment everything started falling apart. The possibility became real. A new baby Chimera became something that could happen. Caelan couldn't deal with having a child who might one day outshine him. He made me think I'd give birth to a—" My voice broke. "A monster. He made me feel like I was nothing, like anything that came from me would be tainted."

Tears streamed freely from my face. "It broke something inside me, and I thought I was flawed. When Rowan came along, I resisted for so long because I thought I might bring him down, that I couldn't give him what he deserved. I wondered if I could even have children, and if I did, I wondered if they'd be exactly what Caelan said they'd be—monstrous."

Moira's face was stone. Her eyes burned with rage. My lower lip wobbled. I couldn't stop the hot tears from flowing, all the anger I still felt over everything that happened, spilling over into physical form. I'd gotten my grief out a while ago, but seeing this child brought the fury roaring back.

"This child just showed up a few hours ago, and everything I thought I could never have suddenly became a real possibility." I wiped my tears away. "I'm not a monster. I've never been one. I've allowed other people to dictate my thoughts about myself, and I have no idea why."

I pressed the spot in my chest where the bond between Rowan and I grew every single day. "I almost mated with Rowan today."

Mom sucked in a shocked gasp. "Evie. That's—" Tears brimmed in her eyes. "So wonderful. He is a good male. A very good one."

Moira nodded. "You deserve the best of everything, Evie. Never let someone tell you what you are. You define your fate. Not me, not your mother, not Rowan or Caelan. No one can dictate your life." She brushed a kiss over the top of the baby's head. "She was brought into your life for a reason. Her mother or whoever brought her wants her safe, and she trusted you and Rowan to keep her that way. A mother would never trust their baby with a monster."

Mom smiled. "We can be monsters when it comes to protecting the people we love, but there is a difference between us and those who care for nothing but their own power."

Something tight loosened in my chest, a knot that had been

there for years finally withering away and dissolving into nothingness. "Thank you. Both of you. I promise I'm done spiraling."

Moira's smile was sad. "You, of all people, deserve the occasional spiral." She tapped the baby's nose gently. "Now, how about you stay with Auntie Moira tonight?"

I blinked in surprise. "Moira, she might not be sleeping through the night. Are you sure?"

Moira snorted. "I'm a vampire. We don't need to sleep all that much. It will be nice to have some company. Ash and Tess are in their own little world right now." She rolled her eyes. "I don't know what's going on over there, but I haven't seen either one of them in days."

At my look of alarm, Moira laughed. "They're fine. I can hear them sometimes when I'm passing by. But I think they're very busy." She winked.

"Eww," was all I could say.

"Yeah. Crazy kids. I don't know if they're gonna make it, but they're sure having fun trying."

"Aaagh. Gross." I shook the images away and adjusted the baby's blanket. "If you want to take her tonight, you can. But you might have to bring her by the other dorms. All the other shifters are dying to meet her."

"No problem." Moira brushed the baby's bangs to the side. "We'll need formula and a few other things, but we'll be just fine."

The baby cooed.

"Should we call her something?" Mom said.

My mind was blank, and Moira was too busy cooing back to respond.

"How about Missy? Short for *misneach*, a word that means courage."

She pronounced it like *mish nah*. "Beautiful. Misty is pretty, too," I said.

"I like Misty better. It's an older name. Now everyone is Ashley or Kristen or Maddy." Moira rolled her eyes. "Misty is both descriptive and pretty."

"Misty it is," Mom said. "Hope bought a few things for the baby. There's formula and—" she dug through the bags, "lots of adorable clothing and binkies and bibs."

"Ooh," Moira cooed to Misty. "We get to play dress up tonight!" She rose and snapped the baby into the car seat. "Let's leave Aunt Evie and Miss Cliona alone. They have grownup business to talk about." Moira winked and picked the seat up. "I'll keep you updated on any cute things she does and bring her back over tomorrow sometime."

With a wink and a wave, she slung the bag Hope had brought over her shoulder and breezed away.

When she was gone, Mom shook her head. "If that baby is around for any length of time, she's going to be spoiled as all get out."

"I hope so," I murmured. "Her mother is gone, and she's been abandoned in a place full of strangers."

Mom's face sobered. "She is lucky to have you and everyone here as caretakers. Her circumstances might be unfortunate, but love saturates this land and Keep. Such will find its way to her."

"Thanks, Mom."

Mom smiled, but her eyes were filled with unfathomable sadness. "Every choice I made was to keep you safe. If I could go back and keep you with me, I would. I missed you every single day when we were separated, and every day I woke up without you, I lost another piece of my heart."

She brushed my hair away from my eyes. "She is not old enough to remember any of this. If her mother does not come back, and she is fated to stay here, she will be raised with love and kindness because you and everyone else here knows no other way."

I brought Mom in for a tight hug. She froze in surprise, and it took her a moment to soften. A shuddering breath rattled her chest, and her arms tightened around me. "I will never be able to make up for what your father and I did, even if we did it out of love, but I hope you will allow me to spend the rest of my days trying."

Why was I crying so much today? I nodded against her shoulder. "You don't have to make anything up to me. You've already shown me how much you regret everything that's happened. I hope you always come around. Wherever I am, you will be welcomed."

Mom gave me a gentle squeeze. "And you as well. My realm is always open." She stepped away. "The Lord is pacing back and forth by the door, waiting to return to you. Do not make him wait too much longer, darling. The male and the bear inside him are getting very antsy."

She disappeared in a swirl of light. The door opened immediately, and a moment later, Rowan's head peeked around the corner. "Everyone gone?"

I nodded. "Finally. Moira took the baby, but I expect you will be slammed with visitors this evening."

Rowan's jaw tightened. "I expect you're right." A ring of gold appeared around his iris. "I can think of far better things to do than entertain visitors."

I laughed. "Patience. We have the rest of our lives, don't we?"

Rowan let out a frustrated growl and reached for me just as the outside door opened.

He closed his eyes and let out a soft curse. "I'm about to lose it," he whispered.

Dad's magic reached us before he did. I stifled my sigh. Everyone was bound and determined to keep us apart today.

"He's bound to be hungry," I said, extricating myself from Rowan's tight grip. I brushed a quick kiss over his lips and turned to face my father.

"Hey, Dad."

Cernunnos was in his full-on god form today, complete with ceiling scraping antlers. He appeared like this when he was on official business, had come from official business, or just wanted to be scary that particular day.

Unfortunately for me, I never knew which one it was until he told me.

He had to duck to pass through the hallway to get into the kitchen. When he rose to his full height, I noticed his eyes swirling with power.

I willed myself to be calm. "You hungry?"

Dad stared at me for a long moment, and I waited, silently, Rowan still and quiet beside me.

After a moment, he blinked and his eyes bled to his normal greenish gold, only a little swirly. The antlers retreated into his head, and his outfit morphed from buckskin to a pair of dark trousers and a pullover sweater, more formal than his usual joggers and t-shirt, but still normal enough not to freak me out.

"There you are," I said lightly. "Want a grilled cheese?"

Dad nodded and sank into one of the chairs with a groan. I turned away to fix him some lunch, giving Rowan a sharp shake of my head to warn him to give my Dad time to decompress.

Rowan went to the fridge and got the sandwich fixings out while I readied the pan.

Dad didn't say a word the entire time. When I set two sandwiches in front of him with a glass of tea, I sat across from him, Rowan to my right, and waited.

He scarfed the entire thing down and drained his tea. I got

up and refilled his glass, keeping the pitcher next to me in case he needed another refill.

Dad drank the second glass too. When he finished, he closed his eyes and let out a deep sigh. "Thank you."

"Of course." I said nothing else.

Dad remained quiet for a few moments. He looked at Rowan and narrowed his eyes. "Ah. I see."

I resisted the urge to squirm uncomfortably.

"This is why I'm here, actually." Dad let out a sad laugh.

I straightened. "Because of Rowan?"

"Our people are not...enthused about the potential for a shifter king."

Rowan froze beside me.

"Granted, they think Rowan is a much better choice than the other Lord, but they wish to be led by someone who is of pure fae blood."

Rowan started to rise from the table, his face an expressionless mask. "I'll give you two some time to discuss."

I took Rowan by the hand and tugged him back down.

"Evie, it's fine—"

"It is not fine," I said quietly. Rage roared through my veins.

"The bond can still fade."

I turned to face Rowan. A crimson light washed over his face. Rowan swallowed and went still.

"Be. Quiet." When he gave me a sharp nod, I returned my attention to my father.

"The people that abandoned me now dare to make demands of me?"

Dad blinked, a furrow appearing between his brows. "Evie, you are the queen—"

If I heard that one more time, I was going to set something on fire. "I am fully aware of what I am and what I am not. I am also fully aware of what you made me to be and know you are the reason I currently wear the fae crown. Under duress, by the way. And I know that you did not answer my question."

My father's eyes narrowed. "There is required decorum, a set precedent of past kings. I was reminded so earlier today by a few well-meaning friends."

I snorted. "Well-meaning. I can see how you might say that since every single fae I've met so far has been nothing but *well-meaning* to me."

"You're angry." The words were a flat declaration.

"You seem to be under the impression I should roll over and do what they want. You think I should abandon Rowan and take some poor fae male who, by the way, would not know how to deal with me, nor would he want to, as my husband."

"You'd be surprised by who would want to deal with you," Dad said under his breath.

I bared my teeth. "That is not the point. I might be the fae queen, but there is no law on who I take to my bed or mate with, correct?"

Dad's jaw tightened. "There is no law, only an expectation—"

"*I do not give a shit about expectations!*" I rose from the seat and paced back and forth. "I am happy for the first time in my entire life. Truly happy. Things will never be perfect. That's not how life works. But they are good. I love Rowan."

Rowan's irises glowed at my declaration.

"I plan to finish the bond. Not today, maybe not even tomorrow, but soon. And that is not all."

Rowan blinked. He tilted his head, an animalistic gesture, all his focus on me.

"A fae bond forms between us."

Rowan sucked in a shocked breath, surprised at my admission to my father.

"I am not inclined to deny it." I met Rowan's gaze. "If

Rowan allows it, I plan to bond with him in both ways—the animals and fae sides of my nature. If he will have me."

Rowan blinked several times. "I've felt the tug for a while now and couldn't figure out what it was," he said hoarsely.

Dad's face took on a contemplative look. "You'd shun your people over this?"

I leaned against the counter and crossed my arms. "They are my people in blood only. The only fae who've ever stepped in to assist me with anything have been you and Mom, and that was only recently. As far as I'm concerned, they can take their opinions on who I choose to love and shove them right where the sun don't shine."

Dad looked at Rowan. "And you?"

Rowan chuckled. "Would you let someone like her walk away from you?"

His words seemed to be the right answer. Dad dipped his head. "Unfortunately, I have, and I regret the decision every single day."

"Don't make me choose," I said quietly. "You know how it will go, and I will never look at you the same. This is not up for debate. I will not allow people to choose how they feel I should be happy. That's forced servitude. If I am to be their queen, I will make my own decisions on this matter. As they should make those decisions for themselves."

Dad's eyes began swirling again. "Is this your final answer?"

"It's always been my final answer. When are you going to stop asking the question?"

Dad's lips twitched. He rose and held out his hand. "Come. Both of you."

I let him lead me outside, Rowan following behind. Dad led us to the middle of the Keep, close to where we trained. He stopped and let go of my hand. "Rowan, will you briefly drop your wards?"

"Why?" Rowan's tone wasn't angry, more curious than anything.

"I need a few witnesses."

Rowan glanced at me. I shrugged. "No idea," I mouthed.

"Thirty seconds enough?" he asked.

Dad nodded.

Rowan's eyes flashed gold. The wards shimmered away. Dad's form morphed back into his god form, his eyes swirling with multiple colors. Several flashes of light appeared.

Mom stood beside my father, and a couple of the people I met in the Hall of Fae arrived next. Birch showed up, and strangely enough, Ethan was there as well, looking decidedly nonplussed.

"Call for Moira," Dad murmured. "And your banshee and dryad friend."

"I will do it," Rowan said. Our gazes locked, and he gave me a short nod.

I shot a hurried text to Moira.

Leave the baby with a trusted person.

The wards went back up. Moira, Ash, and Tess appeared a few minutes later, quizzical looks on their faces. Moira came up beside me. "What's going on?"

"I think Dad might be about to strip my crown," I whispered back.

Moira's attention snapped to me. "What happened?"

"I won't marry a prancing fae male." I said it a little louder than I should have.

Dad shot me a dark but amused look. I wiggled my fingers at him. He shook his head and looked away.

"Evie. Rowan. Please come."

Rowan held his hand out. I interlaced my fingers between his, and we walked to my father.

"Do you know what's going on?" he whispered.

"Not a clue. I might not be queen in a minute, though."

Rowan slid me a look of surprise. "Is that a bad thing?"

"Not even a little bit," I murmured. One less thing on my plate. I hadn't even started my duties yet, nor had I told Rowan about my deal with my parents.

One thing at a time, Evie.

I squared my shoulders and stopped before my father. A silvery light appeared above my head. Rowan glanced up and hid his smile. The fae crown swirled and glinted around his tousled hair.

"Thank you to everyone who answered my summons today." Dad's voice boomed across the land.

The flutter of hundreds of wings sounded in the air. Birds of all sizes and colors settled on the surrounding trees. Fee and Poe were somewhere on Rowan's land, but they wouldn't come around if Mom was here. Even after everything, Poe remained wary of Mom and protective of Fee. The raven had an excellent nose for magic. He'd keep the phoenix away until everyone was gone.

Seymour was somewhere around, too, though he'd taken a liking to dorm life and preferred spending his time with Declan and the others. I visited him occasionally, and sometimes he'd find me. As long as he was happy, I left him to his own devices. He was still grieving Caelan, and though he'd come to me of his own volition, I knew he missed the other Lord.

Seymour liked Rowan and was often affectionate to him, but he wasn't ready to completely let go of Caelan. I understood and let him grieve on his own schedule.

Foxes and coyotes of the natural kind sat at the feet of the fae. Snakes slithered through the grass and curled up on exposed stones. Insects and other creepy crawlies waited around the edge of the semi-circle we made.

My heart lurched with nerves. What was Dad doing?

Above us, the sky churned, stirring up a sharp wind. The temperatures dropped by at least twenty degrees. I took a step closer to Rowan. He let go of my hand and wrapped his arm around my waist. His face was blank, but his eyes burned with curiosity even as they swept across the fields monitoring for threats seen and unseen.

Mom stood next to Dad and didn't look alarmed, but she'd had thousands of years to perfect her poker face. Rowan and I, on the other hand, were flying blind.

Magic thrummed through the air, thick and heavy. Power flowed in the wind, soaking my veins and bones. This was ancient magic, that of the universe long before any of us gained flesh. The fae bond tugged me forcibly. It wanted the male by my side. Rowan's hand clamped against my waist was warm and possessive, sending a strong flood of desire through my bones.

His nostrils flared and he glanced down at me, surprise lighting his gaze. "Evie?" His whisper was quizzical yet amused. "Are you alright?"

My fingers itched to tear his clothes off, take him to the ground and make him mine.

Rowan's eyes began to glow.

Dad spoke again. "You are here to witness the official crowning of my daughter."

Hmm. I thought we'd already done that. My foot tapped impatiently, and I had to sing a song in my head to keep from molesting Rowan.

"I can smell how much you want me," Rowan murmured, his voice so low only I could hear him.

"It's the bond," I whispered back. "There's so much magic in the air I'm having trouble controlling it."

Rowan stared at me. "Then don't."

I let out a soft laugh. "Funny."

Ignoring everyone else around us, Rowan turned me to face him and lowered his forehead to mine. "Don't."

Dad cleared his throat.

"Though my daughter has already been crowned, she has never stood before the most important of her people, nor has she brought forth a king."

Rowan blinked. His attention jerked to my father.

"Are you sure?" I whispered. "I can leave. Right now. I can hurry back to the cottage and calm this thing down. I'm so sorry."

"My daughter has chosen Rowan Beithir to stand as your king." Cernunnos swept a hand out toward us. "He is loyal and stronghearted and will serve both us and my daughter well."

Rowan cursed under his breath. "Evie. Did you mean for this to happen? I can get us out of this. I can—"

I put a hand over my chest. The magic was unbearable now. My eyes cast an azure glow over his face. "If you want out now, say the word," I gasped. "I don't think I can hold this in for much longer. This bond is not the same as a shifter bond. It's—"

Rowan let out a soft laugh, cupped my face in his hands, and gave me a searing kiss. He teased my lips open and claimed my mouth. With one hand tangled in my hair, the other yanked me against him.

Applause rang out in the clearing.

Magic exploded between us, a song of pure, primal power, encompassing us in a silver and pink haze. That bond reached toward Rowan, flooding his body with ancient magic.

He gasped, his eyes wide with surprise. The bond between us allowed me to feel Rowan, know him down to his bones, his wants and dreams, his hopes and failures.

He was everything I ever wanted. Beautiful and perfect and

flawed and so utterly in love with me it almost brought me to my knees.

I closed my eyes against the flood of sensation, tears streaming down my face.

I heard my mother gasp. Moira's cool touch against my arm before she drifted away.

Right now, it was only Rowan and me. No one else existed in this time and space.

"Evie," Rowan whispered, his hand tightening in my hair. "Gods above. You are so fucking beautiful. Inside and out." Tears slipped from his eyes. "I've never felt anything like this."

I laid my head against his chest and wrapped my arms around him, so overcome I couldn't speak.

Gasps rang out. I lifted my head to see a matching crown of silver swirling above Rowan's head.

This was borderline ridiculous, a voice said in the back of my mind. A fae spectacle spearheaded by my father. And Rowan was here with his arms around me, and he smelled and looked so delicious, so why were we still participating?

The fae bond settled into our hearts, right next to the budding shifter bond, a spot of silver and pink, almost touching the other.

And with it came a roaring hunger to taste every inch of Rowan's skin. "Will this wear off?" I whispered as my fingers crept up his chest.

Rowan snorted. "Gods, I hope not." He tilted my neck back and pressed a hot kiss to my throat.

At that moment, feeling his hardness press insistently against my thigh, I had had enough of this constant theater.

"Get out," I said.

A feminine snort of laughter before Moira called, "Speak up!"

Rowan dotted kisses along my collarbone.

"LEAVE." My voice boomed throughout the keep. Thunder rolled above us. Lightning cracked and sizzled, smashing to the ground. The scent of ozone rose around us. I flicked a careless hand out. Screams sounded all around us before silence clanged like a bell.

Dad or Mom, someone had sent them all away. Or me. Who the hell knew? We both had enough magic flooding our bodies to take down the entire state.

Rowan chuckled against my throat.

"Reset your wards," I whispered.

I felt the wards settle around us. With a whispered command, a thick layer of roots and vines rose from the ground, tangling around each other in tight knots. I sent them high enough to prevent prying eyes, giving us enough room to navigate, and left the area above us wide open.

Rowan tugged my shirt up and over my head and tossed it to the ground. I called up a soft bed of grass and leaves behind Rowan and gently pushed him down.

His wicked chuckle made me shiver. Rowan settled against our makeshift bed and watched as I removed my clothing. His eyes glowed a strange silver and gold, mixed with a trace of familiar watermelon tourmaline.

"It's been long enough, don't you think?" I murmured, shimmying out of my pants.

Rowan unbuckled his belt in response.

"No. Let me."

A smile curved his lips. His hands fell away. Vines slid from the ground, wrapping around his buckle. Rowan sucked in a breath before releasing it with a soft laugh. The vines made quick work of his buckle, but I took over, sending the vines to wrap around his wrists.

"Evie."

I didn't want to talk. Other, more pressing things took

precedence. "No more waiting, Rowan. We're already bound forever. You are my friend, my lover, my king. Such a relationship requires consummation."

His eyes burned with emotion and desire. "I want to touch you."

"Me first."

I made quick work of his clothing until Rowan was bare beneath me. I'd never get enough of him, never tire of the way he looked at me.

"You look at me like you want to devour me."

In response, I straddled him, his tip at my entrance.

"*Evie.*"

"No more waiting," I said and sank onto Rowan, claiming him as mine for all eternity.

He sucked in a sharp breath. A low moan escaped my throat as he filled and stretched me. Muscles corded in his arms when he tried to reach for me, but the vines held tight. Release tingled at my spine, and I hadn't even moved.

A golden light bloomed in our chests. I smiled down at my mate and began to move.

CHAPTER

SIXTEEN

ROWAN

I lay tangled in Evie, her hair spread out like a fan over my chest. Words could not describe what I felt right now. Everything about the last few hours had been perfect. We'd have to come out and face everything that had happened eventually, but for now, I was content to stay here with her, with my mate.

Both fae and shifter. The two bonds had tangled together sometime during our first mating. Our next two encounters solidified the bond into a completely fused thing of light and magic.

All my life I'd never dreamed I'd be so lucky. Never had I thought I'd end up with such a ferociously independent, beautiful, powerful woman lying beside me, completely sated and knowing her, ready to go again the second she opened her eyes.

I couldn't help the grin spreading over my face. The last few days had been a whirlwind. I regretted none of it, not the stress, not the worry, not Cernunnos' obvious attempts to manipulate Evie, though I planned to speak to him later about that. I couldn't regret anything because it had led me to this moment with Evie curled against me.

129

Stars glittered above us, casting Evie's bare body in silver moonlight. The silent evening was shattered by the sound of hundreds of wolves howling. Evie's eyes flew open. She took a second to get her bearings.

I dropped a kiss on her nose. "Hi."

Her eyes glowed a bright silvery azure blue. "Hi."

All the screaming had made her voice a little hoarse. The bear in me preened at that.

She snorted. "I recall you were a little noisy too."

"Mmm. Yes. I'd like to do that again and again and again."

Her cheeks went pink making me laugh. "Do you think everyone heard?"

"I try not to lie to my mate," I said primly.

"Gods." Evie buried her face in my chest.

"They would have felt the binding. Every one of my shifters is bonded to me. Now they are bonded to you as well. I'm not sure if they felt the fae bond, though I wouldn't be surprised, but they definitely knew when the shifter bond was finalized."

"That's what it is," Evie murmured, rubbing the spot on her chest. "I feel you most of all, but there are threads—many, many threads. Those are your people."

"Yes. You will know when someone is hurt and needs their Lady."

Evie blinked. "Oh shit. I forgot about that."

I laughed. "You were too busy ogling my perfect form."

Evie smacked me on the chest. "The fae bond is powerfully sexual. We're going to be tired if that one doesn't calm down."

"You underestimate my prowess and how much self-control it took not to take you against every flat surface we passed by over these last couple of months."

Evie snorted, but as she stared into my eyes, her face sobered. "I never asked you if you wanted children."

I picked up her hand and pressed a kiss to her palm. "Bears

are not especially fertile. Our kind tends to have few children, one to two usually. Some of us are more fortunate. I once knew a mated couple with four cubs." The chaotic memory made me smile. "They went through three couches a year and couldn't keep a kitchen table because of all the wrestling."

Evie chuckled.

"They were so blessed." I let out a heavy exhale. "I love children. I'm in no hurry to have them, but if we were blessed with a cub, I would be the happiest man in the world." I tugged her closer. "If it's possible for me to be happier than I am now."

Evie cupped my cheek. "You are the king of the fae. Are you okay with the title?"

"Too late to do shit about it."

Evie groaned.

"If we mated, I expected to claim the title. Your father went about this in an underhanded way, but I'm not upset. I would walk through a forest fire for you, what are a few fae? If being king keeps us together, bring me my scepter and guillotine."

She laughed. "I think they stopped using the guillotine several hundred years ago, but let me know if we need to buy another one."

"Mmm. I'm sure we could think of a few people who deserve a beheading."

Evie pressed a soft kiss to my lips. "Word about this will get out. Are you going to be okay with how the Lords might react?"

"I don't give a shit how anyone reacts. But I think most of them will be ecstatic. They've been worried about your influence the second they saw that automaton at Caelan's party. Now that we're mated, they'll know our goals are aligned."

"Which might make it worse if your goals are aligned with the fae," Evie observed.

"Would it?" I wasn't too bothered and already figured there would be times when my interests as a Lord and a King clashed.

I trusted Evie and knew she wouldn't put us in a precarious position of loyalty if she could avoid doing so.

"Not if I can help it." Evie blew out a breath. "But there's something else I need to tell you."

I toyed with a dark strand of her hair, desire stirring in me once more.

"Once my training is complete, I agreed to spend a week out of the month in the fae lands."

"Unsurprising. How else could you rule the fae if you're never there?" I stroked a hand down her back and felt a flicker of desire along the bond.

"You aren't mad?"

"I'll come with you."

Evie blinked. "Really?"

"You're my mate. Of course I'll go with you. Mom will be ecstatic."

Evie gasped. "Oh! Oh no." Her voice was filled with dismay. "We mated without your mom here."

My eyebrows rose. "Can't say I would have wanted my mom here for this."

"Rowan!" She snickered. "I meant for the ceremony or whatever the hell Dad did out there. I'm sure she would have loved to see you crowned."

"Mom doesn't care much for the trappings of politics." I kissed her shoulder. "She might be horrified."

Evie watched me. Her eyes were still glowing. "Do you think she'll like me?" Her voice sounded so hopeful.

I rolled over, trapping her between my arms. "She'll love you. But even if she doesn't, I don't care. You're my mate, and you're stuck with me."

She touched the side of my face. "I never thought I'd be here, Rowan. With you, doing this." Her cheeks went pink.

"We're mates." Evie sucked in a breath. "I can feel you inside my heart. How will I ever get used to that?"

"I hope we never get used to this," I said as I slid down her body, teasing and tasting.

And soon we weren't speaking at all.

WE SPENT the rest of the night under the stars. In the morning, Evie dismantled the structure we'd consummated our bond inside. I didn't tell her the entire Keep was outside waiting for her. If I had, I'm not sure she would have come out.

I tugged her close, Evie's permanent floral scent washing over me, along with that ever-present hint of desire. Whoever or whatever created that fae bond deserved a kiss on the lips because it had turned Evie feral last night. Mates already held an extreme attraction to each other. Her magic had taken it to a completely different level, one I would never, ever complain about.

I was the luckiest man on the planet.

Evie's sharp inhale as she tried to pat her hair into some semblance of sanity almost made me laugh. "Shit, Rowan. I must look like—like—" She sagged against me.

"Like you've been thoroughly mated," I said quietly. "Stand proud, Evie. They're here to greet their new Lady."

Declan and Hope stood in front of the crowd. Once the last of the barrier came down, they both stepped forward, huge smiles on their faces, then went to their knees, their heads bowed.

"Welcome to the Keep, Lady," Hope said.

Evie pressed her hand against her chest. "Oh, Hope. Thank you. Thank you both. Please don't kneel." She touched them both on their heads. "Stand up and give me a hug, okay? That's a much better way to welcome me."

Both of my shifters rose. Declan whooped and scooped Evie up into a hug, spinning her around to her surprise. Her laughter rang through the clearing. When he put her down, he smacked a loud kiss against her cheek and ruffled her hair. Hope shoved him away with a laugh and brought her in for another hug.

Simone and Garrett came next. Their faces were a little more somber than everyone else's. Garrett came forward first and bowed his head deeply.

"You deserve this," he said in a low voice. "Rowan is a good Lord and is worthy of all that you are."

She brushed her knuckles against his cheek. "Aren't you glad you didn't kill me?"

I started in surprise, but Garrett flashed her a savage grin. "I think you were humoring me back then. We both know who the better beast is here." Garrett brought her in for a tight hug and stepped away. He nodded and stuck out his hand. "Lord Rowan. Congratulations."

We shook. "Come by and visit me in the next few days. Declan's been bitching about all his additional duties, so if you're interested in taking on some things around the Keep, we'd all appreciate it."

Garrett's eyes glittered with interest. "I'll do that, Lord."

"Rowan, please. No one calls me Lord unless the other Lords are around."

The wolf dipped his head in acknowledgment. "Alright then. See you in a few days."

Simone stepped forward and dragged Evie into a hug. "Gods above, you do love to make a scene, don't you?"

Evie snorted. "What? You didn't like my open-air wood and grass love shack?"

Simone grinned. "Well, from that epic bedhead and swollen lip look you have going on, I have to admit it must have been effective."

Evie blushed. "Ass."

Simone winked and stepped away before turning to me. "King," she said with a grin. "And Lord. Moving on up in the world, aren't you?" But there was no sting in her words.

I winced. "No idea how to be a king, but I'm sure Evie and I will figure things out together."

Simone stood on her tiptoes and kissed me on the cheek. "I'm glad it was you," she whispered.

I brought her in for a hug. "Me too," I whispered back.

Once she stepped away, it was endless congratulations from what felt like a never-ending line of shifters. By the time the last one had said their piece, Evie looked completely frazzled.

"Hazards of the job," I murmured. "This only happens once, thankfully."

"Your people are wonderful," she said before chuckling under her breath. "And there are *so* many pregnant women here." She sighed. "I don't know how, but I can sense them now. Life beats inside of many of your females, some of them who don't even know yet." She lifted those beautiful eyes to mine. "You are a wonderful Lord."

My breath caught. "I am only as good as my people."

She wrapped her arms around me. "Can we maybe get some sleep?"

I burst out laughing and scooped her into my arms, taking off for the main house in a loping run. "Of course we can."

Her laughter bloomed across my skin as I ran. Happiness warmed my heart, the bond between us strong and healthy.

CHAPTER
SEVENTEEN

We slept all the way through to the next morning. Muted sunlight streamed through the curtains, highlighting the golden hue of Rowan's skin. I was still having trouble believing he was here with me, permanently etched onto my heart and soul.

But alas, the real world had to intrude someday. I toyed with Rowan's hair, tracing my fingers down the edge of his jaw.

Rowan awoke with a smile. He nipped at my finger and growled.

I grinned at him. "Are you always this cranky in the mornings?"

He hauled me on top of him. "Yes."

I pretended to bite his nose. "Thorvin has already texted twice asking what time I'll be there."

"Want company?"

I loved the way he sounded in the morning, all sleep deprived and husky.

"Never stop looking at me like that," Rowan rumbled. His hand swept down my back, stopping at the curve of my hip. His eyes began to glow that strange new color.

"Your eyes are different." I traced my finger down the curve of his cheek.

"Yours are too."

I blinked. "Really?"

Rowan grinned. "Yup. They're still blue, but there's a touch of silver and pink and green in them now."

I frowned. "Weird. Think it's the bond?"

"What else could it be?"

The evidence of his growing desire rested against my thigh. I wiggled a little bit.

"What time did you tell Thorvin you'd be there?" His fingers tightened.

"I didn't." My voice was a little breathless.

In one elegant move, Rowan turned and trapped me underneath him. "Good. You're booked for a last-minute appointment with me."

He tugged on my earlobe with his teeth, setting my nerves on fire.

"You got twenty minutes," I breathed.

Rowan's eyes burned silver. "Challenge accepted."

WE WERE JUST ABOUT to head out the door when Rowan's phone went off. His jaw tightened when he saw the caller.

"It's Caelan."

My stomach lurched with dread. "Do you want to take it? I can wait outside for you."

He shook his head. "Come to the office. You should be here for this."

Rowan took me by the hand and led me to a room off the living area. Once we were shut inside, he answered the video call.

"Caelan."

"Are you sitting down?"

"No, but I can't speak for long. I have a prior engagement."

"You should. There's something I need to tell you."

Rowan's eyes glimmered with amusement. "Just so you know, Evie's with me."

A long silence, then, "Good. This concerns her."

Rowan sat on the small loveseat and patted the space beside him. I sat down and watched Caelan. He sat in his office, his face a mask of stone. Our eyes met.

Fury turned his eyes golden.

"Evangeline is cheating on you."

I pressed my lips together to keep from laughing.

"Oh?" Rowan said, not a hint of concern in his tone. "By the way, she doesn't like when anyone besides her parents call her Evangeline."

Caelan leaned forward. "Did you not hear me, Rowan? Evie is a faithless bitch."

The words felt like sparks of fire touching my skin, each word a burn.

Rowan straightened. "I've warned you before about speaking of Evie like that."

"I'm trying to save you from making a huge mistake!" Caelan bared his teeth. "We were friends at one time, weren't we? Or was everything a lie?"

I was beginning to feel bad. "We should tell him," I murmured.

"When did you see this supposed infidelity?" Rowan asked.

"Evie was in Joy Springs a couple of nights ago with Moira and her mother. She had another man with her."

Rowan's form shifted into the male from the other night. I sucked in a breath. I'd forgotten he could do that. Mom never had to spell him with a glamour, but she'd done so anyway, probably so Caelan wouldn't smell anything off about Rowan's power.

"Is this the male you speak of?" Rowan asked.

Caelan sucked in a sharp breath. "It was you," he growled.

"Guilty as charged."

"Evie's magic has grown in leaps and bounds, it seems," he said, wrongly attributing Rowan's shift to me.

"Every single day," Rowan agreed.

"You encroached on my territory," Caelan said.

"Evie's lands do not belong to you," Rowan reminded him. "As she is now officially my mate—"

Caelan's obvious flinch made my chest hurt. Even after everything happened, he wasn't completely guilty. He was a victim as much as I was, though everything that had happened during the time we were together made me see other things he'd done or said to me in a different light.

We were not good for each other. We never had been. And now that I was here, sitting beside Rowan, my chest warm with the bond between us, I felt grateful for Caelan in a strange way. If it wasn't for him, I'd still be working in my flower shop, totally ignorant of how wonderful love could be when it was right.

"Evie holds domain over my territory as well," Rowan continued.

"Mates," Caelan said softly. "Truly?"

Rowan let out a soft, regretful sigh. Not regret for us, but the situation, I knew. "Yes. Truly." He said nothing of the fae bond.

I stayed silent. There was nothing more I needed to say to Caelan.

"You are the fae king, I take it?"

Rowan nodded.

Caelan's eyes burned. "Will you be renouncing your position as Lord?"

Rowan's brows lifted. "Why would I do that?"

"You now have a conflict of interest. A Lord cannot be beholden to another people other than his own."

"True," Rowan mused. "Evie's people are now my own. By your own account, if this is true, you should resign as well. There are numerous fae living in your territory, including Evie at one time."

"We are meeting soon," Caelan said in response. "At that time, I will ask for a vote."

He clicked off the call without another word.

Rowan shook his head and tucked his phone back into his pocket. "That went better than I expected."

A surprised laugh bubbled from my lips. "Yes, he seems enthusiastic about the future."

Rowan chuckled and rubbed his chin. "This will get worse before it gets better. He's pissed off enough to force a vote. There's no way to tell which way Ethan will go. Ben might side with me. Thorvin should. Soren is always a wild card. Caelan will obviously vote against me. It's possible they could force me out."

I leaned against him, my hand touching his heart. "Do you still want to be Lord?"

"I never wanted it in the first place." His fingers toyed with my hair. "Power doesn't discriminate. Magic like ours becomes a beacon. I had no choice. Once that first ring of gold appeared around my iris, I couldn't hide it, and the other Lords eventually found me."

Rowan pressed a kiss against my hair. "I've gotten everything I wanted, Evie. If they force me out, I won't mind too much for myself, but this would affect my people. They are the ones who would suffer."

I thought about his predicament and how I might be able to

help. A slow smile curved my lips. "Well," I said slowly, "I might have a plan for that one."

Rowan's brow furrowed. I gave him a quick kiss. "We can talk about it later. I'll need your people's permission before we do anything. In the meantime, I want to go smell the baby's head before we go to Thorvin's, so chop chop."

I slid off the couch and headed out the door.

Moira, Ash, and Tess were almost to the house when I walked out. Moira carried Misty's car seat and handed it off to Ash when she spotted me. She took off at a run and stopped a foot before me, dark eyes searching my face.

"You really did it," she breathed. Tears swelled in her eyes, and she jerked me in for a tight hug. "Holy shit, Evie."

Moira was overwhelmed. Her almost too slender frame trembled as she held me. "I was so afraid for you," she whispered. "I'm so happy you let yourself have this."

My throat clogged with tears. "Me too." It was all I could say in the moment. "I mean, how could I say no to that guy, right?"

Moira sniffed. "Yeah. Hot. Kind. Turns into a fucking bear?" She pulled back and shook her head. "You'd be crazy not to grab that with both hands and hold on tight."

We grinned at each other until Ash passed the baby to Tess and shoved his way in. "My turn!" He grabbed me around the waist and swung me around, planting a smacking kiss on my cheek before setting me down. "Congrats. Rowan for the win."

Rowan had come up behind me a second ago. Odd feeling him through the bond, but he felt good, all warm and calming. Tess floated over and handed the baby back to Moira. She wasn't a big hugger, so I was surprised when she reached in and enveloped me in a cool embrace.

"You deserve the most love," she said in her tremulous voice. "We are happy here and can see you are, too." Tess turned to Rowan. "Thank you again for allowing us to stay here. Ash loves it so much he finally took my virginity. Apparently, Joy Springs wasn't green enough for him, but ever since we got here, he hasn't been able to keep his hands off me."

Ash choked. "Tess. *Gods.*"

Rowan burst out laughing, his amusement a bright and sparkling thing through our bond. Moira gaped at Tess. I put my hand over my mouth, hopeless to contain my snicker.

"What?" Tess demanded. "It's true."

Ash's face had turned crimson. "Yes, but talking about your sex life isn't really done."

Rowan brushed his words away. "You are in a Keep full of shifters. Do not be surprised if you occasionally run into some couples enjoying their outdoor time, if you know what I mean. Especially with Evie's presence."

Moira grinned. "You might want to contact the record keepers. I've never seen so many knocked up shifters in one place."

It was my turn to blush.

Rowan put his arm around my waist and tugged me closer. "Her presence makes the land content, but her magic encourages life. Of all kinds. In a few months, our Keep will be overrun with children, an auspicious blessing for the future."

If he was still Lord. A trickle of unease ran through me at the thought. I had a backup plan, one I didn't want to use until absolutely necessary because it would make me enemies.

I had more than enough of those these days.

Moira smiled down at the baby. "Did you hear that? You're going to have so many friends in a few months."

I slipped away from Rowan and unbuckled Misty from the carrier, cooing to her as I picked her up. She gave me a gummy grin and waved her chubby hands at me.

My heart melted. "Aren't you the sweetest thing?"

"No news?" Moira asked.

"Not a peep." I straightened the baby's cap and touched her

cheek. "No one has stepped up to claim her or asked any questions. Whoever dropped her here did so in complete secrecy."

Moira frowned. "What will you do?"

Rowan made a silly face at the baby who let out a loud belly laugh. "We'll keep her here," he said. "Everyone here loves babies. She'll have all the love she'll ever need." He glanced at me. "And we have a Chimera who will help her control her magic."

I winced. "Once your Chimera learns to control her own."

Rowan waved away my reservations. "You're already controlling your shifts and transformations. The rest is a matter of practice."

Too bad the practice wasn't going well, fae or Chimera. I'd been practicing every day, trying to master the art of moving from one spot to another instantaneously. All I felt was a slight tingle and absolutely nothing else. "We can't bring Barrett back," I said. "He'll scent the baby. His senses are more finely honed than mine." Yet another thing I was working on.

"Your mother or father could help," Rowan said. "We can ask. Barrett isn't due back for a day or two. We can delay him until we figure something out. Or we could move training somewhere else. We're already having a baby boom." A sly grin made the edges of his eyes crinkle. "We could tell him my people are tired from all the sex you're encouraging them to have."

Moira chuckled then sighed. "Man. I need a boyfriend." She blinked and grimaced. "No. Scratch that. I need a silent man who knows how to shut up and use his penis. Preferably at the same time."

I barked a laugh and covered the baby's ears. "You shouldn't say penis around the baby."

Moira rolled her eyes. "Please don't tell me you're the kind of mom who gives private parts weird names like nur nur or tooter."

Ash groaned. Tess had floated off to investigate something within the trees.

"Uh no. I'm way more sophisticated than that. A vagina is a va jay jay and a penis is a peen."

"Dear gods," Moira muttered. "I like nur nur better."

I grinned and waved her away. "She has plenty of time before we talk about any of that stuff."

I buried my nose in the baby's downy hair. Misty smelled like sugar and baby shampoo. I adjusted her so she could see over my shoulder. Her big blue eyes took in everything, and she cooed happily with every new thing that appeared.

"We need to go," Rowan said. "Thorvin just texted me."

"Aww." I rubbed my cheek against Misty's and handed her back to Moira, already missing her sweet warmth. What would it be like to have a baby with Rowan? To have a sweet little thing made from both of us?

Rowan's hand swept down my back. "We'll find out one day," he murmured.

I blinked and glanced up at him in concern.

"Don't worry," he said, eyes sparkling with amusement. "We can't read each other's minds. That one was kind of obvious." Rowan winked and turned to my friends. "We'll return shortly."

"How about dinner tonight?" It'd been a while since we had been together.

"As long as you two crazy kids can keep your hands off each other long enough to eat," Moira said with a grin.

Color heated my cheeks. "I can't wait until you find your silent penis," I grumbled.

"Me either," Moira said with a laugh. "How about seven tonight?"

I looked at Rowan, who nodded.

"Good with us." I pulled out the potions from my jacket pocket. "How's your supply looking?"

"Excellent." Moira nodded to Rowan. "Your territory is wonderfully abundant with most of the things I need for my work, and I haven't walked more than ten percent."

"With Evie here, I'm sure that will only get better."

Moira winked at me. "Have fun you two. And if Thorvin acts up, tell him he's overdue for another glittering."

"Will do." I gave her and Ash another quick hug. They wandered away to find Tess while Rowan and I continued on to a safe space far away from the prying eyes of the Keep. We both trusted Rowan's people—my people now, too, but shifters didn't always love magic. They seemed fine with my particular flavor—earth magic—though growing flowers and making people randy was vastly different than disappearing into thin air.

Rowan suggested easing them into power like this. They've never had a fae living on Keep grounds and things had been a welcome but big adjustment for everyone.

When we were out of sight, Rowan snagged me around the waist and kissed me senseless. I sagged against him, hands clutching the soft fabric of his sweater.

"Mm. What was that for?"

Rowan kissed me once more. "Because I can and because I want to."

He never held anything over my head, never teased or cajoled me without following through. Rowan never made me feel weak. My breath caught.

Concern flashed in his eyes. He tilted my chin up. "What's wrong?"

"I'm sorry it took me so long to find you." I swallowed hard and looked away.

Rowan's arms gathered around me. "It took exactly as long as it was meant to take."

He always knew the right thing to say.

"Seeing me with Caelan must have been difficult for you."

Rowan nuzzled my hair. "I didn't know you were my mate back then. I knew there was something between us, more than an easy friendship. There were moments of jealousy, but those were tamped down by your feelings for him." His sigh was deep. "As time went on, my feelings grew, and there were a few times I had to stop myself from beating that idiot to a pulp when he was casually cruel to you."

Rowan shook his head. "These things are all in the past. We've gotten to where we need to be." He clasped our fingers together. "You never have to apologize to me for your feelings, no matter what they were."

I lifted our joined hands and pressed a kiss to the back of his hand. "I'm glad I found you."

He squeezed my hand. "I'm glad we found each other."

I handed him a potion. "To Thorvin's?"

"Hopefully this goes quickly," Rowan said. "The Lords are a buzzing annoyance right now."

I grinned. "Maybe we'll get there and everything is fine."

Rowan laughed and tilted back the potion, swallowing the contents in one go. I did the same.

"One can wish," he responded.

A tingle of magic washed over us. I closed my eyes and thought of Thorvin's Keep.

Not ten seconds after, I opened my eyes to a barren wasteland.

EIGHTEEN

Revulsion washed over me, the taint of dark magic seeping into the air and ground all around us. Winter always tinged everything in white and brown, but life was circular and when spring came, the land would rebound. Today, everything looked dead with zero chance of recovery.

Rowan took an involuntary step back. "What the fuck?" he breathed.

I swayed on my feet, my gaze sweeping across Thorvin's land. "You stubborn ass Lords," I swore under my breath.

"As your mate, I hope I am excluded from that generalization."

I stomped toward the Keep, every step sending my senses spiraling with grief. The land didn't just look dead, it *was* dead. I didn't dare place my fingers in the ground, not yet. Not until I got a better read on things.

Rowan hurried behind me. "Evie." There was a warning note in his tone.

"Stubborn, foolish, selfish men," I muttered to myself. "Thorvin let his land die because he didn't trust me not to take his territory for myself." I stopped and speared Rowan with a glowing gaze. My eyes cast a haze over his skin.

Rowan's eyes were soft but concerned. "They are less powerful than you."

"So?" I demanded. "They're also a hell of a lot dumber."

Rowan snorted and gently took my arm. "Taking their land will weaken their standing with their people."

Anger bubbled in my veins. "Do you see what we're standing on, Rowan? Can you feel the earth's grief like I can? I offered to help weeks ago, and your Lords treated me like I had the plague. Instead of accepting and maybe drawing up some sort of agreement to make them feel better about this, Thorvin allowed the land to die."

My voice broke as I swept a sharp hand out. "All of this is *gone*. Those trees. This grass. At least a foot of dirt, all the earthworms and grubs, and all the insects and snakes that keep the world turning are gone. I can sense their remains rotting below. He allowed the magic to poison the land because he was afraid of losing power." My voice deepened, magic booming around us. "TELL ME WHY I SHOULD NOT STRIP HIM OF EVERYTHING."

A sharp wind blew around us, whipping my hair into a tangle around my face. Magic snapped over my skin, hot and wild. Rowan took my other arm and peered into my eyes, his own glowing that strange new color. "I cannot justify what he did," he said softly. "But I do understand the urge to cling to the only thing you know, the only thing protecting you from the evil things in this world. For people like Thorvin, that is his power."

I had to take a few cleansing breaths before I could speak again. "His people are not limited to humans and paranormals. Lords are stewards to this land. He has broken his covenant with earth."

"I know."

"Then why are you discouraging me?" Tears thickened my voice. Agony and grief rose around me.

"Evie." Rowan huffed a breath. "I'm not discouraging you, only asking you to show some restraint. Your power is growing in leaps and bounds, and if you come here and strip his land from him, none of the other Lords will agree to work with you. Diplomacy, as shitty and unfortunate as it may be, is the only way I've been successful in dealing with some of these asshats."

His words got through. Somewhat. I was still staring at him, my magic lending a faint blue and silvery glow to his skin. His eyes turned wary. "Evie?"

"I'm thinking."

He stroked a finger down my cheek. "Take all the time you need."

I chewed on the side of my lip. "Why are you so reasonable?"

He laughed and brought me in for a hug. "Trust me. I really don't want to be."

"But someone has to do it?"

"Can you see Soren or Caelan being reasonable?"

I snorted. "There's always Ethan."

"The bastard has a kill first, ask questions later rule. He's quite maddening when we're trying to negotiate anything."

"I thought Thorvin might be reasonable."

A long pause. "Thorvin is driven by intellect. Sometimes, when someone is extremely smart, they suffer from what's called analysis paralysis. Knowing him, he saw exactly what happened and threw himself into research on how to fix the problem. He probably has twenty potential solutions and can't pull the trigger on any of them."

"And he couldn't call me, either, because I was in the pool of potential solutions."

"Exactly."

"Everything is dead, Rowan." I stepped away from his embrace and touched my heart. "I hurt. Right here. I feel the land's agony. There should be repercussions. There have to be repercussions to stop this from happening again in the future."

Rowan nodded solemnly. "Suggestions?"

"Taking his land, stripping his ability to ever be a caretaker again."

Rowan saw my face. "Perhaps something a little less severe?"

"Can I kick his ass?" I muttered.

A thoughtful look crept over Rowan's face. "Lords and shifters respond to physical violence," he mused. "Can you promise not to kill him?" His eyes glinted.

I thought about it. "I won't kill him," I said after a moment.

Rowan's chest rumbled with amusement. "That was a long pause, my darling."

"Yes, well, he deserves to feel exactly what he's done. I want him to feel his land's agony…" My voice trailed off. The idea had merit. Hmm.

Rowan and I locked gazes. "Is it possible?" he murmured.

"Give me a bit." I held up a finger. "I'll get back to you in a minute or two."

Rowan nodded. "I'll go on up to the house. He knows we're here."

I hurried away to find a clean spot on the ground. My plan wouldn't work without a little help.

CHAPTER

NINETEEN

ROWAN

"She's pissed, isn't she?" Thorvin scrubbed a hand over his face.

I liked the scholarly Lord, though like all of us, I knew not to underestimate him. Evie, after almost getting Garrett killed when she trespassed on his land, had learned the lesson the hard way. Thorvin was a crack shot with a weapon, so good I always wondered if he had a touch of magic. Or, like me, a lot of carefully hidden magic.

Regardless, Thorvin was one of the gentler Lords, only retaliating when someone pushed him. He, like my territory, maintained peace and a good relationship with his people. He wasn't loved like some of us, but respected. And that seemed fine with him. Thorvin was introspective and introverted, and difficult to get to know. I'd known him for years and still couldn't figure out what made him tick.

Learning was his passion, but I always worried the Lord was letting his books get in the way of his social life, if the poor bastard even had one. We respected each other and had a good relationship, but today, based on the fury and heartbreak in my mate's eyes, would determine whether it stayed that way.

The shifter looked like he hadn't slept in a week. Dark bags had moved in under his eyes and made themselves at home. His hair and skin were dull, and his clothes looked like they'd been slept in multiple times over. Empathy filled me, but Evie wasn't wrong. He'd been insanely neglectful of his territory.

"If you could feel what Evie could, you'd understand," I said quietly.

Thorvin sighed. "Shit, Rowan, I couldn't control this. This magic...it's completely unfamiliar to me. I feel like I'm an intruder on my own property. This shit seems sentient, like it's watching me and waiting." He shook his head. "This power wants something and I don't have a clue what that might be."

Thorvin leaned against the side of his vehicle and studied me, sharp intellect and realization in his light brown eyes. "You mated." A quick flash of smile. "It looks good on you." Thorvin chuckled under his breath. "You were always good at fucking up a plan, weren't you?"

I couldn't help my wince.

"I assume Caelan isn't taking things well?"

"Understatement," I agreed. "Though he spearheaded how this came to be and is too shortsighted to see it. One day he will understand why Evie left him, and when he does, I hope he has a friend to go to."

Thorvin eyed me. "That friend won't be you?"

My magic spiraled. Thorvin gasped and took a step back. "Rowan. Your eyes."

"He abused Evie until she broke." My voice sounded not of this world, a side effect of joining with Evie and one I'd have to learn to manage. "Caelan no longer has a friend in me."

Thorvin's slow, thoughtful nod calmed me.

"I hope when Evie is through with you that you still call me friend."

Thorvin's jaw tightened. "You won't step in?"

I laughed. "I keep reminding everyone she is not a Lord. Evie might be my mate, but she is an earthbound goddess. I could no more stop her than I could stop the sun from rising."

She came over the hill, dark hair dotted with daisies flowing behind her like a banner. Her azure eyes glowed with magic, and flowers rose behind her as she walked toward us, healing the land with every step she took. She'd removed or lost her shoes somewhere along the way, no way to tell with her.

Desire tightened my skin. I couldn't tear my eyes away from her. She moved like an assassin, silent and lithe.

Thorvin cursed softly before letting out a sigh of resignation.

"Is she going to kill me?"

I was so caught up in watching my mate walk toward us it took a second for his words to register. "Not today."

Thorvin let out a soft snort. "You got it bad, man."

I did and life was finally as it should be. "She's magnificent. I hope one day you experience this."

Thorvin was silent for a long moment. "Me too," he said quietly and pushed off from the vehicle to meet his fate.

CHAPTER

TWENTY

My mate stood beside the man who'd allowed his land to die and watched me like I was water in the desert. Magic rode me, spilling from my hands and feet into the ground. Life sprang up behind me, not enough to heal the land, but enough to begin the process. Healing what this spell had done would take me a while.

But first, Thorvin would know what he had done; he would see and feel what I felt the second I stepped into his territory.

The Lord left Rowan and started toward me. I said nothing, only threw my magic into the ground, opening a wide, deep hole. Thorvin's eyes widened when he saw what I was doing. His steps hitched, and I thought for a moment he might turn and run. But the Lord squared his shoulders and kept walking.

"LORD THORVIN. AS A STEWARD OF THIS LAND, I HAVE FOUND YOU LACKING."

Thorvin bowed his head. "I am aware. My power comes from books and knowledge, and I waited too long to heal this cancer on my land. For that, I cannot be sorry enough."

Vines rose from deep in the ground, struggling to rise through the dead parts of Thorvin's land. I encouraged them to

157

break through, healing them as they rose. They wrapped around Thorvin's arms and legs, lifting him high into the air.

Thorvin did not struggle or beg. Instead, his face turned stoic. "If you kill me, there will be war."

"YOUR DEATH IS NOT YOUR DESTINY TODAY. SEE WHAT YOU HAVE ALLOWED TO TRANSPIRE, LORD, AND KNOW HOW YOUR LAND SUFFERS."

Without further ado, I directed the vines to gently deposit Thorvin into the hole. I made a pocket of air to ensure he would survive and sent dirt pouring back into the hole.

Danu would take care of the rest.

Once he was buried deep inside the earth, I opened my eyes, my magic draining into the ground.

Rowan stood before me, eyes glowing. "The voice thing is new." Amusement and a touch of wariness colored his tone.

I'd noticed too. "My power keeps growing. Dad did something the other day at that ceremony." I grimaced. "Haven't felt the same since."

A scream rumbled through the ground. One of Rowan's eyebrows rose. "Should I ask?"

"Plausible deniability."

He nodded. "He'll be alive when he comes out?"

"Should be. I asked Danu to ensure he can...recover."

Rowan winced. "Do we need to have the Keep medics respond?"

I lifted a shoulder in an unconcerned shrug. "We'll see when he gets back. I asked Danu to keep him for a couple of days."

"Days," Rowan said slowly. A dark chuckle, then a shake of his head. "When you teach a lesson, you do it well."

I tugged him down for a kiss. "Killing him would have been more merciful."

Rowan smiled against my lips. "No one has ever accused me of being merciful."

How in the world could I have ever looked past this glorious man? I ran my hands over his chest. "I'll be here for at least a day. If you have business to attend to, I have another of Moira's potions in my pocket."

Rowan frowned. "I don't want to leave you in another Lord's territory alone."

We'd have a ton of fun being naked in a hole together for a day or two, but Rowan was still a Lord. He'd sacrificed many things when he took me into his territory, and I wouldn't keep asking him to sacrifice more. I smoothed the wrinkles I'd put in his sweater when I grabbed him. "Send Moira. She's always up for some fun, and I know she'd love seeing Thorvin come up from the ground."

"Hmm. Your friend is a bit of a masochist."

I laughed. "Moira is definitely bigger on the inside. We see very little of her on the outside. She'll protect me, though I don't anticipate anything going wrong. Thorvin is contained, and the other Lords are preoccupied with other things, I assume. No one should know I'm here."

"More than likely they do," Rowan corrected. "Caelan is in his territory."

My eyebrows rose. "You have a spy in Joy Springs."

He flicked my nose. "Darling, I have spies everywhere."

"Of course you do. He's the one we need to worry about most. We should be fine. If Moira can't come, see if Ash is available."

Rowan still hesitated. I kissed him again. "It's fine. I promise. You have things to do, and I have to fix the mess Thorvin caused."

When he saw I wasn't going to back down, he nodded. "Fine. Text me when you come up for air." He winced. "Or whatever happens when the earth releases you."

"I expect a full twenty-four hours, possibly forty-eight."

Anger rose inside me once more. "The land needs a lot of attention."

"I'll check in with Moira enough to be annoying," he promised.

After a kiss that left me breathless, Rowan disappeared. I touched my lips and sighed, laughing at myself when I realized I was wearing a dopey smile.

Guilt still touched me sometimes but quickly became overshadowed by what I'd found with Rowan. Love waited for no one, and sometimes it hit you like a freight train. I'd been doubly blessed and vowed to never take it for granted.

A shimmer appeared before me several minutes later, revealing a slender, grinning vampire holding a cooler. "Hey, hot stuff. Heard you put a dude in the ground."

I pointed to the mound of dirt. "If you listen hard enough, you can occasionally hear him scream."

Moira's eyes lit with vicious delight. "I'll have to put on my listening ears, then."

Her face changed the moment she took in our surroundings. She blinked and let out a vicious curse. "I didn't think Rowan was lying, but gods, Evie. Are you sure you can fix this?"

Moira swallowed hard and shook her head. "This should be criminal." Her jaw tightened as she came to sit beside me. "I'm glad you put him in the ground. Wish it would have been permanently."

"Killing a Lord could have disastrous consequences." I quoted the words I'd heard a dozen times over the past year or so.

Moira rolled her eyes. "Don't they know who your dad is?"

Dad seemed disinclined to get involved in most things, unless it happened to be my love life. "Sometimes, I think it might not matter if I killed all of them. People, especially our kind, can be self-governing. We might have to deal with a despot here and there, but that happens with humans too. If the Lords were gone, would we even notice after a few weeks?"

Moira stared at me, amusement sparkling in her dark eyes. "Careful. You're sounding awfully Libertarian there. You might offend the masses if you accuse the people of—" She let out a dramatic gasp, "having sovereignty over their bodies, emotions, and property."

"Only a closet Libertarian would know that's what they believe." We grinned at each other. "The world would run so much better if the world operated under the principles of doing what's right versus what's right for them to line their pockets or their egos. The Lords are a mess, and people shouldn't have to suffer because they can't get their shit together. Would it really matter if we allowed them to self-govern for a little while?"

Moira shrugged. "Power abhors a vacuum. Someone will step into the empty spaces the Lords leave and claim they'll do a better job. Even if we know it's bullshit, people tend to flock to charismatic leaders." Her lips twisted. "We need to think about this deeper. The fae are tricky bastards and have been for eternity." She smiled at my look. "We have to start asking more serious questions."

"Like what?" As I was one of those tricky bastard fae, I knew better than most the games my kind could play.

Moira's expression turned somber. "Are we being led by our noses to walk a certain path?"

I'd thought the same thing a few times but didn't have enough evidence to prove such a thing was happening. "There's no reason a fae would design a spell like this if it didn't have a purpose. All of us are harmed when the land suffers. The fae may not feel any ill effects immediately, but they would after a while. I can't figure out why someone would do something like this if all of us would suffer."

Moira's lips twisted. "Perfect example of collateral damage.

Any fae who suffers the fallout might not be the intended target, but whoever cast the spell considers the end result worth the potential loss."

I stared at Moira for a long moment, disturbed to my core. When I opened my mouth to ask her why she would know something like this or automatically think this was the purpose of the spell, Moira makes a downward slash with her hand. "Don't ask," she said in a clipped voice.

I pulled my knees up and rested my chin on top of them. "A burden earned hurts half as badly when it's shared," I said lightly.

"As much as I appreciate your colloquial wisdom," Moira said dryly, "I like my burdens secured tightly behind a closed door in my mind." She softened her words with a smile.

Didn't make me hurt any less for her, though.

"One day I hope you find someone you can unlock that door for," I said softly.

Moira shook her head and scoffed. "Gods, I hope not. That poor bastard will be opening Pandora's box and have no idea what's about to hit him."

I nudged her with my shoulder. "I thought Caelan was it for me. For a while, he was everything. I would have torn the world apart to keep us together. When I was floating in that gods-damned tree, all I could think about was all the mistakes I'd made and wonder if I'd ever make it back to the people I loved. When I did and I saw you all there, I thought I had everything I'd ever wanted. I'd been given a second chance."

Moira bowed her head.

"The moment I stepped out of the tree and saw Caelan, I wanted the rest of my life to start right then, with me as his wife." I spread my hands out to encompass Thorvin's land. "But here I am now, with Caelan nowhere to be found. I have a mate, someone I love more than I could have ever loved Caelan, and you, Ash, and Tess are still with me." I scooted over and slung an arm over her shoulder. "Life isn't linear, Moira. Sometimes a second chance means doing something different than before. It means taking chances, even if it's opening up a little bit to the people you love so we can help share your burdens."

Moira let out a heavy sigh. Her fists clenched at her sides. "I'm not ready," she said after a long silence.

I reached up and stroked my fingers through her silky dark hair. "That's okay. One day you will be. Until then, I will be right by your side."

She laid her head on my shoulder, relaxing bit by bit, until she finally exhaled and sat up. "You better get in the ground and do your fancy woo woo stuff. Rowan won't wait too long before he's chomping at the bit to have you back."

I smiled at her and stood to undress. Going underground unclothed would be unpleasant at first, but I didn't want to have to travel home naked, and this type of magic always destroyed my clothing.

Moira turned her back and waited. When I sat back down and hissed at the freezing ground on my bits, she laughed and turned. "I'll be right here," she promised.

"Thorvin will be under for the next forty-six hours."

Moira raised an eyebrow. "Specific, but okay." She looked at her watch. "Good luck down there."

I frowned. "Remind me to punch Thorvin a few times once I'm awake."

"No problem," Moira promised.

I closed my eyes and let the magic sweep me under. Lots of work to be done to give Thorvin's territory a fighting chance.

And the work had to be done even if I didn't think he deserved it. The land was the victim here, not Thorvin's ego.

CHAPTER

TWENTY-ONE

MOIRA

A full twenty-four hours had passed, and I was bored out of my gourd. I'd brought snacks, a couple of puzzle books, and my e-reader, but I hadn't been this alone in years, and the silence was starting to weigh on me.

I wasn't like Evie. That chick could get buried under twenty thousand pounds of dirt for months, and I don't think she'd bat an eye. I liked noise, bustle, music, action. No one had shown up at the Keep. Thorvin was the type of Lord who preferred solitude, so no one was overly worried about his absence yet.

The screams underground had gone from horror to the occasional shout, to a deep, soul shaking cry. I almost felt bad for the guy. My friend wasn't vindictive, but if you pushed her past the point of anger into straight outrage, she would find a way to pay your ass back in spades.

When Thorvin came out of this, he would not be the same man. Whether it was for better or worse...only time would tell.

I paced around the clearing, careful to keep clear of the mound Evie had buried herself under and ate a handful of nuts. I'd rather it was cake, but cake was hard to transport. I'd brought the necessities—nuts, dried fruits, cookies, and water.

If this went much longer than tomorrow, I'd have to risk breaking into Thorvin's house to raid his fridge, but the Lord should be out tomorrow, anyway.

He might not be in a sharing mood once Danu was done with him, but I could be very persuasive when necessary.

A branch cracked behind me. I spun, nuts spilling from my fingers.

No one was there. I knew the sound of an animal moving versus the sound of a human. This was no animal.

"I know you're there. Reveal yourself," I said, putting as much menace in my tone as I could.

"Or what?" A cultured male voice touched with amusement responded. "Will you throw nuts at me until I beg for mercy?"

I looked at the handful of almonds in my palm and frowned. The voice was familiar and yet...not. Not Caelan or Rowan, definitely not Soren. Thorvin was in the ground, and Ben...no, it wasn't him either. He had no sense of humor.

"Ethan?"

The Lord appeared from nowhere, making me jerk in surprise. He should not have been able to do that.

I narrowed my eyes. "Why are you on Thorvin's land?"

Ethan was one of the Lords I couldn't get a read on. To everyone else, he was rigid, unfeeling, and too formal. If I hadn't broken into his Keep and spied on him, I might have thought the same. Standing before me was a carefully crafted persona.

He was handsome as all the Lords were, but Ethan held himself tightly leashed. Violence lurked just underneath the surface. I would know. I saw myself in him.

He was older than the others, though not old. Shifters were blessed with immortality. Silver edged Ethan's temples, either as a result of age or a deep trauma his DNA had not healed, something that had permanently altered him. I suspected the latter. No fine lines or wrinkles marred his handsome features, though the edges of his eyes held the faintest of shadows, as if he used to smile frequently and his skin hadn't forgotten the memory of his happiness.

Against my better judgment, I wondered what life had done to Ethan to erase his joy.

He was shorter than Caelan and Rowan, but he still hit right at six feet, maybe a touch taller, forcing me to tilt my face up when I looked at him. Compared to the other Lords, Ethan was smaller, leaner, built for speed rather than brute violence. His eyes were dark, though I knew they were not brown, more of a midnight blue, reminiscent of a starless night sky.

I found him breathlessly beautiful, and if Evie knew, she would laugh her ass off and beg me not to pursue this madness. Not that I could pursue anything. Ethan stared at me with barely concealed distaste.

To be fair, he looked at most things the way he was looking at me, but I couldn't fathom how I, a woman who hated just about everything and everyone, could find someone so profoundly stunning only for that person I secretly admired to stare at me like I was moldy leftovers forgotten in the back of the fridge.

He was not the kind of man you slept with and walked away from.

He was the kind who'd burn an image in your mind, one that you saw every time you closed your eyes, whether you wanted to or not.

I'd cursed myself over and over for trespassing on his property and getting a glimpse at his private life. Doing so had made me want things, unattainable things I knew I'd never have. I wasn't Evie. I was no secret goddess, and my powers weren't the blessing of life Evie had.

My powers were haunting and varied, and almost always

ended in death. And now, thanks to the exposure to fae magic on Caelan's property, they were even more fucked up than usual.

"A better question," Ethan drawled after a drawn-out and uncomfortably long silence, "is why you're here."

His eyes flicked to the mound I stood by. Realization made him flinch. "Where is Thorvin?"

I crossed my arms and said nothing.

"Moira."

The way he said my name made the hair on the back of my neck stand up.

"This does not have to come to violence." His voice was cajoling, but his dark eyes were flat.

"You suck at charm," I drawled. "And I am immune. Try another tactic. Let's see what you got."

His lips thinned. "If we brawl, you will lose."

"Ah. So you went for arrogance. A way better performance than when you tried charm."

He let out a sharp breath of annoyance. "Spending so much time with Evie has sharpened your tongue."

I laughed. "Other way around, though I have to give you Lords credit. Your shenanigans helped her hone her devastating sarcasm into an art." I smiled. "Her magic, too. She's way better at things than she used to be."

His eyes flickered with annoyance. "Why is she in the ground?"

I gestured. "Have you not seen what your precious Lord allowed to happen to his land?"

Ethan stared at me with those flat eyes. I wondered what would happen if I touched him?

He would kill you.

That voice in my head that never steered me wrong whispered through my mind. The few times I'd failed to listen to that voice, I'd come close to dying. Sometimes I thought the voice was mine alone, but there were times in the deep of night when I wondered if something else lived inside my head, something separate from me.

Those nights I got little sleep.

To my surprise, Ethan grunted. "Fool." He sighed and came closer. "Got any more of those nuts left?"

I blinked at him. "Err. Yes. I have fruit and cookies, too."

Ethan had not noticed the other mound yet. When he did, I expected our truce to be shattered in a flurry of tooth and claws.

"Cookies?" he questioned.

Did the handsome Lord have a sweet tooth? "Scottish shortbread. I've been out here for twenty-four hours and needed something that would hold up."

"Any preservatives?"

I studied Ethan, biting down a smile. Interesting. "No. I made it. Grass-fed butter, Italian sourced flour, and raw sugar."

He blinked in surprise. "Then yes, I would be honored if you shared your sustenance with me."

Good gods. He spoke like an old-timey gentleman sometimes. I fucking knew he'd hold the door open for me if we went on a date.

Shaking my thoughts free of that ridiculous thought—Ethan would never take me out on a date—I opened the cooler and pulled out the vintage metal tin filled with the homemade shortbread and passed it over.

A flash of something burned in Ethan's eyes as he took the container and opened it. The sweet, buttery smell of shortbread filled the air. A faint tug at the side of Ethan's mouth made my breath catch.

Note to self. Carry shortbread and homemade, no-preservative cookies everywhere you went, just in case you ran into Ethan.

Be still my beating heart. This dude was a stone-cold fox.

He didn't even complete the smile, and my lady parts were standing up singing God Bless America at the top of their tiny lungs.

Snap out of it, you stupid bitch, the voice said. *Ethan is not the type of man to settle down.*

I should know. I'd stalked him relentlessly after returning to Joy Springs. The handsome bastard had no record of ever having a girlfriend, never been seen on a date, was rarely spotted out anywhere, not even for dinner, had never been married or linked to anyone and was, essentially, a social media and internet ghost.

Maddening, I tell you. It made me itchy and far more curious than I should be.

Ethan reached in and hesitated.

"Take as many as you want," I said, my voice a little huskier than it should be.

Ethan, even with my permission, showed great restraint, and took three cookies out, carefully replacing the lid after he did. "Thank you."

"Sure." I opened the tin back up and took two out. "This is Hazel's recipe," I said, wanting to fill the silence. "True Scottish shortbread." A thought tugged me. "I asked her about adding vanilla, and she smacked me with a wooden spoon." My lips curved at the memory.

Spending time in Hazel's cottage had been a breath of fresh air. The woman was a lot of things, but she knew how to make a damned good shortbread.

Ethan said nothing, only put the cookie to his mouth and took a small bite. The flash of his teeth and the crumble of the shortbread into his mouth made me swallow and look away.

Good gods. I needed to find that silent penis sooner rather than later.

But I couldn't help myself. I looked at him again and saw he'd closed his eyes as he chewed. His throat worked as he swallowed.

Alright. Shit. That made it worse.

Cookies were not supposed to be erotic.

I shoved the entire cookie into my mouth so I couldn't say anything stupid like, "Take me now, you big handsome powerful beast."

Seriously. I needed to get a grip.

Ethan focused on those cookies like a soldier focused on the battlefield, with intense concentration and attention to detail. Every bite was planned, but his enjoyment was obvious. He ate all three cookies slowly and in silence.

By the time he finished the last cookie, I was about to leap out of my skin and right on top of him. Keeping a stoic face and pretending I was completely unaffected required using all my skills.

"Those were delicious, Moira. Thank you."

I passed the tin back over, even though I might die if this fucker tortured me by eating another cookie. "Want some more?"

Was that amusement sparkling in his eyes? I watched him warily.

"Maybe when I'm ready to leave. For now, I am sated." He turned to me, spearing me with that beautiful dark gaze. "With food, at least."

Holy fucking hell. Was Ethan *flirting* with me?

He looked away and exhaled a deep breath.

No. He wasn't. What the hell was wrong with me?

"Where is Thorvin?" he asked.

If I lied, I suspected he would know. He was not as flippant as the other Lords. I pointed to another mound behind and to the left of me.

Ethan didn't catch it at first, but when he did, he froze. Violence sparked over his face. "Do I dare ask why one of my Lords is in a grave?"

I stayed perfectly still, feeling like a mouse hiding from a predator. "Not a grave," I said quietly. "A punishment."

Ethan jerked his attention away from where Thorvin lay. "Elaborate," he snapped.

"Thorvin delayed asking Evie for help until it was almost too late. When she arrived and saw his territory in this state—" I swept my hand across to encompass the destruction of the land, "she was understandably furious."

Ethan's granite jaw tightened. "And she thought that gave her the right to punish one of my Lords?"

I couldn't help it. I laughed. "Evie is a goddess. She is very close to being Mother Earth, Gaia, whatever the hell you want to call her. It hurts her when the earth dies. Thorvin made a deliberate decision not to call her. So yes, she thought he deserved punishment."

His irises ringed with magic the color of burnt gold touched by a tinge of that delicious, dark blue. "And what do you think?" His beast rode his voice, turning the already deep timbre into something rough and violent.

I thought I wanted to take him by the collar, push him to the ground, and do terrible things to him. "I agree with her. He is responsible for everyone in this territory, and we know the magic can infect its inhabitants. If allowed to spread, it's possible he would have harmed or even killed the people who rely on him to help them."

His fingers elongated into claws. I braced myself, waiting for him to leap toward me, but he turned away and stalked toward Thorvin's makeshift shelter. When he went to his knees and shoved his claws into the ground, I rose and walked over.

"I wouldn't do that," I warned him.

A snarl rumbled in the back of his throat. He flashed his teeth at me, elongated canines gleaming in his mouth, and kept digging.

I watched him for a moment before trying again. "Ethan."

"Do not dissuade me from this task, woman."

Woman. Le swoon. "Evie could not release him from this cage even if she wanted to."

His hands stilled. "What."

"Danu holds him," I said quietly. "Despite your blatant dislike of Evie, she has always been reasonable. From what I understand of Danu, she is…less so. This punishment was taken out of Evie's hands the moment he went into the ground."

Ethan swore under his breath and removed his hands from the dirt. "How long?"

"Another twenty-four hours," I said.

"Will he be released alive?"

"From everything I know, yes."

Ethan peered up at me. A smudge of dirt marred his perfect cheek, lending him a decidedly human and rumpled look. Yum.

"Will he be the same?"

I lifted a shoulder in a shrug. "Leaning no on that one, Ethan."

At the flash of magic in his irises, I held up my hands. "Sometimes the lessons we learn are hard ones. You can see the evidence of his neglect. Perhaps it's better if he comes back changed."

He rose to his feet, not bothering to dust off his slacks. His knees and perfectly shined loafers were covered in icy mud.

Ethan Flint, why am I so obsessed with you?

The Lord looked to the horizon, where the sun was slowly beginning to set, then back at me. "You're staying here?"

I nodded.

"It's freezing out here."

A tiny, hairline crack appeared in the stone surrounding my heart. "It is," I agreed. "I brought a blanket."

"And cookies."

"And cookies," I agreed.

"And nuts and fruit."

"Yep. This shouldn't go over two days, and I needed food that would keep."

He shook his head. "I know you won't agree, but I can stay with them."

I stared at him.

He let out a sigh. "Fine." Ethan fished his wallet out and handed me a heavy, embossed card with his name and a phone number stamped in silver foil across the middle. "Call me the moment he wakes up."

I lifted an eyebrow.

Ethan rolled his eyes. "Please."

Not waiting for my response, he stalked back over to the cookie tin, opened it back up, and took a handful of my shortbread.

He held a cookie up to his temple and did a little salute with it before turning to walk away. Just before he disappeared, he turned around, his irises ringed with magic.

"Oh, by the way, Moira?"

I tilted my head.

His eyes gleamed. "Wolves have an extremely acute sense of smell. I had no idea food was your...*thing*."

A wicked grin slashed his face, sending my loins into overdrive before he disappeared in a mist of blue and gold.

Oh my gods. I'd forgotten. Not a single person had made me feel desire like he had in *years*. HOW THE FUCK COULD I FORGET WOLVES COULD SMELL SHIT LIKE ME BEING HORNY?

Maybe because I hadn't been legitimately horny in probably ten years.

I let out a bloodcurdling scream of horror.

Several hours later, I awoke in the middle of a black night, stirred from a deep sleep by something unknown. My eyes focused immediately, spotting the large brown paper bag six inches away.

I froze, all my senses on high alert, but there was no one around for miles.

Wary, I pulled the bag closer and peered inside. A folded note lay on top of something that smelled delicious. My mouth watered as I unfolded the paper.

Thank you for the cookies. I hope these help ease the pain of a cold winter's night.

Ethan's bold signature was scrawled below.

Warmth filled me. If I ever saw him again, I'd probably die, but there was food in this bag. Hot, delicious smelling food. With no shame, I dug in to investigate.

Chicken fried steak, mac and cheese, and roasted broccoli, still hot, lay in the first container. The second held a massive slice of coconut cake. The third held banana pudding.

Gods. Was it possible to fall in love via food delivery?

I frowned as I fished around the still-not-empty bag. I pulled out a large, flexible parcel wrapped in brown paper and tied with a long string of blue twine, then a separate, smaller parcel wrapped in the same.

The first held a battery-operated electric blanket. The other was a blue cashmere cap with ear flaps and a stunning cashmere scarf in blue and gold.

I'd never look at the two colors the same again.

Ethan must have spent several hundred dollars on this. I

wrapped the scarf around my neck and pressed my nose into the deliciously soft fabric, inhaling Ethan's unique, spicy scent. No one else had handled this. There was the faint tang of several scents, older now and probably belonging to the people who'd made and packaged the item, but Ethan's scent was the most prominent. The cap and blanket smelled the same.

Knowing he hadn't outsourced this to a company or a personal assistant made another tiny hairline fracture around that stone surrounding my heart.

I scarfed down the food, moaning at how good it was, and snuggled up with the warm blanket when I was finished. I'd have to get it dry-cleaned when everything was done. Staying out in the wilderness wasn't good for any fabric, but terrible for cashmere. The thought of wiping away his scent bothered me, and I squirmed uncomfortably.

Falling in love with a Lord would be all kinds of dumb.

I was not dumb. All the foolishness inside of me had died many years ago. I was no longer that tender girl, the one made of curves and soft edges. Life had honed me until I was only teeth and claws and fury. There was no room in my heart anymore for something silly like *love*.

But I could definitely get behind a bad case of lust.

My eyes drifted shut, the image of Ethan emblazoned in my mind as sleep claimed me.

TWENTY-TWO

By the time the earth freed me, I hated Thorvin with the fire of a thousand suns and wanted to punch him in the face over and over again. I lay on my side, completely drained of magic, the first time I could remember this ever happening.

Moira's cool hand rested on my back. "You're safe," she promised.

"Why are you wearing cashmere?" I croaked, spitting out a clod of dirt that had gotten lodged in my teeth. Moira was a thrifter, but the scarf and cap she wore looked unfamiliar and brand new. Very high quality from the look of it, and I made a point of knowing my cashmere.

Moira grimaced. "Long story."

"Is Thorvin awake?"

"Not yet."

"Then I have time before I have to punch him in the face. Spill."

She gave me an exasperated look. "Ethan stopped by."

Alarm rattled through me. I tried to rise and couldn't.

"Shh," Moira said, rubbing my bare back in comforting circles. "Everything is fine."

"What does he have to do with that scarf?" I must have spent too much time in the dirt. My thoughts were completely scrambled. Moira couldn't possibly be saying...

"Holy shit," I wheezed. "Ethan gave those to you?"

She closed her eyes and sighed. "Yes."

I rolled onto my back and let out a cackle.

"Shut up," she begged. "That's not all."

I squinted at her. "Did you sleep with him?"

Moira squawked. "Evie! No! Gods."

"But you wanted to, didn't you?"

Two spots of high color rose on Moira's cheeks. "I am obsessed with him," she admitted in a quiet voice.

Even though I was lying on the cold ground butt ass naked, it didn't stop me from yanking Moira down to wrap her in a hug.

"Gross," Moira said with a rasping chuckle. "Get off me, you perv."

I laid a smacking kiss on her cheek. "You have a crush. This is wonderful news!"

"You hate Ethan." Moira pushed me away and sat up, brushing herself off.

"Hate is a strong word. If it helps, I hate Thorvin more right now."

She rolled her eyes. "There's something about him. He's wounded, damaged, and yet, he makes me want to know more about him."

Moira told me about the cookies and Ethan's teasing when he left. I could see she was horrified, not only by her reaction but by Ethan's reaction, too. The way she spoke about him made my heart hurt. I thought for a while she and Soren had a thing going, but after this, I knew whatever it was had been nothing compared to this.

But Ethan? Gods. The man was a walking pair of heavily starched pants. He was uptight, rigid, and he clung to his ideals like a Remora to a shark. Yes, he was hot. All the Lords were, but Ethan was older or appeared that way, at least. My mind ran through a dozen things about Ethan that I didn't like until I suddenly stopped.

I didn't know Ethan. At all. He and I had never said a non-angry word to each other. I had no idea what colors he liked or if he watched television, or if he had a girlfriend or had ever been married. But Moira...

Moira knew he loved shortbread and ate it with the slow ferocity of a starving man in the desert. She also knew he liked feeding people and keeping them warm.

Ethan would have left my ass in a frozen tundra and tried to steal my clothing to boot, so Moira was already far ahead of me in the getting Ethan's approval category.

I ran a muddy hand down Moira's cheek. Her nose wrinkled but she laughed. "Asshole," she said fondly.

"I can't claim to know a single thing about Ethan, but I know he isn't evil. He's been surprisingly reasonable lately." I lifted a shoulder in a muddy shrug. "If you want him, go after him."

She shook her head. "No. I want to sleep with him. That's all."

My best friend in the entire world was lying to herself. Super hard. The same way I had for so, so long. I yanked her down again and curled my arm around her waist.

"You're getting my new scarf dirty."

"Rowan has a great dry cleaner. She'll make it look brand new. Now shut up and let me hug you."

Moira sighed. "You're naked. This is weird."

"This is the way the gods brought us into the world, Moira. Don't be such a prude."

She patted my bare thigh. "I love you, you fucking weirdo."

"Love you too, you delusional vampiric swan."

Moira's bark of laughter made me grin.

I sobered, worry for her simmering inside my gut. "If all you want is sex, you can get that from anyone. You're smart and gorgeous and sometimes even more unhinged than I am. If you want to pursue him, you should. But I don't think Ethan is the kind to go for short-term dalliances. I don't know his situation, but I've never seen him with anyone. Thorvin might be the most secluded Lord, but Ethan is the most private. You're in for a challenge. Soren is a good candidate for a one-time thing. Or four or five times. Whatever. I expect Ethan might not be that kind of man."

Moira lay still underneath me. "Evie?"

"Hmm?"

She let out a soft breath. "I want you to stay out of this one, okay?"

Hurt speared my heart. Tears pricked the back of my eyes. I opened my mouth to say something I knew I might regret, but closed it a moment later. Then I did the thing I might not have done a few months ago.

I took a deep breath and said, "Alright. I'm here if you ever need to talk."

The drop in her shoulders told me how relieved she was. "Thank you," she whispered.

"Of course," I said back, my throat thick with unshed tears.

Things were changing. Such was life, but I didn't have to like it.

A shrill, panicked scream of horror shattered the quiet.

"Thorvin's awake," I growled, sensing the rumble of earth below us. "He'll be up in a minute."

Moira rolled away and rose. "You should get dressed."

"I dunno," I mused. "Getting your ass kicked by a naked woman is a little more embarrassing than if she were clothed, isn't it?"

She shook her head. "Yes, but I'm sure Rowan doesn't want all the Lords seeing his mate in all her glory."

"Fine," I grumbled, rolling to my feet to grab my pants. My well of magic was slowly refilling, but I needed at least a day's worth of sleep before I recovered all the way.

Thorvin was still rising through the ground a few minutes after I got dressed.

"Danu must have dragged him down pretty far if he still hasn't surfaced," Moira mused.

"Be prepared," I warned her. "Danu is not known as one of the kinder goddesses."

Moira glanced at me. "She's literally Mother Earth, isn't she?"

"No idea. I assumed so until I met her. She's...a lot."

Moira laughed. "As long as he comes up alive, we're in the clear."

A few seconds later, the earth spit up a naked Thorvin. He was curled in the fetal position, completely nude. I winced. Probably should have warned him about that beforehand.

Moira had her cell out, typing a message.

I strode over to Thorvin and nudged him with my toe. The Lord's body held a fine tremor. His hands were clasped together, and silent tears rolled down his face.

Thorvin cracked open an eye and flinched. His mouth worked, opening and closing like a fish gasping for air.

"Evie?" he croaked.

I punched him right in the face, the satisfying crunch of cartilage beneath my fist enough to soothe the violent urge to kill him.

A choked scream rang from the Lord. His hands flew up to cover his face. Blood spurted through his fingers and flowed down his neck.

Moira whistled low. "Ouch."

"Hello, Thorvin," I said.

The Lord broke into soft gasping sounds. "I—I'm sorry, Evie. I didn't realize. How could I? I do not have your sensitivity to the land. There was no way for me to know the damage I was doing until..." His voice trailed off. "There's no way I can ever apologize for what I allowed to happen on my territory. I can promise you it will never happen again."

He went to rise and stumbled, jerking in surprise when he realized his clothes were gone.

I let out a sigh and gripped him by the arm. "Come on. You need to see a medic."

Thorvin let me pull him along, but he shook his head. "I don't keep medics on staff. The Keep is empty."

I shot him a disbelieving glance. "What the hell, Thorvin?"

He let out a heavy sigh. "I like privacy."

"So do I, but you must have someone you can trust."

His lips thinned. "You wouldn't understand."

I let out a crack of laughter. Even Moira chuckled.

"Out of everyone you know, Evie would understand the most," my best friend said dryly. "We had to damn near bully her to get to know anything about her. She was the most untrusting person on the planet."

"She's not wrong," I agreed. "The question is why don't you trust anyone?"

Thorvin stayed silent. "My nose will heal overnight. Danu did not physically injure me, Evie. I will be fine." But there was a haunted look in his eyes I didn't like.

"How about you show me and Moira to the kitchen, and we'll make you a sandwich?"

Thorvin's brow furrowed. "You literally just punched me in the face and now you want to feed me?"

I shrugged. "I never said I was easy to figure out. Just hard to get to know."

Thorvin let out an aggrieved sigh but didn't deny us. We trudged in silence to what I assumed was his main house and let us in.

I blinked in surprise. Thorvin's place looked like dark academia had knocked on the door, stamped the dirt off its boots on the front stoop, then moved in and decided to make a few changes. Everything was deliciously dark, but not in a depressing way, more in a dark and stormy night spent reading by the fireplace way.

Bookshelves were everywhere. The walls and ceiling were color-drenched in the most beautiful jewel tones. Deep, forested green living room walls. Purple-burgundy walls in the kitchen. Copper pots hung neatly on a rack above an island made out of—

"Holy shit," I said as I ran my fingers over the cool stone. "Is this a labradorite slab?"

He looked at me in surprise. "Yes. I had to source it from—"

"Madagascar," I murmured. The stone whispered to me, a new trick I had no idea I had. It...missed Thorvin. Was I going mad?

Thorvin blinked. "Err. Yes. How did you know?"

"The stone told me," I murmured.

Moira shot me a concerned glance.

I shook off the strangeness and went to the fridge. "Any preference?"

Thorvin shook his head and sank onto one of the kitchen chairs with a soft groan. He sighed and crossed his arms on top of the table, then laid his head down.

Moira stared at him for a moment. "Do you want to talk about it?"

Thorvin took a shuddering breath. "No."

Danu was true to her word. The Lord was physically whole, minus the broken nose, and seemed to still have all his faculties. A successful mission, all in all.

Thorvin lifted his head. "You healed my land."

"Yes," I added a large chunk of ham to the sandwich. "That is why I came."

His shoulders slumped. "I wasn't sure you would. After..." Thorvin lifted light brown eyes to mine. "I'm sorry again, Evie."

"You're lucky," I told him, adding a large slice of Butterleaf lettuce. "Any later and it might have been too late."

Thorvin's eyes squeezed shut. "Any chance that poison will come back?"

I pushed the sandwich over to him. Thorvin eyed it for a moment, so long I snorted. "If I wanted to kill you, I wouldn't have bargained with Danu for your life."

Thorvin flinched, then nodded in thanks.

"No," I said, answering his question. "Not until I drop my claim on your borders."

Thorvin's hands stilled in the act of picking up his sandwich. "Just the borders?"

I passed Moira the second sandwich I made. "Unlike you, Lord, I keep my word."

Anger at the situation rode me once more, and magic colored the sound of my voice when I next spoke. *"You've angered the fae today, Lord Thorvin. This is not a slight we will soon forget."*

Thorvin went white as a sheet. Moira gave me a curious look and rose, taking her sandwich with her. "I think it's time we head home." She took me by the arm and tugged.

I glanced at the sandwich stuff in mourning.

. . .

"We'll be there in a hurry. I've already told Rowan to heat something up for you."

I swayed and pressed a hand to my temples. "Thank you."

Moira nodded to Thorvin. "We will leave you now. Take care nothing like this ever occurs again. Evie will not be so magnanimous next time."

Thorvin's lips thinned, but he nodded. Moira was the only one who believed I'd been magnanimous today.

Once we were outside, Moira paused. A tall, lean male sauntered toward us, hands shoved in the pockets of his jeans. My friend's breathing patterns changed and her scent went sharper.

Oh gods. This...I did not want to know certain things.

"Moira," I hissed through my teeth. "Get it together."

She shot me a sharp glance, horror widening her eyes when she realized. Her desire drained immediately.

"Better."

Ethan nodded to me, but his eyes changed when he looked at Moira. "Thank you for contacting me."

Moira shrugged. "Thank you for the delivery yesterday."

Ethan stared at her for too long.

Whoo boy. Was this how Caelan and I were in the beginning? Because I could light a match off Moira's arm right now.

"It is the least I could do," he said after a moment. "Thorvin's inside?"

I nodded. His land was healed, far greener than it should be for the season. The air was fresh once more, and life bloomed under my feet.

"You've done him a great service, Evie." He touched his hand to his heart. "You have our thanks."

I inclined my head. "I can visit your property at your convenience."

Ethan's eyes burned. "I'm managing," he said.

I straightened, power blooming along my skin. "Do not make Thorvin's mistake," I warned.

His teeth pulled away from his lips in a smile very close to a snarl. "And do not assume I take orders from the fae." Ethan said the word with ill-concealed disgust.

"Ethan." Moira watched him, anger sparking in her dark eyes.

His strange gaze flicked to Moira. A muscle in his jaw feathered.

"Thorvin is one of the younger Lords. He's still prone to mistakes." He turned his attention to me. "I am not. If I need your assistance, rest assured I will contact you. Until then, you will not enter my territory unless you have my permission." With a nod, he strode past us and jogged up the stairs to Thorvin's front door.

Moira let out a slow breath.

"I think that's the friendliest he's ever been to me."

Moira snorted a laugh. "He won't ever get an award for his personality, that's for sure."

I eyed the door Ethan went into. "Soooo," I drawled, "he's the kind of man who gets you all hot and bothered."

Moira shoved a bottle in my hand. "Drink that and shut up. We're going home."

I grinned at her and downed the potion in one go.

Time to see my guy.

CHAPTER

TWENTY-THREE

The Lords postponed their emergency meeting for two weeks, citing an undisguised illness. Rowan got the message while we were sitting at the breakfast table the next morning.

He held my foot in his lap, stroking an idle hand over the back of my foot. "Do I want to ask what you did?"

"Mmm. Well, I didn't do much at all. Danu gets most of the credit."

His eyebrows lifted. "But you did do something?"

"I healed that asshole's land which more than makes up for his broken nose," I said primly.

Rowan blinked. "You broke Thorvin's nose?"

I took another bite of my pancakes. "Mmm hmm. He's lucky that's all I did." Chocolate melted over my tongue. Rowan knew I didn't like dark or semi-sweet chocolate, so he always made my pancakes with milk chocolate chips. I don't recall ever telling him my preference, but the guy just noticed things. Tiny things no one ever noticed about me, he'd tucked into his heart and saved.

It made me want to jump his bones all the time. The fae bond had shown no real signs of slowing down, and I couldn't exactly ask my mom or dad about why I was so hot for Rowan all the time.

Not that Rowan minded. Goodness. Dude had the stamina of a fleet of Navy men stepping off the ship for the first time in months.

"He deserved it." I took another bite of pancake and watched Rowan.

His lips twitched. "I suppose he did."

"How's the baby?" Moira had brought me home, shoved me at Rowan and told him to feed me, then hurried home, her cheeks still crimson after seeing Ethan.

"Adorable." Rowan dug a thumb into the arch of my foot, drawing a deep groan from my throat. He flashed a grin.

Yesterday's magic drain hadn't completely resolved yet, and I still had some body aches and overall soreness. I felt like sleeping another twelve hours, but Dad was due for training today, and he wouldn't be so easily fobbed off.

Rowan had made excuses with Barrett but had a thoughtful expression on his face when he hung up the phone. "He seemed a little agitated over the cancellation."

I lifted a shoulder. "Barrett is difficult to read. He followed me all the way here, so he seems invested in helping me learn my powers."

"Mmm," Rowan responded. "Is it possible he already knows about the baby?"

I blinked. "How?"

"No idea. This is only a theory. You're supposedly the last female Chimera, which we both now know could be a lie. Barrett is the Chimera's de facto leader."

My mind whirled. "You think Barrett might be looking for the child and is using me to do it?"

Rowan tilted his head. "You did come out quite fantastically in Joy Springs. Most paranormals know who you are. Who better to keep their child safe than a female Chimera safe in a shifter pack?"

I wanted to wave his concerns away, but I couldn't. If I'd learned anything over the past several years, it was that sometimes people wouldn't stop until they realized their goals, whether they were for good or evil. Barrett might be on the up and up, but he did drop into my lap rather abruptly and claim I should be the one to lead our people.

Not that I'd done much of that. I preferred staying out of the limelight, first because I was still hiding my Chimera identity at that time, and second because I had issues with the Chimeras after what Finn had done to me, followed by his psycho companion, Rhona.

Barrett had helped me, no question about that, and he'd asked for nothing in return. Rowan's words made me examine his actions under a closer microscope now. Very few people in my life, minus Rowan and my friends, had helped me without wanting something in return.

Was Barrett the exception to the rule or was the baby in danger once he found her?

"I can see the wheels turning in your mind," Rowan murmured.

"Maybe we should test the theory," I mused.

Rowan's wicked fingers rubbed the knots from my calves. "Always willing to engage in some shenanigans," he said with a quick smile. "But first, I want to talk about something else."

My eyebrows lifted. "Oh?"

He patted his thigh, silently telling me to lift my other leg. I closed my eyes as he started working on the other leg.

"Mmm hmm. I was thinking we should get married."

My eyes flew open. I watched him for a long moment,

looking for the familiar twinkle of mischief in his eyes when he teased me, but there was nothing but a somber expression on his face.

When I said nothing, his lips twitched. "We're mated, on my people's side and on yours. Our laws see us as together for the rest of our lives."

I nodded, still struck mute by his proposal.

"We don't live in your world, and many humans claim citizenship in my territory. They do not often get to celebrate with us. Would it be such a bad idea to have a wedding here at the Keep?"

Tears swelled in my eyes. "You want to marry me."

Rowan snorted. "If I haven't made that painfully obvious by now, I've been remiss in my duties."

He sighed when I stayed silent. Rowan leaned forward, gripping my thighs with his large hands. "Evie, I am perfectly content to be your mate, but I'd also like to be your husband. Legally. I want you to wear a wedding ring so everyone, human and paranormal alike, knows you are taken. I want to introduce you as my wife and mate to anyone who asks."

A vision of a gold band on Rowan's finger flashed in my mind.

"What happens if you shift?"

His eyes lit from within. "We'll have two rings, one we wear on our finger, and one we wear around our neck. Just in case we lose the one on our finger." Rowan shrugged. "We'll commission ten of them if we need to. I don't care. I just want you to be my wife."

I slowly put my legs down. A moment later, I launched myself at him.

With a grunt of laughter, Rowan caught me, but not before he tipped over backward, the chair cracking in several pieces.

I claimed his lips in a heated kiss, my fingers already busy unbuttoning his shirt. Rowan's fingers tangled in my hair, his lips dragging down my neck.

"That's a yes?" he murmured against my throat.

"Yes," I whispered. "Always, Rowan."

And then there were no more words.

TWENTY-FOUR

ROWAN

Declan burst out laughing when he walked into the house and saw the scattered remnants of broken dishes and breakfast scattered all over the table and floor, and the destroyed chair.

"Looks like the mating is going well," he mused, eyes sparkling with mirth.

Gods. I know I'm mussed, and I caught a glimpse of my shirt earlier and hadn't fixed it before Declan interrupted me. It's buttoned wrong.

I ran a hand through my hair. "We're fae bonded, too."

Declan's eyes went comically wide. "Shit." He sank onto an unscathed chair and swept a hand out. "Is that what all this is? A normal shifter mating isn't quite so...volatile after the first twenty-four hours."

I grinned. "Yep. It's fucking amazing."

Declan's low chuckle made me laugh. "Good for you, man. Evie is exactly what we hoped you'd find. More than we ever expected, actually." He eyed me. "You sure you can handle her?"

I eyed my friend and Second. "Why, you in the market for a wife?"

Declan grinned. "Most of the shifters in the Keep are vacillating between jealousy and euphoria. Evie is a powerhouse."

My mate was so much more than that, but I understood what he was saying. "We're getting married."

Declan blinked before a wide grin settled over his face. "Sonofabitch. That's awesome." He scrubbed a hand over his chin. "The Keep hasn't had a big celebration in a long time."

He nodded and slapped his hands on his thighs. "Is Hope planning the shindig?"

I got up and made us both a cup of coffee. "No idea. I just asked her to marry me."

Declan's wicked chuckle dragged an embarrassed grin up.

"So that's the real reason for all of this," he said, gesturing to the debris all over the floor. "You did well, brother."

I had. "Touch and go there for a while," I admitted.

The smile slid from Declan's face. "I know seeing her with another man must have been devastating, even if you didn't realize what she was to you yet."

More than devastating. I struggled the entire time, trying to be what she needed while not trampling all over my own needs.

All I could do was nod. "I knew she'd come around in regard to Caelan."

Declan watched me. "But you weren't sure if she'd come around to you."

I shrugged. "Turns out she has great taste, too."

Declan snorted. "We couldn't be happier for you. There's a sense of...happiness in the air." A sharp shake of his head. "No. That's not the right word. Evie brought a sense of contentment to our home. She's blessed our lands and our women."

"We're probably going to have to build more houses," I said ruefully.

"You might have to build an entire subdivision if Evie keeps pumping the air with that fertility juju."

A happy laugh burst from me. "A blessing none of us expected, for sure."

"And you?" Declan asked quietly.

I knew what he wanted to know without directly asking. "I would be blessed beyond all I deserve if we had children."

"Are you taking precautions?"

I clamped down my anger. The question, asked by a Second, was valid. By virtue of his position, he had the right to ask. A Second was responsible for ensuring the safety of a Keep's Lord, and if that Lord mated, that protection flowed to the mate, and, eventually, any children born of the union. Him asking the question was not the problem, but Evie was asleep a few rooms over, and I knew her well enough to know she would not be comfortable with Declan having that level of knowledge about our sex life.

"Whoa," Declan said. "Easy, Rowan." He leaned away, his eyes wide. A silvery blue light reflected over his face. "Your..." His voice trailed off. "Have you gotten a gander at your eyes lately?"

I let out a slow breath, allowing the fury to drain away. "Sorry." My voice is rougher than usual, my bear riding on the edges of this new bond, and the touches of Evie's magic I seemed to be inheriting. "Bonding with a fae has altered some things."

Declan pressed his lips together for a moment. "Yeah," he said after a long moment of silence. "No shit."

My eyes shifted back to their normal color, allowing Declan to relax a hair, though his eyes still held a wary look I didn't love. Even now, in a place where I was loved beyond all I thought I deserved and after Evie had given us more than we could dream of, my people were still wary of her power. The thought both enraged and exhausted me.

When would it be enough? When would the world stop

draining Evie, taking and taking, and rarely giving her anything but heartache in return? Would Evie have to give every bit of herself before anyone gave her any credit? She would, I knew it. I'd do anything to stop her, but Evie had always been a giver, far more than many people deserved.

The look bled away a second later. My shoulders slumped. Declan was one of my oldest and dearest friends, and he'd known how long I'd wanted what I had with Evie, so for him to look at me like that crushed something inside of me.

Declan's lips twisted. He shook his head, as if arguing with himself over something, and finally spread his hands out. "Hey, man. You don't have to answer that. I understand that Evie is not a shifter, not the same way we are. There will be different boundaries." He dipped his head in apology. "I didn't mean to violate those boundaries. I wasn't thinking, and it won't happen again."

"You're scared of her." The words came out hard and flat.

Declan met my eyes. There was no amusement or mischief in his gaze. "She is a fae goddess, Rowan. Her power is tremendous. We should all be a little afraid of her, I think."

But I shook my head and rose. "She saved us all, Declan. And not only that, she gifted us with children. So many children." My hands trembled. "She saved me. You know how long I wandered this world searching for something like this."

Declan looked stricken. "Gods, Rowan. I know. Of course, I know. It's just—"

"What?" I demanded. "You can't see past her fae parts into her heart?"

"I am not her mate," Declan said softly. "We all feel her." He touched his chest. "We know her power and her love for you. But we don't know her."

My Second sighed and rose.

"You do know her," I said quietly. "The moment we bonded, all of you knew her. You may not know her likes and dislikes or her family or her history, but you know her heart."

Declan opened his mouth and thought better of speaking. His gaze flicked to the hall.

The door creaked open. Evie stood there, blue eyes brimming with grief. She tied her robe closed and slid a pair of slippers on. "I just wanted some coffee," she said quietly as she glided into the kitchen.

We watched, dead silent, as she poured herself a cup of coffee from the pot, but Evie didn't go back to our bedroom. She walked outside and headed to her cottage, her head bowed in defeat. I hadn't seen her look like that since the night I carried her out of Joy Springs. My heart cracked at that moment, and I turned to my Second.

"Get out."

Declan took a step forward. "Rowan, I—"

"**GET. OUT**." The full force of Lord power boomed through the kitchen.

Declan winced and turned on his heel, unable to resist the command. The door slammed shut leaving me in bereft silence.

"GODSDAMMIT," I roared, swiping my hand across the table. Ceramic shattered, the metal candle holders slamming into the opposite wall, damaging the sheetrock. The tablecloth lay half on, half off the table, dripping with spilled maple syrup and half melted chocolate.

I needed to go to her. The mating bond tugged at me, Evie's grief roaring through our link.

She'd heard everything.

I started toward the door, only for it to open.

Garrett stepped inside, a telltale hint of gold ringing his irises.

"Don't," he said, holding a hand up.

I stopped in my tracks. "What did you say to me?" My words were low and deadly, and completely out of character for me, but Evie's grief compelled me to go to her, to comfort her.

How much more would she have to give before the world finally gave back to her?

I'd known Garrett for years in his capacity as Caelan's Second. He was a good man, quietly violent when necessary, but loyal and intelligent.

"You are in no shape to see her right now."

"You are standing in the way of a Lord!"

Garrett's eyes were calm and steady. "Not my Lord."

Thick claws slid from my fingertips. "Get out of my way." My voice was an almost indecipherable snarl.

Garrett didn't move an inch. The bastard crossed his arms over his chest and stared, still not angry. "My loyalty is to your mate, Rowan. Not you. Not right now. I am oathsworn to her and feel her grief. She is not angry at you, only the situation. Give her some time. She will seek you out."

My anger drained. I sank into an unbroken chair and let out a heavy sigh. "Fuck," I muttered. "Apologies, Garrett."

He leaned against the wall, arms still crossed. "No worries. I can't say I know what a mating bond feels like, but I imagine the urge to comfort one when they're hurt is close to over-whelming."

I closed my eyes for a moment. "Understatement."

When I opened them, I took in the surrounding carnage and shook my head. "You said your loyalty wasn't to me. Not right now."

Garrett nodded.

"What do you mean by that?"

Garrett poured himself a cup of coffee and rummaged

through the cabinets for a second mug. Mine lay broken in several pieces on the ground.

He set a cup in front of me and pulled a chair over to sit. "Simone and I felt the new bond, but it does not compel us." A rueful smile. "Her oath is open-ended. Evie is not one who wishes to control anyone. I've cautioned her against giving us so much leeway, but she refuses to adjust her wording."

I hadn't heard this story. "Mind sharing the oath?"

Garrett rolled his eyes. "Protect the people I love, or some such romantic nonsense."

I winced. "Far too lenient and open to interpretation."

Garrett's eyes lit. "Yes! Simone wanted to strangle her."

The laugh was a release. The rest of my anger drained away, and with it came a realization. The man before me had walked a rough path. Splitting from his Lord, and losing his pack, to becoming the guardian of a reluctant fae queen, the wolf before me had risked it all to do what was right. "Garrett, would you consider becoming my Third?"

Surprise lit his face, followed by immediate wariness. "Is this how you earn my loyalty, Lord?"

I shook my head ruefully. "The decision is yours. Having you as my Third would be an honor, Garrett. You've served Evie well, and Caelan before her."

At the mention of his former Lord's name, Garrett grimaced. "It's no easy decision leaving a Pack, but I could not serve a man who would treat someone he supposedly loved so horrifically. There were other factors, and I certainly had no love lost for Evie in the beginning, but there comes a time when a man must do right by himself and his honor or face his lack of courage in the mirror."

I'd made the right choice. The position of Third had never been filled inside my Keep. Plenty wanted the role, but I was looking for someone who offered more than the minimum. The man sitting before me possessed all the qualities I wanted and needed in a Third.

"Serving a fae queen is interesting, but I do not know if any oath you offer me is binding since I'm already sworn to her."

"You swore to protect the people she loves, correct?"

A small smile played over his lips. "I did."

"Evie loves me. She loves this land. She loves my people. Our people now. Any binding you have with me would require the same."

A ring of gold outlined his eyes. I nodded to myself. "You could be Lord one day, Garrett. Is that something you'd want?"

Garrett's eyebrows flicked up. "I've never been offered the opportunity."

"They offered it to that shit Dario."

Garrett's bark of laughter made me grin. "He was far too pretty to make it as a Lord."

I leaned forward. "What if there was an opportunity to run a Keep. Would you want it?"

A silence fell over the room. "I don't know that I would. A comfortable prison is still a prison."

I wasn't surprised by his words. "You've spent far too long in Caelan's company. Speak to Evie. See what she thinks of my proposal. Get her blessing if need be. If she agrees, I'd like you to spend some time with Declan. He will show you what it means to be in a truly free Keep."

Garrett inclined his head in a nod and rose. "I'll bring your cup back later. Evie will find you when she's ready, Lord. Don't make me find you again."

I snorted and waved him away.

As difficult as it was to admit, Garrett was right. Evie needed time to process.

I wasn't Caelan. She'd have all the time she needed.

My phone rang with a video call. I swore under my breath when I saw who was calling.

"Ethan," I growled. "What do you want?"

"Permission to enter your territory."

I did not want to deal with Ethan tonight. "State your case," I barked.

At least this would keep my mind off of Evie for a while.

CHAPTER

TWENTY-FIVE

Mom's booze proved popular with the locals. Hours later, Moira and I had claimed a table toward the back of one of the downtown pubs, our glasses filled with her newest brew, some type of delicious berry ale.

I was half-drunk already, idly munching on a handful of spiced nuts. Moira was a little drunker and flirting outrageously with every shifter in the bar.

"Hey!" she called to a devastatingly handsome one who'd been eyeing her all night. "Come over here and sit on my lap, and I'll tell you a story!"

I snickered.

The shifter's eyebrows lifted. An amused grin tugged his lips up. He set his pool cue down and sauntered over.

"Oooh," I said under my breath. "He's a beaut."

"Eight out of ten," Moira whispered. "I reserve the right to adjust the scale up or down based on what's behind that zipper."

I choked on my ale or mead, or whatever the fuck Mom had cooked up this time.

"Shit," she breathed as the male came closer. "He's fucking huge."

I gaped. "Huge-mongous."

Moira barked a laugh. "It would be a crime if I had to adjust the scale down."

"The gods would never be that cruel."

"Shit," Moira said. "They'd definitely be that cruel, but the gods didn't make the shifters, so maybe I'll pray to their gods instead."

I slid a glance toward her. "Do the shifters have gods?"

Her lips curved in a smile as the enormous male stopped at our table. "That's what this handsome fella will be screaming for in a few hours, so I'll let you know."

I burst out laughing and clinked my beer glass against hers. With a wry look at the shifter, undoubtedly one of Rowan's from the warm tug in my chest, I patted him on the arm.

"Good luck."

The shifter grinned. "Hope you wished your friend the same," he said good-naturedly.

"Moira?" I laughed. "She's not the one who needs it."

Just as I was walking away, I saw Moira patting her slender thigh.

"Come sit on Mama's lap," my best friend cooed, dark eyes sparkling from drink and mischief.

The shifter's eyes widened with alarm. I gave him a cheery grin and walked away.

Someone shouted my name as I navigated through the thick crowd. I turned to see a mop of red hair and a friendly face.

"Evie!" Hope called again. "Come sit with us!"

I swayed her way, trying unsuccessfully to keep from spilling my ale and failing. Hope snapped her fingers at someone, and by the time I made it to the table, someone had taken my glass and pressed another full one into my hand. Hope shooed some people over to make room for me to sit.

At first, I was happy to be taken in, but the memory of earlier today crept in. Some of Rowan's people—my people now—were frightened of my power. The same thing happened with Caelan's people, leading to our eventual sundering.

Rowan was my mate. We couldn't be separated. But how could I live in a place where I knew his people wondered if I could control my power?

Hope leaned in. "Evie?"

I blinked. "Oh. Sorry. Hi!"

Rowan's Omega touched my arm. Her soothing magic flowed into me, washing away my doubts. She smiled and leaned her forehead against mine. "Rowan called me earlier."

At my look of alarm, she shook her head. "He didn't tell me what happened, only that I should keep an eye out for you if I saw you."

The other shifters were ignoring us, well into their cups by now. Hope had kept her voice low enough for only me to hear. "I know how difficult it is to be different in a place where everyone is the same."

"None of you are the same."

"We are all shifters. Not all wolves, not all bears, but shifters just the same. Different animals, same biological urges, for the most part." She winked. "Unless you are a Lord mated to a fae queen."

I blushed.

"But you, Evie, are different from everyone. You are not a shifter by definition of the word, nor are you a true fae as we know them to be. Your power is unknown, stranger than anything we'd ever seen before. Some of us will be fearful." She cupped my chin. "But that is why you have to show them your heart. Show us who you are. Shifters have too much love not to want to share it. We already love you because we love Rowan. We love you because you have given us the gift of children. But we want to love you because we know your heart. Show it to us, Evie, and your life will never be the same."

My lower lip trembled. "Rowan is my heart."

A soft smile but Hope shook her head. "No. Rowan is in your heart. Show us what your heart is made of." She pressed a kiss to my cheek and clinked our glasses together. "Also, we love your mother. We would like her to move into the Keep. Tell her we will build her a brewery to rival the gods as long as she keeps producing whatever this deliciousness is." She raised her glass. "To Cliona!"

The shifters around the table roared. "TO CLIONA!"

I lifted my glass and cheered with them.

TWENTY-SIX

ROWAN

Ethan standing on Keep grounds bitching about my mate's best friend was not on this year's bingo card. His rant was very un-Ethan-like, and I struggled not to laugh.

So far, he had yet to point out anything Moira had done that might have made him this annoyed, other than her presence on Thorvin's property without permission. Thorvin hadn't said a word about it, and if he didn't make a claim, the point, as far as I was concerned, was moot.

Ethan sounded a lot like...

I went still.

Ethan sounded like Caelan when he first met Evie.

I had to remember Ethan was not Caelan, not even close. The Lord standing next to me had always been difficult to get to know, which was why I found it so surprising he asked for permission to come into my territory. We weren't friends and never had been.

I wasn't sure Ethan had friends, to be frank. After everything with Evie, I wasn't his biggest fan, but he had pulled back on his vitriol the last few months. Whether he realized Evie wasn't the one in the wrong or had gotten a deeper look at Caelan's behavior, Ethan had toned himself down and pulled back on his demands concerning my Floromancer.

He'd been downright decent lately, something I was nervous about.

But listening to him bitch about Moira lent me more of an insight into his personality.

Ethan, the usually unflappable Lord, was completely bothered by Moira's complete disregard for authority or rules or pretty much anything. But he wasn't bothered by her in the same way he was bothered by Evie.

This was different.

And *very* interesting.

Ethan had always been smart, and I could tell the moment he realized he'd said too much. He cleared his throat and stopped talking.

"Well, fuck," he muttered, surprising me into a laugh. He sat on the edge of the porch, long legs dangling over the edge. "This is the first time I've had any dealings with Moira. Is she always like this?"

I chuckled. "No."

When he nodded and let out a sigh of relief, I added the rest. "Usually, she's worse."

Ethan snapped his attention to me. "Worse?"

"Yup." I didn't plan to tell him who'd fucked up Thorvin's pipes or any of the other mischief she'd gotten into because it could get her and Evie into trouble, but I felt bad for the bastard and had to give him something. "She and Evie are thick as thieves, and Moira is loyal to the point of her own detriment. If you do something to someone she loves, she will retaliate swiftly and viciously. Moira has her own sense of justice, and it might not agree with the mainstream. She's difficult to read and unpredictable."

Ethan slowly nodded. "Do you like her?"

I thought about it and ended up shaking my head. "I can't rightly say, Ethan. She's been a wonderful friend to Evie. For that alone, I'd say yes. But I don't know who Moira is. She gives me nothing. I know she likes to bake, and she likes babies. Other than that, she's a blank slate. If you want to get to know her—"

Ethan scoffed. "No. Absolutely not. I just don't want another problem like the Floromancer."

I slid a glance his way. "You mean, my mate."

Ethan waved a dismissive hand.

"Who, I might add, never did anything to you or any of us other than exist. The problem you had with her lies with Caelan."

Ethan's jaw tightened. "I realized that some months back." He turned to look at me. "For what it's worth, I'm sorry. I can be insistent on things when I think I'm right."

Ethan hadn't apologized for a godsdamned thing in the entire time I'd known him. I could be a dick about it, but this was a rare olive branch. "As long as you respect Evie as my mate and know I will protect her as I would anyone in my Keep, even more so, you and I will not have any problems."

Ethan nodded. "Where is she?"

I chuckled. "A pub downtown. My Omega is with her."

"Moira with her?"

I nodded. "They both needed to blow off some steam."

Ethan opened his mouth, then closed it, a furrow appearing between his brows.

"Ask," I said quietly.

Ethan shifted, the first sign of nervousness I'd ever seen from him.

"How is it having a mate of a different kind?"

"You mean her being fae and me being a shifter?"

Ethan nodded. Telling him the entire truth would divulge a hard-kept secret about my own identity. We weren't there yet and maybe never would be. But I could throw him a bone and see what happened. He deserved that much at least. Most people were different between work and home.

"That's why she's at the bar, actually," I admitted.

Ethan's eyebrows rose, but the Lord stayed silent.

"Evie's magic is awe-inspiring to see in person. Being affected by it is something out of this world. When I took her out of Joy Springs, she was extremely careful about how she used my land because her type of power urges her to protect and nurture by claiming. When she couldn't use her magic as it was meant to be used, her power reservoir grew too full. I had to take her far outside Keep boundaries so she could release some and not inadvertently claim my territory. While she was busy siphoning, she spotted that spell and healed the area, which resulted in a massive boom of magic. Now we have over a dozen pregnancies."

Ethan choked. "A dozen?"

I nodded. "Those are the ones we know about. There might be more."

"Gods, man." Ethan scrubbed a hand over his face. "That's unheard of."

"With that sort of power comes misunderstanding."

Ethan's eyes flashed. "Your people are afraid of her."

"Some," I corrected. "Evie overheard my Second speaking. It threw her for a tailspin, and Moira invited her to blow off some steam."

"I bet she gets that a lot." The words weren't accusing, more thoughtful than anything.

"Caelan tanked their relationship due to fear of the unknown and his own insecurities."

Ethan let out a heavy sigh. "I suspected. When you took her

out of his territory, I fielded half a dozen furious phone calls from him. His rage was something to witness."

"Every bit unjustified. Evie took weeks to come out of her room. He'd broken her."

He swore under his breath. "I'm sorry, Rowan. I wondered about their suitability. You know I had my own issues with Evie, but I'm sorry he treated her so poorly."

"Had?" I questioned.

A flash of a grin. "Caught that, did you? Yes, had in the past tense. I have my own reasons for distrusting the fae, but none of them are Evie's fault. But all the Lords will still be wary about Evie coming onto their property." His eyes sparkled. "Besides Ben."

I glared at Ethan. Ben had professed his intentions toward Evie some time back, but thank the gods he'd screwed that up all on his own. Once he shunned Evie due to his own prejudices, she'd turned her back on him. If there were ever a threat, it would be Ben. He was a good man, an even better Lord, and an off-the-charts healer. They would have made a good pair.

I'd be eternally grateful he couldn't get over himself.

"Ben made his own bed." I grinned. "Now it's far too late for him to do anything but be jealous."

Ethan laughed. "I'm here for another reason."

"Caelan wants to oust me."

A nod. Ethan figured I already knew.

"What are his chances?" I asked.

"Hard to say. We aren't as tight knit as we used to be. Ben might vote against you because of Evie."

Shit. I hadn't even thought of that.

"After Evie threw Thorvin down a deep hole and delivered him to a goddess as retribution, he might vote against you too."

I pinched the space between my brows.

"Caelan is obviously against you. There's no way to tell with Soren. He hasn't been as close to Caelan as usual."

"And you?"

His expression sobered. "I'll hear Caelan's case and make a determination at that time."

As usual, the odds were against me. Would it be so bad to be stripped of a title I never wanted?

The urgent ring of my cellphone jerked me out of my reverie.

TWENTY-SEVEN

ROWAN

Evie and Moira had one of the most admirable friendships I'd ever been exposed to, but sometimes, their friendship turned from cozy familial bickering into chaos incarnate.

The pub was a madhouse when we walked in. Shifters of all kinds crowded around us. Everyone recognized me right away, but few knew who the man beside me was. Even so, they gave us a wide berth, opening a path to guide us to where Evie and Moira were.

Evie was at a small circular table, about two dozen shifters standing around her intently, concentrating on what was going on between her and the male shifter who sat on the opposite side. A large potted plant sat on the floor right beside her, one that was growing at a fantastic rate, one far faster than nature allowed for.

Unless that *nature* was my mate arm wrestling a Navy vet shifter named Rick.

I choked down a guffaw of laughter, put my finger up to my lips when the other shifters spotted me, and watched. Ethan stepped up beside me and gaped at the scene.

My mate had lost her sweater somewhere and wore a blue, strappy tank top. She had on a thin bra underneath, but even so, her curves were highlighted in the low light, moisture casting a golden glow over her skin. Evie's hair had long abandoned any sense of decorum and had sprung into a wild mess of wave and curl. I don't think she noticed, but when she was expending a lot of magic, her hair responded accordingly. A thin line of sweat dotted along her brow, and her eyes glowed azure and watermelon tourmaline.

Her smile was edged with savage glee, and her eyes sparkled with the thrill of the win.

Evie, like the rest of my shifters, was quite drunk and having a grand old time.

She sat with her posture perfectly straight, her right hand clasped within Ricky's. Both of them glared at each other, but neither was angry. The glare was one of effort and intimidation. I smelled desire thick and heavy in the room, though it wasn't coming from the participants, only some of the other shifters watching their Lady arm wrestle someone who could snap someone's neck with a twinge of his thumb.

The only reason I didn't interfere was because I liked Ricky. He wouldn't hurt Evie.

Plus, I wanted to see who'd win. I wasn't sure it would be my shifter.

"If I win, you have to weed the roses for a month," Evie growled.

Rick bared his teeth. "And if I do, you get latrine duty for a month."

Evie snorted. "Hardly fair. Weeding is far different than cleaning up wolf piss."

Several of the shifters burst out laughing.

"You forgot bear piss!" Someone shouted.

Evie's grin was evil. "Bear piss. Wolf piss. Cat piss. It's all the same. There's no piss on my roses. Come up with something else."

Ricky's eyes narrowed. "Fine. Dishes for a month."

"For a dormitory of a hundred? Your ass. No. How about you weed the roses for a month, do the dishes at the main house for a month, and chauffeur me around when I need a ride?"

"You haven't learned to fucking drive yet?" Someone shouted from the back.

"I know how to drive," Evie called back. "I just don't want to."

More laughter. "Passenger princess!" someone shouted.

"Damn right," Evie called back. "Someone give me a crown!"

I liked seeing her like this, talking shit and completely relaxed.

Ricky mulled it over. "And you get latrine duty for a month?"

Evie nodded and flexed her hand. "You skeered?"

Ricky's teeth pulled back in a grin. "I ain't skeered of nothing." He inhaled. "Alright, Lady. You got yourself a deal."

Hope, my unruffled, unflappable, capable, and usually sober Omega let out a whoop. She'd stripped her overshirt off and wore a white tank top and a pair of tight jeans. Every shifter in the room cast the occasional glance at her. Good thing Declan wasn't here. He'd lose his shit and their fun would be over in an instant.

Staring was a lot different than action. As long as Hope didn't mind, I didn't mind. And if she did mind, she could take care of herself. I'd only step in if she needed me to.

And right now, this seemed to be overall, pretty innocent fun.

Evie held up her hand. "Wait! I need another plant." Her

eyes narrowed. "Large. Same size as this guy if you have it." She pointed to the tree on her other side.

Someone scurried away and came back less than a minute later toting what I assumed to be a Ficus tree. Why the fuck a bar had real Ficus trees was a question for another time. The shifter set it beside her and stepped back into place.

Evie flashed him a grateful, sloppy smile, and touched her fingers into the soil. Her eyes flashed and the tree grew several inches. When she was done, she wiped her fingers on her jeans.

"Alright Ricky Bobby, let's go." Evie's grin held an edge of violence.

Ricky returned her crazy smile and nodded his head.

Like everyone else, I was captivated.

Hope raised her hands. "One! Two! Three! Begin!"

Both trees burst with blooms they shouldn't have. Evie bared her teeth, her smile edged with the promise of pain.

Desire prickled over my skin.

Ricky grinned at her and leaned forward. "We're having tacos and burritos every single night."

Evie snorted. "I'm going to purchase bat shit from the local farm and fertilize my flowers."

The veins in Ricky's arms bulged. Evie's Ficus trees kept growing.

"I'm going to buy the worst piece of shit beater I can find and tote you around in it," Ricky promised.

"Who gives a shit. A passenger princess is still a princess no matter what car she's in."

Ricky cracked a laugh. "I'm going to have all the toddlers potty train in our bathroom."

Evie's eyes narrowed. "Dirty pool," she accused. "I'm going to plant the thorniest roses I can find and cross breed one of them to be poisonous." Her smile widened. "And not tell you which one it is."

Ricky's hand tilted about twenty degrees the wrong way.

Everyone went nuts. Shouts of encouragement, shit talking, and insults flew every which way. A wild, delighted laugh broke from my mate.

"If I win, a round for the entire bar on me!" she shouted.

The entire bar went nuts this time. An even larger crowd gathered, this time fae mixed in with the bunch.

I wished every single day could be like this for her. Maybe minus the drunk part. I'd never seen Evie so relaxed and free. She was stunning, the most beautiful thing I'd ever seen.

"Well shit," Ricky rasped, "a free round makes me want to lose."

"You're losing already!" someone shouted.

It was true. Ricky slipped another twenty degrees. Those plants grew another few inches and lost a few inches, back and forth as Evie and Ricky struggled.

But there was a sparkle in Evie's eyes.

Was my mate playing him? A slow grin spread over my face. Her muscles were bulging but not as much as they should be.

Just how much extra energy and strength were those plants providing her? The lights flickered above us.

"Ricky?" Evie said.

"Hmm?"

"Do you prefer bat or cow shit?"

Ricky's brow furrowed for a second until he made the same realization I had.

He opened his mouth just as Evie cackled and slammed his hand down to the table's surface.

The bar went wild. Shifters shouted with glee, money changed hands, and Hope was screaming with laughter. She reached over and ruffled Evie's hair.

Ricky sat back in his chair and let out a good-natured laugh.

"Well shit, plant lady. Good match." He reached over the table and stuck his hand out. Evie shook it.

"Rematch one day?" she asked.

He nodded. "You bet your ass."

Ricky slapped the table and rose. Our eyes locked. The shifter went pale. "Erm. Umm."

I walked over and clamped his shoulder with my hand. "Thank you," I said quietly. "That's the most fun I've ever seen Evie have."

Ricky blushed. "You brought us an amazing Lady, Lord." He rubbed his elbow. "And a surprisingly good arm wrestler."

We grinned at each other. I turned and brought my hand up and made a circle with my finger. "Two rounds for the bar on the Keep Lord and Lady!"

I'd been so focused on Evie I forgot Ethan was with me. He had an odd look on his face.

"I wish you all the happiness possible, Rowan."

We locked gazes for a long moment. The bastard was sincere. Huh. How about that. I grinned. "I hope one day you experience the epic level of craziness I get to."

Ethan snorted. "I'm not sure about that one, but maybe one day I'll experience this." He gestured around the bar.

I turned to see Evie watching me with parted lips and wide eyes. Her hair was even worse, if possible.

"Hi," she breathed. Color heated her cheeks.

I stalked over and hauled her from the table for a searing kiss. Evie melted into me, boneless and tasting of berries.

Wolf whistles and catcalls rang out.

I grinned against her lips.

"You aren't mad?" she whispered.

I reared back. "Mad that you singlehandedly united my shifters and kicked one of their asses in an arm-wrestling contest?"

Her color deepened.

"Absolutely not. They'll be talking about this for years."

Evie snorted and shoved her hair out of her face. "I am quite drunk, Rowan."

"Oh, I know it, darling. I brought drops for you."

"Thank the gods," she breathed.

"Are you ready to go?"

She nodded. "Wait. Moira is somewhere around here."

I hadn't seen her, but when I turned and saw Ethan go predator still, I winced.

He'd spotted her and whatever he saw was bound to cause trouble.

Evie sucked in a breath. "Why the hell is Ethan here?" she breathed.

"Lord business," I said, not wanting to get into the weeds about Moira just now.

She smacked me on the chest when I started to walk. "No. Wait. I gotta see this. Turn around."

I grimaced and turned to see Ethan stalking toward a dark-haired woman sitting on top of an enormous shifter.

Oh. Fuck. Moira had met Kelton, arguably the randiest of my shifters. From the looks of it, Kelton's hands had been busy.

"Ohhhhh shit," Evie whispered, blue eyes wide. "Kelton needs to get the hell out of there."

Ethan wasn't the type to start a bar fight. He didn't need to. He was a Lord. Kelton would recognize he was beaten the second Ethan came within a foot of him.

He stopped right by Moira and crossed his arms over his chest. Moira, busy dotting kisses over Kelton's face, looked up and went completely still. Her face went expressionless.

Kelton tried to drag her back down, but Moira shoved his hands away.

I couldn't hear what was said, but whatever it was wasn't good.

"We should go," I murmured.

Evie clicked her tongue. "Hell no! Moira never gets into trouble. This is way too good to leave."

I stared down at her, but Evie gave me a guileless smile. "One more minute," she pleaded.

I was helpless to resist her. "Fine."

CHAPTER

TWENTY-EIGHT

ETHAN

Unexplainable, yet pure, unadulterated rage pumped through my veins. Seeing Moira on top of the shifter had brought out all the violent tendencies I worked so hard every day to suppress.

Remembering I wasn't in my own territory took great effort. I could not kill the shifter, no matter how much I wanted to. Seeing his enormous mitts wrapped around Moira's slender waist made my vision haze red.

"Moira," I said quietly. The familiar ring of blue and gold around my irises cast a watery shadow over her face.

She was disheveled, her silky dark hair tossed into a careless bun on top of her head. She, like Evie and Hope, had lost their overshirts somewhere. Seriously, what was with women losing articles of clothing after a few drinks? She was still decent in a strappy tank, but gods above, the woman had foregone a bra today, and the creamy, pale skin displayed was driving me to distraction.

Her face turned to stone when she pulled away from the shifter, his skin still moist from her lips. My fists clenched at my sides.

"What are you doing here?"

"Business," I said through clenched teeth. "Having fun?"

A wicked smile curved her lips up. "As a matter of fact, yes, I am. Mind if we talk later?"

The shifter's hands slid up her waist, pushing up her tank to expose a flat abdomen. He hadn't looked up yet.

"You heard the lady. Get lost."

Moira's eyes widened in alarm.

I smiled, enjoying Moira's flinch as she sucked in a stunned breath. "*Kelton.*"

"We're busy," the shifter insisted. "Everyone else in here knows not to interrupt us." He smiled at Moira, a smile tinged with an insinuation I didn't care for. "What do you say we get out of here?"

Moira swallowed and glanced up at me. One of my eyebrows rose.

On a normal night, If she wanted to go, I wouldn't like it, but I would acquiesce. Tonight, based on the amount of beer glasses scattered around the table, Moira was inebriated. Kelton would not be taking her home tonight, even if I had to piss Rowan off in the process of detaining him.

"Moira won't be going anywhere with you tonight, I'm afraid." The words sounded regretful, but there was only ill-concealed violence in my voice. Only Moira was intelligent enough to hear it, even through the haze of Cliona's magical booze.

Kelton jerked his head around, teeth bared, only to halt. His eyes widened.

"Umm."

His hands slid from Moira's skin. My shoulders fell a hair.

"Leave," I said, locking eyes with Kelton.

He couldn't hold the look for more than a few seconds. Kelton dropped his gaze and removed Moira from his lap, depositing her on the seat beside him. He slid from the booth and ducked his head, not even bothering to say goodbye to the woman he'd been...molesting for the gods know how long.

I drew in a deep breath.

"How. Dare. You," Moira hissed. Her black eyes flashed with something, a spark of light I'd never seen before. Magic rumbled through the area.

I took a step back. She was not what she said she was. Or, like Evie, she was far more than she pretended to be. I bent down, ensuring we were at eye level. "Whatever this is, button it up," I growled. "We are in a bar full of people."

"You had no right." Her lips pulled away from her teeth, exposing elongating canines.

Vampire then, true to what she claimed. But that's not all this woman was.

I let a little magic slip and curl around her skin. "Want to bite me, Moira?" I asked quietly. "Have you been thinking about what I taste like and forcing yourself to settle for a weak shifter to slake your hunger?"

Moira's eyes narrowed, that strange power still leaking through her irises. "I hate you," she hissed.

I barked a laugh. "The feeling is mutual, little witch. Now get up. We're leaving."

"I'm not going anywhere with you." She picked up a half full glass of ale and tipped it up. I wrenched it from her hands and slammed it on the table, spilling ale on both of us.

"You've had enough."

Claws slid from Moira's fingertips, wicked lethal blades. "I take orders from no man."

"You're acting like a child and instead of engaging in innocent fun like your friend over there, you chose to drown your anger in a male who would give you nothing but boredom and conversation worthy of a high school lunch table."

Her nostrils flared.

I grinned. "You know I'm right. Now get your damned shirt and let's go. We're leaving."

Moira stared at me for a long moment, fury drowning me in the dark depths of her eyes. "I told you," she said quietly. "I'm not going anywhere with you."

I leaned closer. "Last warning. Get your shit and let's go."

She crossed her arms over her chest and glared at me.

This woman was going to be the death of me. "Alright then."

I reached for her and hauled her over my shoulder, clamping her there with one arm. I turned to see Evie and Rowan watching me with wide eyes. Evie looked a little breathless.

Rowan seemed befuddled but shook the emotion off. He dug in his pocket and tossed me his keys. "We'll get a ride," he said quietly. "Be careful."

I gave him a grateful nod.

Moira, her brain catching up to her body, let out a loud screech.

Evie pressed her lips together. "That is so hot," she whispered to Rowan.

Rowan jerked his attention to his mate. "Evie!"

"What? Being dominated is fun sometimes."

Rowan closed his eyes and his lips looked like they were moving in a prayer. I sailed past them both, and the shifters opened up a path, all silent and staring now.

Moira cursed me, my family line, my children, my children's children, and pummeled my back with her small fists, but she was no match for Lord strength. When she scratched my back with those wicked claws, I raised my hand up and slapped her on the rear-end, the sound like a gunshot in the bar.

A collective gasp, then "Ooohhhhhhhh."

"I. Will. *Kill*. You," Moira snarled.

My hand stung, and I immediately regretted my decision. Moira was thin, almost too thin, but her ass was curvy and fit my hand perfectly, the memory of the shape burned forever into my brain.

"Get in line, darling," I drawled and stalked out of the bar holding her tight.

TWENTY-NINE

Thank the gods for those drops. I woke up a little dehydrated but no worse for the wear.

"Oh shit," I muttered once my eyes focused. "Where's Moira?"

Rowan pressed a warm kiss to my bare shoulder. "Home. I gave Ethan some of the drops before we went to the bar. Whether he gave them to Moira remains to be seen."

Evie snickered. "She was furious."

"Mmm," he agreed.

"She won't forgive him."

Rowan popped his head up and peered at me. "I know she's your best friend, but her behavior last night was destructive."

I tilted my head and studied Rowan, suppressing the flash of anger I felt at his judgment. "How so?"

"Kelton is a known player around the Keep. Nothing would have come of those two getting together."

"Who said Moira wanted anything to come out of it? How is she being destructive? If Kelton is known around the Keep, then women who live here know what they're getting into when they engage him. Moira isn't stupid. She's older than I am by a substantial amount, and she's single. Hopelessly so. If she wants to find a distraction, she's entitled to do so. If anyone comes out of this hurt, I can almost guarantee you it wouldn't be Moira."

Rowan blinked. "I—" His lips pressed together. "Damn. I made a snap judgment, didn't I?"

My eyebrows rose. "Sure did, buddy."

Rowan snorted. "I apologize. I forget Moira isn't young. I assumed I knew her when I don't."

Even someone like Rowan was prone to making snap judgments when it came to women, but the mark of a good man was knowing when to apologize. My anger faded away, replaced by my worry for Moira.

"If anyone can hurt her, it's Ethan." And that's what I was worried about most. She liked him far more than what was good for her.

But...it sure seemed like Ethan had more interest in her than he should, too. I was dying to know what happened, but it would have to wait for a while. My stomach was growling, and I had a handsome, irresistible gentleman who refused to satisfy me last night because of how much I'd drunk.

I rolled over on top of him. "Stop talking," I commanded.

"As you wish," Rowan drawled, his hands already moving.

MOIRA SHOWED up a few hours later, bleary-eyed and grumpy. Rowan made himself scarce, giving me a meaningful wink before he sailed out the door.

She sank into one of the new kitchen chairs. "Coffee," she croaked.

I pressed my lips together to keep from laughing and poured us both a cup. "Want a grilled cheese?" I asked.

Moira grimaced. "Not right now." She curled her fingers around the mug. "Ethan left a little while ago."

My eyebrows rose. I checked my cell phone. "This late?"

She nodded and glared at my look. "Nothing like that. The asshole did a deep dive background check on me and wanted to share what he found."

I sat back in my chair and exhaled. "Shit," I breathed. Moira refused to tell me what she used to do for work, only saying it was "investigative" in nature. "How deep?"

Moira grunted. "He doesn't know everything, but he knows enough." She scrubbed a hand over her face. "He wants me to work for him."

I stilled. "You work at the flower shop." A pause. "When it's open." I grimaced. I had to get back to work soon. There were only a few more things to do before we could officially open up shop again.

"Part-time." She sighed. "He offered me a shit ton of money."

Warning bells went off in my head. "Be careful. That's exactly how things started with Caelan."

A vicious smile crossed her face. "No need to worry about that. This morning, he went into great detail about what a terrible person I was and how much he hated me."

I didn't miss the flicker of hurt in her eyes. Anger flooded me.

She touched my arm. "It's fine."

Magic rose, prickling against my skin.

"Evie." Her cool hand touched my arm. "I'm an adult. He didn't do anything to me. In fact, the bastard was a perfect gentleman." She rolled her eyes. "He brought me back to my apartment. Dug out pajamas for me. Gave me plenty of water and lectured me about hydration, then tucked me into bed and slept on the couch. This morning, he made me a cup of coffee, then pushed a folder full of my past across the table."

But he didn't give her the drops. Hmm. "None of that excuses him trying to manipulate you into doing what he wants."

"Are we surprised? He's a Lord, after all. You seem to have snagged the only good one."

"Ben's decent." I frowned. "A touch of the ol' misogyny with him, but I don't think he would do something like this."

Moira grunted. "I don't put anything past anyone."

"What did you tell him?"

She tilted her face up and pretended to think about it. "It went something like, how dare you, fuck off, get out of my house."

"Seems like the correct order of things. He won't stop."

Her face darkened. "I'm well aware."

"What kind of work has he asked you to do?"

"Investigative again. He said he'd have a case soon." Her shoulders slumped. "I flew too close to the sun and the asshole burned me. I should have kept my head down."

"You did," I said quietly. "If anyone is at fault here, it's me. I'm the one who dragged you into the Lords' world. Soren's already fascinated by you, and Ethan seems headed that way."

Moira shook her head. "It's not like that for Ethan. He sees a tool to be used."

I didn't agree with her. Not after that smack on the ass. That was raw possession. "Hmm. I don't think most men would haul a tool over his shoulder and remove her from a bar for her own safety." I rolled my eyes. "Or what he thought was for her own safety."

Her lips twitched. "Kinda hot, right?"

"Extremely," I agreed. "That ass slap was heard around the world."

Moira let out a loud laugh. "I have an Ethan shaped hand-print on my left cheek."

"All the Lords are attractive." I rolled my eyes. "Must be a job prerequisite. All of them are deadly, but there's something about Ethan." I shivered. "He has assassin energy, the kind of man who will sneak up on you and cut your throat without saying a word."

"He's a puzzle," Moira agreed. "He brought me cashmere and hot food, and now he's blackmailing me."

We looked at each other and burst out laughing.

I got up and brought the coffee pot to the table, refilling our mugs. "Are you going to work for him?"

She lifted a shoulder in a shrug. "The money is hard to pass up. I'm doing well, but Ethan's offer will allow me to permanently retire in a couple of years. Most immortals have to work for the rest of their lives because they spend too much and budget too little. I could probably retire now, but I'd have to follow a strict budget. With the money he's offering me..." Her voice trailed off. "Well, I could do whatever the hell I wanted to."

"Immortality might be boring without something to do."

Moira snorted. "Holding a pink drink with an umbrella and flirting with handsome men is doing something. I could do that all I wanted."

Retirement had never crossed my mind, not for myself. What would I do with myself? Probably get into trouble. There'd be no flirting with handsome men or the like. Not that I wanted to. I had all I wanted outside, giving me some privacy. Seeing the world was appealing, but Rowan was still a Lord. And soon, I'd take up my mantle as the fae queen. Our time for fun would be limited.

"You're smart enough to think through all the pitfalls of accepting Ethan's offer. I recommend putting a time limit on things and a clause where you can bow out for specific reasons. If he wants you bad enough, he'll be forced to agree."

Moira's lips twisted. "There's some wiggle room, but not much."

I didn't ask. He obviously had something on her if he was twisting her arm. "See how far he's willing to bend."

"I have a few weeks to decide."

"Enough time to figure out an easy out if things get dicey."

Moira's smile didn't reach her eyes. "I know you don't want me to do this."

I released a heavy breath. "The situation reminds me too much of Caelan. Ethan is charismatic, I'll give you that, but you two seem like gasoline and a match together."

"I'll insist on professional boundaries. Shouldn't be a big deal since he dislikes me so much." Her lips twisted.

"I don't think that's true," I said quietly.

I went to the fridge and took a small bottle out, passing it across the table. "Take a dropper full. You'll feel better in a few hours."

Moira snatched the bottle like it was the Holy Grail.

"Mom is an evil genius."

She grimaced as she swallowed the drops. "I had a ton of fun last night. The entire Keep is talking about your arm-wrestling stunt."

I grinned. "Probably a good thing Mom's booze is a relatively new invention. The world might be an entirely different place if we had that stuff around the entire time."

We chatted for a little while longer and planned to go see the baby in a few hours. I had a session with Dad today. We were still trying to nail the instant travel thing. I still felt only tingles and hadn't budged an inch.

I waved as Moira let herself out. Rowan came back in a few minutes later and helped himself to the rest of the coffee.

"Moira all right?" he asked.

"Ethan wants her to work for him."

Rowan choked on his drink. "What?"

"I know. It's a lot. He did a background check on her, one of the kinds that digs too deep for comfort and uncovered some things about her he's using to strong-arm Moira into doing what he wants."

Rowan closed his eyes for a long moment. "These Lords never learn, do they?"

A surprised laugh bubbled from my lips. "No, they really don't." My amusement soured a moment later. "This reminds me too much of what happened to me. Moira is probably a little less naive than I am, but I don't want her to have to deal with the things I had to."

Rowan's face turned thoughtful. "Ethan and Caelan are completely different. I think he brings his own unique set of issues to the table."

I gave him a dark look. "That doesn't make me feel better."

Rowan grinned. "Moira isn't as nice as you are."

My eyebrows lifted, making Rowan laugh. "I'm serious! You'd never get hauled out of a bar screaming bloody murder."

"No, I just arm wrestle massive shifters and make dangerous bets."

Rowan laughed, his eyes sparkling. "You're a hit, by the way. The entire Keep is talking about you and Ricky."

I groaned. "He challenged me, and I had a few too many to say no."

"The bar called earlier and said, 'get these mutant Ficus trees out of here before I start charging them rent.' So, I have to go back to the bar around lunch."

"Oops. I had to use them, otherwise it wouldn't have been a fair fight."

"Yes, well, we owe the bar some plants."

"I'll bring them something in a few days."

At his exasperated look, I clarified. "Something tame. Like a pothos or a money tree. And I'll promise not to borrow them again."

His lips twitched. "She's not mad. You brought in more money last night than she made the entire past week. But she draws the line at sentient plants." Rowan winked. "Give her some time, and I bet she'll change her mind. This place isn't used to having a Floromancer around, and certainly not one at your power level."

"I can't say I plan on any more arm-wrestling competitions," I said dryly. "But I also can't promise that will *never* happen again."

"That's my girl," Rowan said.

A FEW HOURS LATER, Dad was yelling at me, and I was sweating buckets.

"Dad! This is not Star Trek! I cannot just pop out of existence the second I want to!"

My father looked like he was about to blow a gasket. "Yes, you can," he said with barely concealed patience. "I've been trying to teach you that for weeks now."

He scrubbed a hand over his face. "You are the master of your magic. You are the one who shapes and wills the power. Get out of your head, Evie. Once that happens, your power will be fathomless."

I choked down a scream of frustration. "Why can't I get this?"

"Fear," Dad said simply. "You're letting your human understanding cloud your ability. We are not made of DNA and atoms, Evie. We're infinite. When you understand that, you don't have to understand magic. You mold your power into whatever you want it to be. The Floromancy and Chimera are extensions of the vast well of your other powers, the magic your mother and I gifted you upon our joining."

My nose crinkled. "Please never refer to you and Mom having sex as joining ever again."

On the sidelines of the training field, Rowan barked a laugh.

Dad waved my disgust away. "Evangeline, you cannot act as the fae queen until you learn how to access the rest of your power. When that self-imposed block fades away, you will be *infinite*. Until that happens, you are diminished, and your enemies will know right now is the perfect time to strike. Your mother and I cannot always be there. You must learn how to turn off that human part of your brain and realize the only limitations you have are the ones you set for yourself."

"I hate it when you're reasonable," I muttered.

Dad rolled his eyes. "Yes, well, when you're involved, being reasonable is difficult."

"Dad! Rude."

The wards tingled against my skin. Rowan rose and walked toward the disruption.

Dad stepped closer. "You must defeat your mind. Enemies press in from all sides. Do not let yourself get complacent."

I stopped what I was doing. "Do you know something we don't?"

Dad shrugged. "Enemies are a natural part of belonging to a powerful position, but you are uniquely suited to having more than normal."

I rolled my eyes. "Thanks, Dad."

Rowan came up over the rise, his face a mask of politeness.

Barrett walked beside him.

CHAPTER

THIRTY

I knew why Rowan had let him in. Refusing him would rouse suspicion. I pulled out my cell and texted Moira.

Keep the baby away from the training field. Barrett is here.

Shit, came the almost immediate response. *Will do.*

Three little dots and then, *Some weird shit is happening in the dorm. Unsure if it's the baby but seems like it. Odd magic fluctuations.*

Fuck.

Try to contain them if you can. He cannot know she's here.

I'll do my best.

"What is it?" Dad asked.

I smiled and waved to Barrett.

"There's a Chimera baby in the dorm," I whispered.

Dad blinked, his head snapping my direction. "*What?*"

"Someone dropped her off a few days ago. No idea where she came from or whose she is."

Dad stared at me for a long moment. "You didn't think this was important to mention?"

"I've had a lot going on," I hissed. "He cannot know she's here."

"You think he might be her father?"

"I don't know. Very few people offer the things he has for free unless there's something in it for them."

Dad grunted. "Fair enough."

"He's about to be within hearing distance. Pretend we're talking about something else."

"If you don't get this down, you'll be useless to us," Dad snapped.

I blinked. "Geez, Dad."

"You asked for it. Now, let's try it again from the top."

"Do I have to?" I whined. Half of the complaining wasn't for show. Mom's drops helped, but they weren't perfect. I still felt like I'd been wrung out and hung to dry.

"Do you want your people to die horrible deaths when others come for your territories and raid them?"

"We aren't Vikings."

"No," Dad agreed. "The fae are worse. Again, Evie."

Barrett seemed relaxed. He nodded to both of us. "I see your father is being hard on you again."

I rolled my eyes, careful to keep my emotions in check. Barrett had a keen sense of smell, and he knew how to use his magic far better than I did mine. I had to pretend like everything was normal. Barrett might be the best guy in the world, but I didn't trust him like I did Moira or Rowan, or my parents. He was still an unknown.

"Always," I agreed. "I'm glad you're here, actually. Once I get through this last drill, I have some questions about Chimera abilities."

Barrett's gaze lingered on me a beat too long. "When you canceled training the other day, I thought I'd done something wrong."

"Not at all," I said with a dismissive wave. "If you haven't noticed, Rowan and I are mated. That took precedence for a few days." The heat on my cheeks wasn't fake. I could still be such a prudish human sometimes.

Rowan's face was apologetic, but he'd done the right thing. If Barrett wasn't here for the right reasons, leaving him at the gate would only rouse suspicion.

His presence put us in a bad position. Barrett had never purposely wandered off or snooped, but we always kept a close eye on him. Garrett and Simone were never too far away when I was wandering the grounds, and Declan and Hope were making their rounds as well. Barrett wouldn't get far if his purposes were nefarious.

A wise man had once told me, "Trust, then verify." Barrett was still in the verification stages.

"Of course," Barrett said with a chuckle. "Mating as a Chimera is supposed to be an intense experience as well. I can't imagine any shifter has it easy during those first few days."

Rowan's smile didn't quite reach his eyes as he came up beside me. "We were pretty busy for a while."

I choked on a laugh. "Rowan!"

His words broke the subtle tension. Barrett sat down on an old tree stump. "Please. I didn't mean to interrupt the middle of a session. We can continue on once you and your father finish."

Dad inclined his head. "There's not much happening right now other than Evie's tingles."

"Is this bully Evie day?" I grumbled.

"When Evie finally gets this part down, worlds will rejoice." My father took a few steps back. "Now. Try again."

WE WERE at it for hours before Dad finally gave up. He said his goodbyes and left me with another lecture.

The moment he disappeared, Barrett rose. "Dusk comes

soon, but we have some time. You up for another practice round?"

I nodded, though exhaustion was set in every line of my body. "Go through the warmups first?"

He shook his head. "Not this time. You should be plenty warmed up after your time with Cernunnos. Let's get right into it."

Everything seemed normal with Barrett. He wasn't acting weird or searching for something he thought we might have. His attention stayed on me. His touches were polite but guiding, and he made no cryptic comments about anything.

I was beginning to feel bad about mistrusting him. Just as I turned to ask him something, magic rocked the Keep.

Powerful magic.

Chimera magic.

Simone and Garrett hurried out of the forest cover and skidded to a stop on either side of me. They'd long ago noted Barrett's presence and said nothing that might reveal our secret.

Barrett stumbled, his eyes sharpening. "What was that?"

The problem with thinking fast is I was bad at it sometimes. "Mom is still on Keep grounds. Maybe she blew up something in her lab."

Barrett gave me an odd look. "No," he said slowly. "That magic is familiar."

A thin stream of crimson magic shot through the air, high-lighting the sky with the color of blood. Barrett sucked in a shocked breath.

"Is there another Chimera on the grounds?" He started to take off, but Garrett grabbed him by the arm

"Apologies, Barrett. This is Keep only business. I'm afraid I'll have to escort you off the grounds."

Declan and Hope walked up just as Garrett was leading Barrett away, but the Chimera dug his heels in.

"Evie! What was that?" His eyes narrowed. "What are you hiding?"

I smiled apologetically. "Sorry, Barrett. He's right. This is Keep business."

His face drained of color. "After everything I've done for you, you'd keep a secret like this from me? Where is the other Chimera? Who is it? Did you find the swans?"

I still wasn't sure if he was playing me or not. Finn had been an amazing actor until he wasn't. Chimeras were born and lived in secret. All of us had the capacity for great deception when it came to hiding our identities.

Rowan gently squeezed my arm. "My mate has spoken, Barrett. Once we have everything under control, we can resume training."

Barrett's genial mask fell away. "I knew you were hiding something from me. Who are you keeping here?"

Simone gripped Barrett's other arm and together they dragged him away. Rowan followed behind. With the three of them, he'd think twice about trying to break away.

"Evie!" Barrett roared. "I WILL find out!"

The sky still glowed crimson. Shifters poured out of the dormitory where the flash of light occurred. Several came running toward us.

"Pick up the pace," Rowan said tightly.

I turned away, confident in Rowan's control of the situation, and hurried toward the dorms.

CHAPTER

THIRTY-ONE

Moira was beside herself when I skidded into the shared living area of the main dormitory. Misty lay in her crib happily burbling away while glowing with an intense red light.

"She seems fine," Moira said, her face stricken. "I—I don't know what happened, but she won't let me near her. Every time I try, it's like she has this field that pushes me away."

Hope came to an abrupt stop and gasped at the scene. "Holy shit."

I moved toward the baby. Hope gripped my arm. "Wait. Me first."

"No. Let me. I'm her kind. If this is the first manifestation of her magic, she might need to see someone like her." I shook my head at the words. No idea if what I was saying was true, but it felt right.

"Be careful," Moira urged.

I shook Hope's grip loose and carefully moved closer.

"Hi, Misty," I said in a singsong voice. "Hey little baby. Everything okay?"

Nothing happened, so I ventured closer, close enough I could peer over the edge and see her.

Misty waved a chubby fist and made a spit bubble. Relief filled me. "You scared the hell out of everyone," I said softly.

And probably made us a few enemies, I didn't say aloud. I reached out and stroked her downy hair. "What is this? You're glowing like an Amsterdam club."

Moira snorted.

"Can I pick you up?" I scooped her up, waiting for something to happen, but Misty seemed content.

A breath of relief escaped me. I tucked her against my hip and booped her nose. "What was all that about?"

Misty let out a loud laugh.

"Mmm hmm. Funny for you. Terrifying for everyone else."

Moira and I locked eyes. "I don't know how far the light can be seen."

"Miles," Hope said grimly. "Maybe more."

"If any of the swans or other Chimeras are out there, Misty just put out a homing beacon."

Hope nodded. "They'll be investigating. Soon. I'll speak with the Lord about bolstering security. In the meantime, is there something you can do to tone that light down?"

Misty blinked slower than normal.

I grinned and looked up at Hope. "I think so. At least for a little while."

The Omega nodded and hurried from the room.

I gently shook the baby's fist. "How about a nap, little monster?"

Misty gave me a gummy smile.

"WE HAVE MAYBE TWO HOURS," I said to Rowan when I got back to the house. "Moira is with Misty, but she won't allow anyone but me near her right now."

It took me a while to get her to sleep, but I had to admit, holding an innocent little baby for any amount of time was amazing for my dopamine receptors. Even with the threat of Barrett hanging over our heads, I felt more relaxed today than I had in weeks.

Poor Moira was a frazzled mess, though.

Rowan pushed a purplish drink toward me. He sat at the table nursing his own amber-colored drink. His hair was a little mussed and there were purple smudges under his eyes.

"Barrett hasn't left." His heavy sigh spoke volumes about how he felt about that. "He's pacing outside the wards, demanding to be let back in."

"Great." I took a fortifying sip and blinked. "Damn. This is delicious."

Rowan's tired smile made my heart hurt. "Spiked lavender lemonade. Hope brought it over earlier and said to tell you there's no time for arm-wrestling tonight."

"I'll never live that one down."

"Nope," Rowan said cheerfully.

We fell silent. "There's more," he said after a moment.

"Of course there is." I took another drink.

Rowan refilled my lemonade from the pitcher. "Barrett is claiming the Chimera is his daughter."

"Not unexpected," I murmured. "Any way to prove it?"

"Unfortunately, the blueprints to build our DNA lab are delayed." He softened his sarcasm with a smile. "I'm hopeful your parents can help. If Barrett is Misty's father, we cannot legally hold her at the Keep without entangling us in complicated politics. Barrett has proclaimed you as the de facto Chimera leader in earshot more than once, and you are my mate..."

His voice trailed off.

"Conflict of interest," I finished.

I pulled my phone out and texted Mom. She showed up, but she wasn't alone. A tall woman with brilliant red hair appeared beside her. Rowan went still.

I sucked in a breath.

"Peace, Lord," Mom said. "She has agreed to help with your...issue."

Brigid, goddess of the home and hearth, smiled at me, the look not especially friendly. She was tall and beautiful, pale blue eyes like ice chips. My father considered her a friend.

I found it hard to believe this woman was anyone's friend.

"Nice to see you again, Evie."

I didn't have to have any special abilities to know the woman was lying. "Likewise."

My smile was all jagged edges.

Brigid gave me the first genuine smile I'd seen from her. "Well, then. Let us not delay. Bring me to the child."

MISTY WAS JUST ROUSING from her nap when she spied Brigid and went completely silent. Even the baby was awed by her beauty. The goddess swept her up and tucked her in the crook of her arm.

Brigid might look like an ice queen, but her demeanor thawed as soon as Misty was in her arms. She swayed gently back and forth and spoke nonsense, gently stroking the baby's hair. Mom still stared at her like one would a poisonous viper.

I clamped my lips together to keep from laughing.

"Where is the male who claims kinship?" Brigid asked.

"Outside of the wards," Rowan said.

One of the goddess's eyebrows rose. "Show me to him."

Rowan's jaw tightened at being ordered around, but he escorted Brigid outside.

Our walk to the front of the wards was silent. The only sound was Brigid speaking quietly to the child. When Barrett spotted us, he slammed his fists against the wards. The impact reverberated through my skull, though not as painful as it must have been for Rowan, who winced with every blow.

We stopped before Barrett. The male always looked well put together every time I saw him, but the baby's presence had shaken something loose inside of him. His hair was mussed from its normal, neatly combed appearance. His irises were ringed with crimson, and his chest heaved with every breath.

"I am trying to be reasonable, Rowan." Barrett's voice was guttural and hoarse. "We both know I can break these wards."

"If you do, you will find yourself in a war with my people," Rowan said mildly. "I'd recommend you maintain your restraint."

Brigid stepped up, smart enough to shadow the baby's face with the blanket. She eyed Barrett for a moment.

The hair rose on the back of my neck. I glanced at Rowan. He straightened, a slight furrow between his brows.

Mom sucked in a breath. Her eyes widened and flashed with azure-colored magic.

"I have to go," she whispered, her face stricken with fear.

Mom blinked away. I stepped forward, my hand outstretched. What was happening?

"HOPE!" Rowan called, his voice booming through the clearing.

Brigid smiled at Barrett, a slow, satisfied curl of her lips.

Barrett smiled back, a roll of crimson magic shining from his eyes.

Rowan's wards shattered, a boom of sound that launched us backward through the air.

Shadows melted from the tree cover. Hundreds of shifters appeared, swans, wolves, and a few others I couldn't make out as I flew through the air.

I flung out a hand, commanding the earth. Vines ripped from the earth and wrapped themselves around me and Rowan, bringing us to a gentle stop. I glanced behind me. Rowan's eyes glowed that strange new color.

Moira, Hope, and Declan came over the rise, my friend in the lead, her dark hair streaming like a ribbon behind her.

The vines released Rowan. He rose, a terrible look on his face. "I've called the others. This will be a difficult fight. Evacuate the children. You know the plan. This is what we've practiced for all these years"

Hope nodded and turned back toward the dorms. Declan shifted, a massive brown bear in the place where the male had just stood.

"The moment they step into Keep territory, down as many as you can," Rowan commanded.

Moira came up beside me. "What can I do?" My best friend wasn't scared, her lovely face set into a determined expression.

Rowan looked to me. "Whatever you say, Rowan."

My mate nodded. "Same instructions I gave to Declan. No mercy, Moira. Kill or be killed. They want to come onto my land and take what belongs to us, we will show them why that's a terrible idea."

Brigid turned, still holding the baby. "Thank you for your hospitality." She started to shimmer away, but Barrett came up behind her. I spotted a flash of black as his arm rose.

Brigid's eyes widened. She tried to spin, but stumbled, blood arcing in a half circle above her back. Her lips parted, crimson streaming from between her lips. The goddess went to her knees, the bundle in her arms slipping. Barrett bent and removed the child, tucking Misty in his arms.

Moira swore. "What the hell did he stab her with?"

"Iron," Rowan said grimly. "Keep your distance."

I shook my head. "No. Iron has never affected me like the other fae. He'll soon find out his weapon is useless." Barrett's attention was momentarily distracted by the child. Whether she was his or not, he would die today.

"This land is yours just as much as it is mine," I said. "Barrett will know our might."

Rowan gathered me around the waist and pressed a fierce kiss to my lips. "Happy hunting, mate of mine."

"Happy hunting," I breathed, my lips tingling from the taste of him.

Barrett turned and handed the baby to one of the swans.

"Moira, change of plans."

"Find the baby," she whispered.

"Find the baby," I agreed. "Secure her somewhere no one can find her. Then come back and kill as many of these fuckers as you want."

Moira's grin held a touch of vicious delight. "Can't wait."

She made an astonishing leap toward the swan, who gaped and stumbled as they turned and ran from Rowan's property.

That bitch wouldn't get far with Moira on her tail.

Rowan took off for the shifters surging onto Keep property. I kept my eyes on Barrett and walked toward him, hands loose at my side.

"Is she yours?" I asked.

"Does it matter?" The Chimera rode his words, his irises ringed with crimson.

Mine had been content since Rowan and I had completed the bond, rising only when I wanted it to. I hadn't thought much about that since I'd been so focused on other things, but I felt overall more settled, more secure in my skin.

"It does," I said simply. We stood a few feet away from each other. "If she's yours, we can work something out."

"If she's mine, you have no claim."

"You tore down Rowan's wards and entered onto Keep property, a declaration of war. I'm within my rights to kill you."

Barrett's eyes lit with surprise and amusement. "You always have been a big talker for someone who can't manage her own magic. You operate at the level of a Chimera child, Evie. What makes you think you have even the smallest of chances of walking out of this alive?"

I smiled. "You always seem to forget I am not only a Chimera."

I brought my hands up. Vines and roots shot from the ground, but Barrett was too fast. He disappeared in a heartbeat, either a trick of the light or a Chimera secret I hadn't yet learned.

I spun around, looking for him, only to see shifters tangled with each other, some in human form, others fighting in their animal forms. Teeth and claws and bladed wings ripping and tearing at each other.

The scene made my heart ache.

So much violence. For what?

I was so sick of these power games, so sick of these people who wanted more than what they were entitled to or what they worked for. Tired of people fighting and dying.

Tears sprang to my eyes. A shift of wind direction was the only thing that saved me. I shifted to the left, just as a bladed wing snipped off a lock of my hair.

Barrett forgotten for now, I spun to face the swan.

"Hello, bitch," a grinning male said. "I can't wait to breed you."

My nose crinkled with disgust. "Sorry. Dinner and conversation before breeding. You haven't even asked me for my number yet."

The swan blinked in confusion. "Stupid bitch."

"Mmm. Yes, you've called me that already. Not the sharpest tool in the drawer, are you?"

A cruel ugliness crept into the swan's eyes.

Seconds later, I was in a fight for my life.

THIRTY-TWO

MOIRA

I rarely used my vampiric abilities to their full extent. Today, the speed at which I flew across the ground felt like stretching a sore, unused muscle. The swan was fast, but it was a fucking bird.

I was a predator.

We both knew who'd win this fight.

Within minutes, I had the swan's scent. Moments after that, I had him in my sightline. I leapt to a treetop and followed, quiet as a cat. If we could find out where he was taking the baby, we could wipe out the rest of the swans once and for all.

They'd be fools if they brought out all their numbers against Evie today.

The swan stumbled out to a small, gravel road where a nondescript silver sedan sat. I leapt to the ground and ran over, but as soon as I came out of the trees, I ducked behind another to keep from being spotted by a male I did not expect to find here.

The swan was having an impatient conversation with a tall, lean man with midnight-colored eyes.

"Man, I don't have time. I need to go."

"Oh, sorry man, sorry. I'm just lost, you know." He stuck his hands in his pockets and affected a good ol' boy air. "New to the city, and I gotta check in with the local Lord. You know about him? That Rowan guy? Heard he's kind of a stuck up asshole."

I pressed my lips together to keep from laughing.

"He's kinda busy right now," the swan said. "You might want to wait a little while."

"Oh yeah?" the man said. "Is he having a party? It's been a while since I've had a hot meal. Wonder if he'll allow me in?"

The swan snorted. "Sure, man. Yeah. Go on up. I'm sure he'd be happy to host you."

"Really?" His face brightened. "Say, that's an adorable baby." He reached over to pull the blanket down, but the swan jerked Misty away.

"Back off, dude. I told you, I don't have time. The Keep's just up the road."

"Can't you give me a ride or something?"

The swan snorted and turned his back.

Ethan turned his head in my direction, winked, and rolled his eyes. He raised his hand and slammed the swan's face into the side of the car door, deftly grabbing the baby as the swan slumped to the ground.

"Fucking idiot," Ethan said with disgust.

I came out from the trees.

"This belongs to you, I take it?"

Ethan looked far too comfortable and far too hot holding a baby. My ovaries caught fire at the way he tenderly supported the baby's head.

One of his eyebrows rose. A soft chuckle rumbled his chest. "Moira, I keep telling you to lock that down."

I slunk toward him, putting a sway into my hips. "It's just you and me out here, and you hate me anyway, so why bother?"

Something flashed in Ethan's eyes, a ring of midnight and

gold circling his iris. I had an incredible sense of smell, but Ethan was a difficult man to read. His emotions were locked down tighter than a Russian prison.

"Guess you're right." He handed the baby over. "Everything alright up there?"

"No. One of the Chimeras training Evie betrayed her. He was working with the fae the entire time. They tore the wards down and came onto the property."

Ethan's eyes widened. "Because of the baby?"

I slowly shook my head. "Partially. I remain unconvinced that's the entire reason."

"Need some help?"

"I'm sure Rowan won't say no to some assistance."

Ethan nodded. "Lead the way, lady vampire."

I flashed a grin. "See if you can keep up."

I shot through the trees like a rocket.

CHAPTER

THIRTY-THREE

My Floromancy hadn't been much help in this fight. Barrett was too quick for me to catch. I bled from a dozen wounds. Sweat obscured my vision, and I still couldn't get a good lock on the Chimera's location. Whatever this ability he was using, I needed it.

I racked my brain, trying to figure out how to catch him, when something occurred to me. No one could ever be completely silent. Such was impossible. When Barrett moved, he would make vibrations in the ground.

I grimaced and shucked off my shoes, fishing in my pocket for a few seeds I dropped onto the ground. I sent a tendril of magic through the earth.

The slightest of sounds. *There.*

I ducked just as a clawed tipped hand swiped through the air. Thorns shot up where the sound came from. Barrett let out a yelp of pain and materialized. I shifted into a leopard and leaped for him.

He swore and moved like quicksilver. I flew past him but not before getting in a good swipe with my claws. Blood sprayed over my fur.

Vines sprang from the earth at my command, tangling Barrett's feet under him.

Chaos rang all around us, the shouts and screams of pain a cacophony of sound in my head. Rowan was still out there, the bond a beating heart between us.

Dark crawled over the horizon, the full moon cresting above the trees. Mom and Dad had not come back. Whatever had distracted them must have been important.

I spotted Moira coming back onto the property, a bundle in her arms, followed by a tall, lean man with glowing eyes.

Ethan. Relief filled me. He'd be a huge help right now.

There was no way to tell who was winning or losing, though the number of swans who'd come onto the property had been substantially diminished.

Barrett sliced through the vines faster than I could make them. Three lines of bloody claw marks marred his handsome face.

"You're learning," he said with a dark chuckle. "But your vines won't hold me."

"I know." I tilted my head and smiled. "Those aren't normal vines."

The first trickle of uncertainty flashed over his face.

I'd been busy in Rowan's greenhouse when I first arrived. At first, I planted normal things—herbs, petunias, some cold weather vegetables, but I also had Dad bring over my plants, the ones I'd made when I was in Scotland, and I managed to coax them into producing seed pods.

I'd planted one of those seeds in the greenhouse and saved the rest. The plants had bred true, and soon enough, I had another wickedly poisonous plant in my possession, one I warned Rowan to stay away from. He wasn't my mate then, but even now, I wasn't sure he'd be immune to the poison.

I made them as a safeguard, never thinking I'd use them, but I kept the seeds with me at all times.

Barrett swayed. A trickle of blood seeped from one of his eyes. "What did you do?"

"I used to try to solve things by being easygoing, peaceable. I made myself small to avoid conflict. But my enemies kept bringing war to my doorstep. They kept poking and prodding like a rotten tooth you can only fix through extraction." I smiled with too many teeth.

Barrett licked his lips. Blood dripped down his teeth. A fine tremor began in his left hand. He squeezed his fist shut.

I came a few steps closer. "Those enemies tried to befriend me under the guise of helping me be the best I could be while waiting for me to reveal my secrets. But I stopped relaxing, stopped trusting as much as I used to. Instead I prepared, ever so slowly."

Barrett swayed. Blood began to pour from all his orifices. He gagged and choked, his hand clutching against his throat as his airway closed.

"Evie," he begged, his voice a hoarse rasp. "I'm one of the last of us left."

"I do not care," I hissed. "I don't care about you or the swans or the rest of our people because not once have you given a shit about me. All you've done is take from me, and I am tired. I will no longer try to be peaceable. If you bring war to me, I will respond with the fury of the gods."

I lifted my hands. Wicked, spiked roots dripping with poison shot from the earth and wrapped around Barrett's neck.

"No! Please!"

I didn't care about his begging, either. I crossed my arms and swiped them apart. Barrett's head separated from his body with a moist thwicking sound, falling to the ground in a heap of blood and viscera.

When his body stopped twitching, I kicked his head away and glided toward the other shifters still fighting, pulling my poisonous thorns with me.

The fight went easier after that. Rowan's people decimated the swans, and I killed with impunity. Maybe later I would feel guilt over this, but right now, magic thumped through my blood in a steady drumbeat. Every swan I saw, I touched with poison. Rowan's people saw what I was doing and disengaged.

When I had cornered the last swan on the property, I surrounded her with poisonous thorns. The shifter took an unsteady step back.

"I wouldn't," I said mildly. "If you touch any of my vines, you will die."

"You have the cure," the shifter said.

I smiled. "I do. But I won't give it to you."

The shifter blinked. "They're right about you," she whispered.

I tilted my head. "Who?"

"The other Chimeras. They said you would kill us when we faced you."

"Then why are you here?"

Her face crumpled. "We just want our curse broken." The swan's lips trembled. "I—I just want to be a mother. Our people will die. Surely you can understand that!"

"Of course, I can. But your people have taken from me. You've taken my people. You've hurt people I cared about, and you've made it difficult for me to move freely within my territory. You would have taken me, chained me, and bred me like an animal. Do you honestly think you are in the right?"

The swan did not respond, but her eyes kept darting back and forth.

"No one is coming to save you," I said quietly.

She began to sob.

I was tired, so tired. I'd come so far only to have to fight again. Discussions hadn't worked. Mercy hadn't either. The only thing that worked was becoming death incarnate, and that was so far away from what I was meant to be. I was meant to bring life to the world. I knew it as sure as I was standing there.

"Return to your people," I said quietly. "Let them know what transpired here today. Tell them if they ever trespass on my property again or try to harm any of my people or anyone I care about, I will destroy every single swan in the world. No one will escape my wrath. I will erase your names from our history. Your curse will be a small problem compared to the problem of me. Do you understand?"

The swan blinked and nodded like a bobble head. "Then go." I made an opening through the path of poisoned thorns, wide enough to allow the swan to run away. When she was off the property, I called those thorns back and turned.

The Keep was quiet. Hundreds of dead lay around us. My shoulders slumped, and I sought out Rowan.

Moira stood next to Ethan, both covered in blood and gore, but they were okay. I shot her a soft smile.

She returned it and touched her heart.

Following the bond, I turned to see Rowan walking toward me, maybe a quarter of a mile away. A deep scratch marred his cheek. His hands were covered in blood, and his clothing was torn, but he was upright.

Mine.

I smiled and started walking toward him, too tired to run. From his pace, I expected he was too.

My smile widened, but a warning tingle brushed against my skin. I stilled, my eyes sweeping across the land trying to pinpoint where the potential threat was coming from. Frustration rose in my stomach when I couldn't see anything.

I kept walking, picking up my pace. Rowan frowned and did the same.

A man came into view behind Rowan, tall and muscled, with familiar storm-colored eyes. He leapt through the air, his right hand tipped with wicked claws, sailing right toward my mate's exposed back.

THIRTY-FOUR

MOIRA

I knew many things about Evie Quinn. I knew she hated cucumbers with the fire of a thousand suns and gagged when someone was cutting one. I knew she liked nature documentaries, especially the ones narrated by men with European accents. I knew she loved my cookies, especially my snickerdoodles, but felt bad about asking me to make them for her because she didn't want to bother me.

I knew she loved the rain and the sound of rushing water and how wet sand felt between her toes. I also knew she felt guilty about hating carnations because she was a creature of the gods and thought that meant she had to love everything that came from the ground.

I knew her fake laugh and her polite laugh, and the one she used when she was humoring someone but planned to verbally eviscerate them later.

I even knew her screams—the high-pitched one when she was frightened, the one that sounded like someone gargling marbles when she was frustrated, and the one she made late at night when a nightmare would drag her from the depths of a restless sleep.

But I had never, in all the years I'd known her, heard a scream like that rip from her throat when Caelan came for Rowan. The sound brought me to my knees, grief spreading like a virus through my veins.

It was the sound of agony, of the earth mourning, of despair and horror, and love shattered far before its time.

I tucked that sound, as painful as it was, into my heart so I would know it if, the gods forbid, she ever made it again.

And as I sat on my knees with my heart shattering, I knew one more thing.

My best friend would not make it in time to save Rowan from the certain death barreling toward him.

CHAPTER

THIRTY-FIVE

I wasn't going to make it. My legs pumped as I ran for Rowan, heart shattering into a thousand pieces and wishing I had seen our potential earlier, seen *him* earlier.

If I had, we wouldn't be here on a battlefield surrounded by the dead.

Time slowed as I ran for him. Rowan hadn't yet realized death was at his back, but I saw the moment he realized my expression had changed from one of relief into one of horror.

He would be too late, too.

An agonized scream ripped from my throat. In a last-ditch effort to save him, I leapt toward Caelan, a spear of hawthorn coated with poison forming in my hands as I flew. Magic tore from my veins, burning through me like a wildfire.

I willed myself closer, promised the universe anything it ever wanted if it allowed me to save Rowan, even if it meant sacrificing my life.

I *moved*, a pop of air the only sound of the magic finally working. A second later I was before Caelan, reaching for his neck with one hand, and spearing him through the chest with the other.

265

Shock crossed Caelan's face, followed by a bark of pain. We flew backward, my momentum carrying us at least a dozen yards back. Finally, we slammed to the ground, me on top of Caelan.

"**HOW DARE YOU!**" Magic thundered through the ground. Trees snapped and cracked under my power. Stones rumbled from the earth, massive ancient pillars of rock rising around us.

Caelan coughed up blood.

My hand was still tight around his throat, claws I'd never seen before dragging ragged gouges down the smooth skin of his neck.

"**HOW DARE YOU!**" I said one more time. My vision was misted in a fine haze of crimson. Dark hair streamed around me, floating in a wind I couldn't see or feel.

"Evie," Caelan wheezed. He stared up at me with wide eyes.

"DO NOT SPEAK, TRAITOR."

A hesitant hand touched my shoulder. I stilled, squeezing my eyes shut when I realized it was Rowan.

"He tried to kill you," I whispered.

"I know." Rowan crouched down beside me, hazel eyes taking in my clawed hand and the spear buried deep within Caelan's chest, along with the starburst black mark where the spear entered.

"Poisoned?" Rowan observed.

I nodded. Tears streamed down my face.

"Will it kill him?"

I nodded once more.

Rowan let out a breath and put a hand on my back. "Do you want to do this, Evie?"

Caelan bared his teeth. "She would not kill me."

Rowan's smile didn't reach his eyes. "Look at my mate's face, Lord, and tell me whether you still believe those words."

Caelan blinked and met my gaze. The moment I saw him

leaping through the air for Rowan's exposed back flipped a switch. Any love I'd ever felt for him died, dried up like a summer drought.

The ground rumbled once more. A wizened woman rose before me, carrying a glowing staff. She was old. Ancient. Her skin was the color of old bark and had the texture of an ancient tree.

"Daughter."

I bared my teeth at her. "Busy right now."

The crone's gaze took in the scene. "I see that. If you kill him, you will reap unfathomable consequences upon your people."

"I do not care," I said through clenched teeth.

"Child," the woman said quietly. "Of course you do. You no longer care for this man, but you care for your people, for the man beside you who will allow you to make whatever decision you think you must, no matter what hell it brings down around his head."

I exhaled. "What do you want?"

"Is that any way to speak to a goddess?" the woman chided.

My dark look did not diminish. She laughed. "Very well. I have a proposal. It would solve your problem and one of mine."

I scoffed. "You wish to bargain. Right now?"

"What better time than when poised on the edge of a knife's blade?"

"Fine," I snapped.

"Good." The goddess snapped her fingers.

I stood in a place of stone and earth.

"My proposal is simple. Take my position, and I will strip the rest of those locks on your magic. You will finally become who you were meant to be, and I can..." The ancient goddess smiled. "Well, I can retire."

I stared at her. "I have no idea what position you hold. Why would I agree to such an open-ended thing?"

"Child, you've already been doing much of my job already."

My eyes narrowed. "Danu?"

The goddess smiled. "It is nice to meet you, Evangeline."

I sighed. "I don't have to kill Caelan, but he's not leaving my territory without punishment."

"The spell is worse on his property. A lesson, if you will, for his treatment of my favorite daughter."

Realization slammed into me with the force of a train. "You," I breathed. "You're the one responsible for all of this? This horrific spell killing the earth?" I stared at her in horror. A goddess responsible for nurturing the world and all the green and wonderful things inside it had gone to extraordinary lengths to bend me to her will.

I was so, so tired. When would this stop? When would all these gods and goddesses and Lords realize I was not their plaything and could not be molded into the shape they wanted?

"You needed a nudge," the goddess said simply.

"A nudge," I echoed. "A *nudge*? You almost got my mate killed, you tree-bark bitch!"

Danu's smile fell away. "I care not for the love lives of others," she snapped. "You are the only one with the power required to maintain this world. I am...diminished."

I resisted the urge to kill this bitch, and it took everything in my power to stay my hand. But as I stood there, horror filling my veins at her sheer arrogance and cruelty, I made a silent vow to myself and to the world. I would take her down. One way or another.

When I'd gotten my fury under control, I crossed my arms over my chest. "What does this have to do with Caelan?"

"I will show you the potential of your power, Evie, something no one but I can do. You will become limitless. Once you have the power you were always meant to, punish him how you see fit, but do not kill him. The Lords play deeper games than many of us can see. I can't see everything, Evangeline, but I can see killing him will cause a chain reaction none of us are prepared for. You are within your rights to punish him. Not even the Lords will argue. But be clever in how you approach it, girl."

"What do you mean, the power I was always meant to have?"

Danu's eyes sparkled. "Someone put a lock on you. There's no telling when or who did it, but that's one of the main reasons you cannot access the full well of your power."

"Dad would have seen it," I argued.

"No. He never looked hard enough. I felt it when you were in the earth with me. We were...joined in a way. Someone doesn't want you to reach your potential. Start there, girl. Your journey, and that of your hated Lord, is not quite over."

The supposed lock aside, Danu wasn't telling me this because she was benevolent or gave a shit about me. "You want me to be Mother Earth."

Danu grimaced. "I hate that name. It makes me sound like a flowery princess. But yes. I want you to become the earth's guardian."

"I'm the fae queen."

"I'm aware. This bargain will only help you more firmly secure that role."

I studied her. "Why don't you just rip off that lock anyway?"

Danu laughed. "Because I am fae. We do not do things for free."

"Don't I know it. Bunch of assholes," I grumbled. "I have no idea how to be a steward of the land. I already am on my own lands, but the world is a vast place."

"The knowledge will come to you when your power becomes unsealed." Danu smiled. "It is not as difficult as it sounds. With the job comes a knowing. You will know where the earth bleeds, Evangeline."

"Will this help my Chimera magic?"

Danu nodded. "Everything is linked. The lock affected everything. Find the one who did this to you and punish the one who broke your heart. They are linked."

I thought about it. "How pissed is Dad going to be?"

Danu shrugged. "Very. But he will be relieved when you rise from the earth once more and he sees you are no longer diminished."

I thought about it. My Floromancy never seemed affected by this lock or whatever it was, but Dad had mentioned something a long time ago. The words escaped me, but a plan formed in my head.

I tilted my head and studied her. "Are you more powerful than my father?"

Danu laughed. "Apples and oranges, girl. We all have different skills."

DAD. I sent a shout and a mental image through the link we'd occasionally shared.

The ground rumbled a second later.

Danu blinked, her eyes narrowing. "What are you doing?"

A golden hand punched through the dirt, followed by my father's grinning head, like an upside-down groundhog. "Need a ride?"

"I've been manipulated by the best, Danu, and I'm tired. I'll have Dad remove the lock."

Dad's amusement drained from his face. "A lock?" His swirling gaze went to Danu, who wisely shrank away.

"Yep. Can you help?"

He didn't answer, but I could tell the answer from the look in his eye. "Take my hand, Evangeline."

I reached up for my father with one hand and flipped Danu

off with the other. "You should have opened an IRA when you were younger so you could retire sooner. Fuck you and fuck your job offer. I have enough shit to do."

Dad's hand clenched in mine and power roared through my body. Something ripped inside my abdomen, a tearing and rendering pain that made me scream in agony.

A second later, sweet, sweet power flowed through my veins, and I was tunneling up through the earth, safe in my father's arms.

THIRTY-SIX

I came back to my body in a rush of magic, my hand still clenched around Caelan's throat, the other still holding the spear. A moment of vicious disorientation made me sway, but it wore off quickly.

"Evie?" Rowan's eyes glowed with concern.

I turned my attention to Caelan. **"FOR THE CRIME OF ATTEMPTED MURDER, YOU ARE CONFINED TO YOUR KEEP LANDS."** Rowan flinched at the power in my voice.

"IF YOU ATTEMPT TO LEAVE, YOU WILL DIE. IF YOU ATTEMPT TO SEND OTHERS OFF THE LANDS TO FURTHER YOUR AGENDA, ALL OF YOU WILL DIE. YOU WILL STAY THERE UNTIL YOU MAKE AMENDS TO ME AND TO ROWAN OR UNTIL YOUR MATE FINDS YOU. YOU WILL SUSPEND YOUR LORD TITLE UNTIL SUCH TIME AS THIS CURSE IS BROKEN."

My eyes had cast a pink and silver glow over his face.

Caelan's face went bone white. "You cannot be serious."

A ball of magic formed in my hand. "I'm completely serious," I said quietly. "You finally went too far. I am no longer the woman you knew before. You *will* stay confined to your lands,

Caelan. As we speak, your territory is surrounded by poisonous thorns. You or any shifter who crosses the boundary with any ill will in their heart will die. If you care about your people, you will heed my words." I released his throat and rose. "You will bear my mark on your chest. Behind it is the poison that will stay inside your body until the curse breaks." I bent over him. "Try me at your peril, Lord."

I yanked the spear from his body and slapped my hand on his chest, healing the wound while still keeping a small capsule of my poison in the area. My power came so easily now it was a simple action.

A dark starburst with a small, stylized flower in the middle was the only sign of the injury. I smiled with too many teeth. "I'll send you a reminder with the details."

Caelan's nostrils flared. "Evie, you cannot do this. I will amass the power of the Lords against you—"

Ethan stepped up. "The power of the Lords only stands with those who are in the right. I saw you try to kill Rowan, Caelan. Evie's methods might be unorthodox, but she's within her rights to punish you."

I winked at Caelan. "How does it feel to finally lose, asshole?" I flicked my fingers at him. "Now get the fuck off our land."

He disappeared with a pop of sound.

Caelan was back home on poison-soaked lands.

Exhaustion caught up with me. I swayed on my feet. My eyes rolled up in the back of my head and darkness overtook me.

EPILOGUE

Spring came early to Emberwood with the help of its resident goddess. Still seemed weird thinking of myself that way. I'd always been just Evie until recently.

Now I was the fae queen, mate to Rowan, and, in a few minutes, I'd claim the title of wife.

Moira fussed with my bouquet, pretending she wasn't crying.

"I'm already mated, Moira. That's a lot more serious than this."

My best friend sniffed. "Yes, I know, but you're in a dress and there's cake and a DJ." She fluttered a hand in front of her face. "It's all so *romantic*."

I brought her in for a hug. "One day, I'll be messing with your bouquet, too," I promised her.

Moira grimaced. "That won't happen for a long time, if ever."

Ethan had left not long after helping us retake our Keep. I never thought he'd be as...

Well, I didn't have the words to describe Ethan. If you asked

Moira, she'd describe him with words like, "asshole," or "misogynist pig," or my personal favorite, "egotistical fucktard."

We all saw people differently, though I suspected Moira would change her mind about him soon enough.

Caelan tried and failed a dozen different times already to break my spell, finally learning his lesson after the third shifter he sent through the thorns died. Nothing would grow on his land either. Nothing would die, but the seasons would not come, new flowers would not grow, neither would the grass or vines. He was trapped in a paused world. A harsh lesson, but one he needed.

What I didn't tell him was the spell had also put his land into a form of stasis. Death would not come for him. Not now.

Tess had confirmed it, staring at me strangely when she did.

Everyone stared at me a little strangely these days.

Everyone except Rowan.

Caelan and I weren't quite finished. Not yet. But he no longer held any power over me.

I was the only one who held the power.

Moira linked our arms together. "Are you ready?"

I adjusted my veil and took a deep breath. "Ready."

We grinned at each other and stepped outside, immediately surrounded by shifters and fae and humans, every single one of them our people. Poe and Fee swooped playfully through the air, their happy cries shattering the skies. Tess and Ash stood together, the dryad holding the Chimera baby dressed in a frilly pink dress. Tess held Seymour, who happily waved his traps around. Everyone I loved was here today. Mom and Dad stood beside them.

Hope and Declan sat in the next row, both smiling broadly.

And as I walked toward Rowan, my mate, the love of my life, my soon-to-be husband, flowers sprang from each step I took, a testament to my power, one I would no longer hesitate to use to protect the people I loved.

No matter how dark a path it might take me down.

~

Keep reading for a look at Book Nine
Final Shift

FINAL SHIFT

BOOK 9, SHIFTER LORDS

Caelan, the Shifter Lord of Texas, is living on borrowed time.

As the fae seek to spread their influence, Caelan's land and his people are suffering. Stubbornly refusing to accept Evie's help, Caelan doubles down to continue fighting a battle he cannot hope to win.

As the other Lords unite, Evie is torn between her duty to her people and doing what is right. But Evie is a child born of gods, raised by humans, and changed by fate. If there is ever a hope to unite everyone, she will have to stand up and command it.

This time, the entire world's fate hangs in the balance, and Evie can no longer deny who she is.

As she rises to power for one final, cataclysmic battle, one of her found family will rise with her and become either a threat no one saw coming or the hope that will unite them all.

Evie's journey of heartache and hope finally comes to an end. But the question remains, will she go out with a world-rattling roar or will she succumb to the force that threatens them all?

ALSO BY S.E. BABIN

Shifter Lords

Shift of Heart

Shift of Morals

Power Shift

Shifting Winds

Shifting Resolve

Shift of Rule

Shift of the Wild

Goddess Shifting

Final Shift

Shift Happens

Shifting Allegiance

Cocktails in Hell

A Twist of Demon

A Shake of Succubus

A Stir of Fairies

A Dash of Vampire

A Touch of Angel

A Whisper of Wolf

A Smidge of Voodoo

A Hint of Hero

OTHER SERIES

A Shelf Indulgence Cozy Mystery Series

Book of the Virago

Trailer Park Transylvania

Psychic Cleaner

The Magical Soapmaker Mysteries

The Goddess Chronicles

Vikings of Virginia

The Deadicated Matchmaker

About the Author

Sheryl likes cake too much and can be found hoarding it while hiding from her children in the pantry closet.

Follow her on Amazon at: https://www.amazon.com/S-E-Babin/e/B00J1J236A

OLIVERHEBERBOOKS